PRAISE FOR ANIMAL

Animal by Munish Batra and Keith DeCandido is a book you will never forget. It takes you into a world of shadows that you knew existed but did not want to admit. It is a book every animal lover absolutely must read. I promise you it will grab hold of you and not let go; it will inspire you, it will anger you and it will live uneasily in your mind for a long time.

— DAVID FISHER, *NEW YORK TIMES* BEST-
SELLING AUTHOR OF *LINCOLN'S LAST TRIAL* AND
NEVER TURN YOUR BACK ON AN ANGUS COW

Animal is a brilliant and ferocious thriller. A tale of hideous inhumanity and very rough justice. Highly recommended!

— JONATHAN MABERRY, *NEW YORK TIMES*
BESTSELLING AUTHOR OF *RAGE* AND *V-WARS*

Animal is an absolute must read that you won't be able to put down. This captivating story will change the way you think about justice and man's inhumanity.

— JEFFREY FOSKETT, GUITARIST AND SINGER
FOR THE THE BEACH BOYS

ANIMAL

ANIMAL

MUNISH K. BATRA M.D., FACS
KEITH R.A. DECANDIDO

WFP
WORDFIRE PRESS

EBook ISBN: 978-1-68057-162-2
Trade Paperback ISBN: 978-1-68057-161-5
Hardcover ISBN: 978-1-68057-163-9
Library of Congress Control Number: 2020949903

Cover design by Janet McDonald
Cover artwork images by Adobe Stock
Kevin J. Anderson, Art Director
Published by
WordFire Press, LLC
PO Box 1840
Monument CO 80132

Kevin J. Anderson & Rebecca Moesta, Publishers

WordFire Press eBook Edition 2020
WordFire Press Trade Paperback Edition 2020
WordFire Press Hardcover Edition 2020
Printed in the USA

Join our WordFire Press Readers Group for
sneak previews, updates, new projects, and giveaways.
Sign up at wordfirepress.com

❧ Created with Vellum

AUTHORS' NOTE

Every instance of cruelty to animals dramatized in this novel is based on documented real-world occurrences, from the use of gorilla hands as ashtrays in Africa to the capturing of dogs to be used for food in Asia to the training methods of orcas in North America. *Nothing* has been exaggerated; more's the pity.

People speak sometimes about the "bestial" cruelty of man, but that is terribly unjust and offensive to beasts, no animal could ever be so cruel as a man, so artfully, so artistically cruel.

— FYODOR DOSTOYEVSKY

The greatness of a nation and its moral progress can be judged by the way its animals are treated.

— MAHATMA GANDHI

Man is the Reasoning Animal. Such is the claim. I think it is open to dispute. Indeed, my experiments have proven to me that he is the Unreasoning Animal … In truth, man is incurably foolish. Simple things which other animals easily learn, he is incapable of learning.

— MARK TWAIN

CHAPTER ONE

3 June 2019

Monrovia Police Headquarters
Monrovia, California, United States of America

DETECTIVE MICHELLE HALLS stared at the monitor on her desk, wondering why she had thought it would be easier to deal with the paperwork first thing Monday morning than last thing Friday afternoon.

Part of the problem was that she didn't factor insufficient caffeine intake into her consideration, and to fix that, she went to refill her mug for the fifth time.

The supervisor of the detective squad, Sergeant Amenguale, was dipping a teabag into a mug of hot water in the small kitchenette-like space just off the detectives' squad room. Without preamble, the balding sergeant said, "I could have sworn that you told me you'd have the Mendoza paperwork done first thing this morning. It's almost noon, so I'd say we're into the third or fourth thing this morning."

"It's almost done," she said as she reached for the glass pot containing the semi-heated brown sludge that passed for coffee.

"You said that an hour ago. What happened to tackling it first thing after a nice, relaxing weekend?"

"That was predicated on my weekend actually being relaxing. I got the last of my stuff out of Bethany's place on Saturday."

"So how long did the shouting match last this time?" Amenguale asked before sipping his tea.

"Oh, no, there wasn't any shouting. That would've actually been cathartic. No, instead she went with silent stares and awkward silence and one-syllable answers to all my attempts to talk to her." She sighed as she dumped a spoonful of sugar into the coffee and started stirring. "So I decided to drown my sorrows in gin and tonic, except I ran out of tonic after the first glass."

Amenguale gave her a half-smile. "That should've let you sleep more soundly, making you nice and rested before you finished your overdue paperwork."

Subtlety was never Amenguale's strong suit. Halls sighed. "Oh, I sleep great when I've had a *little bit* to drink. When I've had a *lot* to drink, I get nightmares. And I shot past 'a lot' around ten Saturday night." She gulped down some of the coffee and realized she hadn't put in nearly enough sugar for it to be in any way drinkable. "Anyhow, don't worry, you'll have the Mendoza file by the time I go to lunch."

"Keep in mind that Mendoza is already closed, even if you haven't finished the file, and that means you're next up in the rotation. If a call comes in, and you haven't finished your paperwork, you will make your sergeant extremely unhappy." Amenguale bared his teeth—Halls couldn't really think of what he was doing right now as a smile—and added, "You wouldn't like me when I'm unhappy."

With a shudder, Halls returned to her desk and stared at her monitor some more. It really shouldn't have taken this long to write up a series of home invasions. But then, there were a *lot* of burglaries involved, and Halls wanted to make sure she got all the details right. Glancing at the screen, she noticed that she hadn't specified which bedroom the jewelry was taken from in the first home to be hit.

She'd also misspelled one of the witness's names.

The real problem, of course, was that the case was remarkably ordinary. Guy broke into several houses, a few people saw him, they put out a description, they found him, and he had the stolen goods in his house. No twists or turns, just your basic legwork leading to an arrest.

At least if the case had some meat to it, she might have been able to engage with the paperwork.

This was the part they didn't show you on television: the drudge work. A TV show only had forty-two minutes, so they cut to the fun stuff, like interrogating witnesses or summing up all the stuff that they'd previously found off camera. In the real world, you had to chase a lot of dead ends and talk to a lot of idiots, and then you had to spend half a day writing *all about it* in excruciating detail.

Which was why Halls hadn't watched a single moment of television that wasn't a news program since she got her badge.

However, at one fifteen, after proofreading the case file for the fifth time, she finally hit SEND and it was in the database, accessible by Amenguale, the other bosses, and whichever prosecutor wound up going after Mendoza in the courts. Then she went to the diner down the street where she would have her first substantial meal since seeing Bethany on Saturday. Relationship stress always made her forget to eat and remember that she used to smoke, both things that were incredibly bad for her. She didn't have any cigarettes on her, at least, but she wasn't hungry, either. Nonetheless, she went to the diner and forced down one of their gloriously greasy cheeseburgers.

At two fifteen, she returned from lunch to see a little old woman standing at the desk talking with Sergeant Malik Whitaker.

Whitaker caught sight of Halls and waved her over to his desk.

"What's up, Malik?"

"This is Winona Jefferson."

Halls wasn't very tall, but she still had to look down to see Ms. Jefferson's face. A short, stout African-American woman, she was clutching a thick canvas shopping bag that was zipped shut.

"I'm Detective Halls, Ms. Jefferson, what can I do for you?"

"I got me a complaint you can listen to, is what you can do for me." Ms. Jefferson unzipped the bag, and Halls felt the cool air poke out from inside it, probably from ice packs.

Ms. Jefferson pulled out a Styrofoam tray half-covered in a tangle of shrink wrap, inadequately covering about two pounds of ground beef. Halls also saw a label with the BurgerBeef logo on the clear plastic wrap.

"I was startin' up the Sloppy Joes I was gonna make for dinner tonight, and I opened up the meat, and will you look at what I found?"

Halls peered at the small tray that was now on Ms. Jefferson's left palm. At first, she only noticed reddish-grayish ground meat, but then she saw it.

The tip of a human finger. Blood-stained, jaggedly cut right below the cuticle, fingernail intact.

Whitaker then added, "I just had a barbecue yesterday at my house, and I used BurgerBeef meat for the hamburgers. Now I'm wondering what in the hell I fed my family."

Ms. Jefferson put the meat back in the shopping bag and zipped it up. "I for *damn* sure ain't makin' *this*. And I want you all to *do* something about it!"

Halls shook her head. As Amenguale had reminded her, she was next up in the rotation anyhow. "I said I wanted a case with more meat to it," she muttered.

"What was that?" Ms. Jefferson asked.

"Uh, nothing, Ms. Jefferson." She pointed to the squad room. "Why don't you come with me, please? The first thing we'll need to do is take a statement from you."

"Long as you find out who tried to put a damn finger in my Sloppy Joes, I'll give you as many statements as you want!"

———

It took about half an hour to take Ms. Jefferson's statement, and also enter the meat into evidence. Halls gave the older woman her card and sent her home, promising to update her as soon as she had something.

Then she did a bit of research on BurgerBeef, which was sold by MCD Meats. The company had several plants up and down the west coast, but Halls figured the local one was the place to start, especially since they supplied all their clients in the Los Angeles area. A two-second Google search turned up the name of the chief operating officer of the Monrovia plant, which was on Royal Oaks Drive, all of a mile away from the police department's office on East Lime Avenue. She hopped into one of the department's Chevrolets and drove over.

The place itself had that giant-factory look that Halls had always found to be incredibly depressing. On top of that, just out here in the parking lot, there was an almost intolerable smell, which got worse as she exited the Chevy and headed to the front entrance.

As she approached the security desk that was right inside the front door, trying very hard to only breathe through her mouth, she pointed at the gold-colored badge on her belt. Before Bethany broke up with her, she hadn't needed a belt with these jeans, but she'd lost weight since then, and it wasn't dignified for a detective to constantly yank her pants up.

"I need to see your COO, Bronson Quinn."

The guard looked up from the copy of *Entertainment Weekly* he was reading and said, "Do you have an appoint—Oh." That last was when he noticed her shield. He quickly handed her a visitor badge, which she clipped to her plain blue T-shirt, and pointed to a small corridor behind him. "Go through there, hang a right, and take the elevator up to the second floor. He's the last office at the end of the hall."

"Thanks."

Unfortunately, the corridor went past the main part of the plant: large metal hooks with deboned carcasses on them, large vats with openings on top and tubes on the sides, people checking on the process of the carcasses going into the top intact and out the tubes in ground form. Halls couldn't see anything beyond that, and she wasn't about to look more closely as she walked briskly toward the elevator.

But what overwhelmed her, and nearly sent her running back to the Chevy, was the stench. As a cop, she was used to the smell of blood, and as a self-professed carnivore, she was used to the smell of meat, but only in small quantities. She generally encountered the former at the site of an assault or the occasional murder, and the latter in amounts of no more than a pound or two—like the cheeseburger that she'd consumed earlier, and which was threatening to come back up right now.

She pounced on the UP button for the elevator and ran in as soon as the doors slid apart to allow her ingress. It lurched upward to the office level, which was a long, narrow corridor overlooking the plant. As she exited the elevator, she saw that the wall on the right-hand side was taken up with doors to offices, some open, some closed. Each of those doors had a desk perpendicular to it, at which sat people (all women) either typing on computer keyboards or speaking on the phone or both. The left wall that faced the offices was one large picture window that gave an expansive view of the plant floor in all its lack of glory. Halls went to great pains to avoid looking to her left as she approached the desk next to the office door on the far end of the corridor.

At least up here, the smell wasn't quite so bad.

"May I help you?" the young woman at the desk asked. The engraved fake-gold-plated sheet attached to the piece of fake wood on the front of her desk identified her as Alyssa Park.

"I'm Detective Halls of the Monrovia Police. I need to speak to Mr. Quinn."

Park scrunched up her nose. "I'm so sorry, ma'am, but Mr. Quinn is in a meeting right now. Perhaps if you make an appointment?"

"This is a little more important than his meeting, all things considered." Halls walked toward the office door, which had a fake gold nameplate attached to the center that read BRONSON QUINN, CHIEF OPERATING OFFICER.

"Excuse me, ma'am, but you can't go in there."

Halls turned and faced Park, who had turned in her chair, but not gotten up. Her nose remained scrunched up.

"That was good," Halls said, "say that louder."

Now the young woman frowned. "I'm sorry?"

"Say that louder."

She looked to the side and then yelled, "You can't go in there!"

Grinning, Halls said, "See? Now you're off the hook."

And then she entered the office, which also had a large picture window, but it looked out onto Recreation Park instead of the meat-packing plant.

The two men in the office both jerked their heads toward the door in surprise at her presence. Sitting behind a large metal desk was a middle-aged white man in a tailored suit, though he did not wear a tie. This was obviously Quinn, and he looked seriously grumpy. Across from him was an African-American man wearing an off-the-rack suit, a visitor badge very much like the one Halls had been given clipped to the lapel of the jacket.

Quinn stood up. "Who the hell are you? I'm in the middle of something. Alyssa!"

His guest, though, noticed her badge. "Detective, what's this about? Who called you in on this investigation?"

Halls blinked. "There's another investigation?"

Park had finally gotten up and was standing behind Halls in the doorway. "I'm sorry, Mr. Quinn, but she said she's the police!"

Quinn waved his hand in front of his face. "All right, fine, Alyssa, get back to work. And close the door." As she did so, he regarded Halls with a pissed-off expression. "What do the police want with me?" Glancing angrily down at his guest, he asked, "Did you call her?"

Holding up both hands, Halls said, "Hold it, please, both of you!" She took a breath. "Hi, I'm Detective Michelle Halls of the Monrovia Police. I'm following up on a complaint made by one of your customers, who found a finger in her BurgerBeef container."

Putting his head in his hands, Quinn sat back down. "Goddammit."

Now the guest rose to his feet, pulling a wallet out of his suit jacket pocket. "I'm Andrew Franklin with the Food and Drug Administration." He opened the wallet to show his FDA ID card.

"Well, I'd ask what you're doing here, but since the complaint I'm following up on involves a woman whose hamburger meat gave her the finger ..."

Again, Quinn said, "Goddammit."

Within a few minutes, all three of them were sitting down. Halls explained about Ms. Jefferson, after which Franklin said, "We were doing a random inspection of meat at a supermarket in Sacramento, and we found human DNA in a package that came from this plant."

"Agent Franklin and I," Quinn added quickly, "have been discussing our options. We will, of course, institute an immediate recall, but we'd like to keep this as quiet as possible."

"Yeah, that's not really possible," Halls said.

Quinn folded his hands together and put them on the desk. "Detective, a public recall will cause a major panic and have an even bigger impact on our bottom line."

"First of all, Mr. Quinn, a public recall and warning will do a lot more to *avert* panic, especially if more people find body parts in their fridge. Second of all, we now have a police report, which is a part of the public record. If you don't call a press conference, we will."

Halls wasn't entirely sure that was true. MCD was a big employer in the town, and she could easily see the mayor telling the department to cool it on going public. But maybe not, and either way, better to intimidate Quinn as much as possible.

She went on: "And third of all, the Monrovia Police Department is interested in serving the public good, not the good of MCD Meats."

Franklin added, "To be honest, Mr. Quinn, the FDA is going to be joining the Monrovia Police in that press conference."

Quinn stared angrily at Franklin. "I *beg* your pardon? Mr. Franklin, I was led to believe—"

But Franklin interrupted. "*I* was led to believe that this was an isolated incident, that some hair or fingernails may have gotten into the meat. However, now we have, not just a fingernail, but the finger that goes with it, and in a different location. I'm afraid I'm going to have to insist on a complete recall."

Halls gave Franklin a quick thank-you nod.

"Perhaps you're right," Quinn said through clenched teeth. "Unfortunately, there's an—an issue."

"What issue is that?" Halls asked.

"Such a recall has to be authorized by our CEO."

"Why is that an issue?"

Quinn let out a long breath, and then ran his palm over his suddenly sweaty forehead. "Because he's been missing since Memorial Day. In fact, both Mr. Lesnick and our floor foreman, Fredi Rodriguez, have disappeared. Neither of them showed up for work on the Tuesday after the holiday, or any day since. Fredi's on the verge of being fired in absentia—he hasn't answered *any* attempt to get in touch with him."

"Have you reported them missing to us?" Halls asked.

Quinn nodded. "For Mr. Lesnick, yes, of course we filed a report. As for Fredi, that's up to his family."

Halls sighed. She spent the next twenty minutes or so querying Quinn about the company, about the process of packing the meats, and about both the foreman and the CEO, filling her notepad with shorthand notes of his answers.

Once that was done, she said, "I'll also need all your security footage from the last month."

"Why?"

Again, Halls sighed. On vanishingly rare occasions when she asked someone for something in a case, they said, "Of course, Detective, happy to help." Most of the time, though, she got belligerent answers like what Quinn gave her.

"Because it's obvious that someone got into your plant and introduced the human body parts that have turned up. It's also possible that either Mr. Rodriguez or Mr. Lesnick caught them and were disposed of. It's even possible that one of those two gentlemen belong to the body parts in question."

"What a horrible thing to say!" Quinn's face scrunched up in much the same way Park's had.

Once she was finished, she exchanged business cards with Franklin. The FDA agent left the office with a sour look at Quinn.

Halls drove back to police headquarters on East Lime. The first thing she did upon arrival was fill Amenguale in. Then they both checked and saw that Alexander Lesnick and Fredi Rodriguez had, in fact, each been reported missing; the former by Quinn, as he'd said, the latter by his wife. The detectives handling the two cases hadn't actually talked to each other, to the annoyance of both Amenguale and Halls, nor had they made any kind of real progress, even though both men worked at the same place, and both went missing after Memorial Day. The sergeant reamed both of them and told them to coordinate their cases.

Twelve hours later, CNN was reporting on the recall. Franklin obviously hadn't wasted any time in making sure that process got started as publicly as possible.

Halls watched the television in the kitchenette while choking down some more of the squad room sludge.

"Now some disturbing news out of Monrovia, California. Random inspection of ground beef processed at a local plant has discovered traces of human DNA in MCD Meats' 'BurgerBeef' product. Over six hundred tons of beef are being recalled after having been shipped to retail stores throughout the US. The Food and Drug Administration is urging consumers to avoid eating beef processed at MCD Meats until further notice."

The co-anchor smiled and added, "I'm glad I gave up red meat years ago."

Exactly what would be revealed to the press was determined over Halls's head. She suspected that Ms. Jefferson's finger was left out of it as a sop to MCD Meats' public image. Mentioning the DNA test of the Sacramento meat gave the public the same impression that Quinn had implied to Franklin before Halls showed up: that this was an accident. The presence of a finger made that impossible, but there was no reason to gross out the general public, as long as *all* the meat was recalled and people who'd bought MCD products threw out what was in their larder.

Whitaker intercepted her as she crossed the squad room to head back to her desk. "Hey, Michelle? Messenger dropped this off for you." He held out a manila envelope.

"Thanks, Malik." The proffered envelope had the MCD Meats logo and address printed across one edge, with her name, misspelled as "Det. Michele Hall," scrawled in the middle. Taking it from the sergeant, she felt a small rectangle inside. Opening it, she tipped it into her hands, and a flash drive came out.

Assuming this to be the security footage she'd asked for, she went straight to her desk and inserted the drive into the USB port. She waited patiently for the computer to run a virus scan on the flash drive, and then, once it was cleared, a folder appeared on her monitor.

There were twenty-eight video files on the drive, each for a twenty-four-hour period.

Halls sighed. One entire month of slaughterhouse footage. Just how she always wanted to spend her work days.

The smart place to start was Memorial Day weekend, right before Alexander Lesnick and Fredi Rodriguez went missing, so she moused over to the video file for the Friday before and double-clicked on it.

After an hour of this, she swore she would become a vegetarian. At first she went through the video feed of the plant floor in real time, but it wasn't long before the mind-numbing and really gross repetitiveness got to her. Cow carcasses were deboned, beheaded, and dropped into the big vats that ground them up and spit them out onto conveyer belts. Then the meat was placed on Styrofoam trays and shrink-wrapped so people like Ms. Jefferson and Sergeant Whitaker could buy them and bring them home to cook for their families.

Before too long, she started moving the video at two times speed, and then four times, and then eight.

According to Quinn, the plant could theoretically go 24/7, but that wasn't cost-efficient given "current sales trends," so they were limited to two eight-hour shifts between seven in the morning and eleven at night. Everything stopped at eleven, and by half past eleven, the plant was shut down, with the lights out. Even on the Friday of a holiday weekend, that held true.

She went through Saturday, Sunday, and Monday at sixteen times speed, but still watching closely. However, the only variation inside the plant, closed as it was for the three-day weekend, was the occasional flash of light through a window from something outside.

Tuesday was business as usual, and Halls went back down to eight times speed. Still, nothing much stood out as she went through the two eight-hour shifts. The lone security camera provided a good overview of the entire plant floor, but it wasn't in high-definition or anything—probably not considered a worthwhile expense for a plant that had already cut back to a sixteen-hour production day from a twenty-four-hour one—so details were hard to make out. But nothing seemed untoward.

As with Friday, the place shut down at eleven, and by 11:23 PM the place was locked down and the lights were out.

At two minutes to midnight, however, someone came into the plant.

The door was too distant, and the resolution too poor, to make out who, but no alarms went off, so whoever it was had to be authorized.

Right before the file ended, she saw a person wearing a white butcher's apron and a mask maneuvering a wheelbarrow, its cargo covered by a blanket.

"Dammit," she muttered as the file ended.

Before double clicking on the next file, which would pick up at 12:01 AM, she put in a phone call to MCD, hoping the place was still open. Given the press attention, she liked the odds that someone would be around to answer the phone.

Sure enough: "Mr. Quinn's office." It was the voice of Alyssa Park.

"This is Detective Halls—I was there this morning? I need to know who entered the building on Tuesday, May 28th at 11:58 PM."

"We're closed at that hour, Detective."

"I know that, but I just watched someone waltz right in the same front door I came in yesterday, and no alarms went off. Mr. Quinn told me that after-hours entry is only possible with a key card."

"That's correct. Hang on, Detective, let me check—Oh."

"What?"

"Well, that doesn't make sense."

Halls rolled her eyes. "What doesn't make sense, Ms. Park?"

"Um, well—according to the log, it was Mr. Lesnick who entered."

Which raised the question to Halls of whether or not it was Lesnick in the mask and butcher's apron or in the wheelbarrow. Or neither.

She also wondered if the detective assigned to Lesnick's missing-persons case knew that his key card had been used after he'd disappeared. She suspected not.

"Has the key card been used since?"

"Let me check." After a moment, and the sound of fingers clacking on a keyboard, Park said, "No, that's the only time it's been used since he went missing. That's weird."

"Thank you, Ms. Park, that's been very helpful."

"But—"

Halls hung up—she wasn't about to give Park anything she could use for office gossip—and double-clicked on the security feed for the twenty-ninth.

The figure in the mask was moving around the floor, turning on all the machinery that had been shut down an hour previous.

Then he went into the freezer and removed several of the cow corpses, and placed them on the hooks attached to the conveyer belt.

Halls watched this in real time. She was hoping for some clue as to who this person was. But the camera was too far away—the best she could tell was that it was a male, or at least someone who presented as such. He was wearing gloves and a long-sleeved shirt under the butcher's apron, and he wore a ballcap in addition to the mask.

It took him the better part of an hour to do the work that a whole shift full of plant workers were able to do in about five to ten minutes.

He also left two of the hooks empty.

Halls's coffee had gone cold, but she sipped it anyhow. It tasted even more like an oil slick than usual, but she couldn't tear her eyes away to get up and fetch a fresh cup.

Especially since she had a feeling she now knew what—or, rather, who—was in the wheelbarrow.

Sure enough, the man in the mask removed the sheet to reveal two people lying in the wheelbarrow, one atop the other. They looked—asleep? sedated? dead? Their hands and feet were bound by something, probably zip ties.

As Halls had feared, the man in the mask hoisted each of the two men—they were definitely men—onto the hooks, hanging them upside down by their feet, just like the cows were. It put the two men's heads right at around the masked man's chest level.

Pausing the video, Halls called up the missing persons files on Lesnick and Rodriguez. Quinn and Rodriguez's wife had each provided a picture that was now in the database.

The video resolution sucked donkey balls, but Halls was pretty sure that the two men on the hooks were Fredi Rodriguez and Alexander Lesnick.

Starting the video back up, Halls observed the man in the mask pull a syringe out of the pocket of his butcher's apron. He injected each of the two men with it.

"Okay, probably not dead, then."

A voice came from behind her. "Talking to yourself, Michelle?"

Turning, Halls saw Amenguale approaching, running a hand over his thinning dark hair. "Yeah, Sarge, it's my only guarantee of intelligent conversation." She paused the playback.

"I'd object, but I couldn't with a straight face." He indicated her monitor with his head. "This our guy?"

"Well, I'm fairly certain that the two he just put on meat hooks are our missing MCD people, and he's about to introduce them as the secret ingredient, yeah."

Amenguale peered closer. "What's that he's wearing? A mask?"

"Looks like. Can't tell what it is, the resolution sucks the wet farts out of dead pigeons."

Looking down at the seated detective, Amenguale said, "You know, Michelle, it may be that you talk to yourself because nobody wants to listen to you make similes like that."

"Actually, that was a metaphor. If it was a simile, I'd have said the resolution was like a fifth-generation VHS tape."

"You also talk to yourself because you're pedantic." Amenguale chuckled. "Anyhow, keep watching, see if you can get a better ID with your pigeon-fart resolution."

Halls nodded and clicked on the play icon.

Sure enough, the two men started to stir after getting the injection.

One of them seemed to be saying something. She jumped the video back a few seconds and turned the volume all the way up.

"I don' unnerstan'," said the one she was pretty sure was Lesnick, his voice slurred as he slowly worked his way back to consciousness, "wha's goin' on? Whyew doin' 'is?"

Rodriguez, meanwhile, was simply staring quietly, eyes wide.

There was a small bag in the wheelbarrow that Halls only noticed because the masked man reached down and opened it. He removed a very large knife from it and held it aloft for a moment before placing it in the pocket of his apron.

Halls let out a long breath. It looked like one of the fancy kitchen knives that Bethany had at their place.

Her place. Halls didn't live there anymore.

Shaking her head, she gulped down the last of the awful coffee and braced herself. She'd studied all about blood spatter, and she knew that things were about to get gory.

That studying did nothing to prepare her for what came next.

The masked man grabbed Rodriguez's mouth and pried it open, pulling out the plant manager's tongue.

Even as he gripped the tongue with one hand, Rodriguez

uttered a strangled scream. Several of the detectives at the nearby desks and the uniforms walking through stopped and turned to look at Halls.

For her part, she didn't only hear Rodriguez's scream, she also felt it at the base of her neck.

As horrible, as mind-wrenching, as dreadful as that scream was, it became several orders of magnitude worse when the man in the mask pulled the kitchen knife back out of his pocket and started slicing through Rodriguez's tongue.

The screams became louder.

The screams became shriller.

The screams became more strangled.

And the blood spurted *everywhere*.

All Halls could hear were the agonized, gurgling cries of Rodriguez as blood poured out of his mouth like a geyser.

After a moment, she realized that the squad room had gone quiet. Everyone was staring at her in horror.

Monrovia wasn't exactly East LA or Compton. They'd had less than ten homicides in the last decade. The Monrovia Police detectives spent most of their time dealing with thievery of some kind— like the home invasions case she'd just closed. And the murders they did get were usually domestic situations that had gone horribly wrong.

Torture was a little outside their wheelhouse.

Hastily, she paused the playback and then opened a drawer of her desk and pulled out her iPod, unplugging the earbuds from it and plugging them into the computer's mic port.

The screams were worse coming right into her ears as opposed to over the tinny speakers in her desktop.

Blood continued to gush from Rodriguez's mouth onto the floor beneath him. The masked man dropped Rodriguez's tongue to the stained floor. Blood pooled around it and flowed toward the drains.

For a long time, Rodriguez just hung there, bleeding. His screams grew ever quieter, eventually working their way down to a wet gurgle.

Apparently, the man in the mask was less interested when his victim wasn't screaming, because once the noise from Rodriguez dimmed, he used the knife to slit Rodriguez's throat. More blood poured onto the floor, and it wasn't much longer before Rodriguez died.

That was when the masked man *really* went to work.

Halls's mouth kept falling further and further open as she observed the man in the mask butcher the dozen or so cows ahead of the two men on the line. He cut each cow into seven parts, deboning six of them and placing them on the conveyer for the grinder, tossing the head into the waste bucket.

The conveyer had already started and it rolled slowly toward the grinder, tossing the cow parts in and slicing them to sizes small enough for properly ground beef.

And then he went to work on Lesnick, who had been muttering something that Halls couldn't make out.

Lesnick's screams didn't last as long as Rodriguez's. That didn't make having to listen to those screams any better.

But the masked man didn't cut Lesnick's throat, instead letting him slowly bleed out and watch as he moved back to Rodriguez's corpse, cutting off each of the man's limbs, then finally severing the head. He put all four limbs and the torso alongside the cow parts on the conveyer, tossing the head into the rubbish.

He did the same for Lesnick, then continued to work on the other cows.

A hand touched Halls's left shoulder, and she let out a yelp of surprise and practically jumped out of her chair.

Ripping the buds out of her ears, she saw that it was Amenguale.

"What the ever-loving *fuck*, Sarge? Don't sneak up on me like that!"

"Fine, next time I'll sneak up on you different. Just got word of something you need to know about."

"What?"

"There was a murder at SeaLand down in San Diego over the weekend, though it's only hitting the press now. Body was cut up, killer wore a mask. Thought you'd wanna know."

With that, Amenguale walked off.

Halls stared after him for a second.

Then she put the headphones back on and finished watching as Alexander Lesnick and Fredi Rodriguez were added to MCD's BurgerBeef mix.

Idly, she wondered whose finger it was in Ms. Jefferson's ground beef. The finger had been sent for DNA testing, but the results wouldn't be back for a while. Rodriguez was already in the system thanks to a stint in the Marines, and the one thing the detective assigned to Lesnick's case had gotten right was obtaining some DNA from Lesnick's house.

When it was done, she stopped it and restarted the video from the beginning.

There had to be a clue here somewhere as to who this fucking lunatic was.

CHAPTER TWO

5 June 2019

An Chang's apartment
Beijing, China

His DREAM of a girl with a flower in her hair was rudely interrupted by the insistent chirp of his cell phone's alarm.

In the dream, he was in Shanghai with Kiara, wearing a button-down shirt and khakis, a cigarette dangling from his mouth. He had found a daisy in the grass outside her mother's estate and given it to her to put in her beautiful dark hair.

As the cell phone played an insistent beep, Inspector An Chang of Interpol dragged himself awake. He snagged the phone off the milk crate that passed for a nightstand, and made four attempts to run his finger across the display before the alarm actually stopped.

Tossing the battered blanket aside, he put the smartphone back on the crate and stared at his studio apartment.

One of these days, he was going to have to unpack all the boxes.

He thought about the dream. The basics were as he remembered them that day in 1989 that he'd visited Kiara right before her mother announced that they were moving back to the United States.

But he was younger then, with a dark crew cut rather than the unruly mop of salt-and-pepper hair that now sat messily atop his head. And the flower he had put in Kiara's hair had been a viola, the same flower she had in her hair in the only picture he had left of her. And he'd picked that from a garden, not a field of grass.

Why did he dream a daisy in the grass?

He clumsily reached for his pack of cigarettes next to his phone, but the pack was empty.

Clambering off the wafer-thin futon on the rickety wooden frame, he navigated clumsily around the stacks of boxes and piles of paperwork that impeded his progress.

The kitchenette took up part of one wall of the dilapidated old apartment. It came equipped only with a sink that provided water of dubious quality and a range with an inconsistently functioning oven and only one working burner. To that, he'd added a mini fridge that he'd bought off a university student, a microwave that someone had thrown out that he'd fixed, and a washing machine that was a gift from the couple next door who had just had a baby and therefore required a larger one for themselves.

His first stop was the mini fridge. Having been denied his morning cigarette, he really needed some food in him before he tried to face another day at Interpol's Beijing office.

All that greeted him inside the fridge were two cans of beer, a tomato that was half-covered in mold, and a takeout container.

He flipped open the takeout container at the same time that Xia Xue, his all-white Shih Tzu, lumbered over. Chang had gotten her from the same neighbors who were the source of the washing machine. The new child whose existence necessitated the bigger machine also didn't get along with the dog. They had given the dog the rather obvious name of "Snow." His attempt to rename her Meyli had failed utterly, as she only responded to Xia Xue.

She looked expectantly at Chang as he took the container out of the fridge. It contained the remains of the orange chicken he'd had for lunch over the weekend.

From the moment he'd taken her into his home, the dog had given Chang unconditional love. Chang had never been able to resist the pleas of those who loved him. As a result, from the moment Xia Xue fixed him with her big eyes and doleful expression, he had no choice but to put the container on the floor in front of her. She wolfed it down eagerly and happily.

Getting to his feet, and wincing as his knees cracked from the action, Chang went to the washing machine, into which he'd thrown his brown khaki pants before going to sleep the previous night. After wringing out the pants over the sink, he clambered back onto the bed, which sat right under the window to the fire escape—also the only window in the place.

Sliding the screen upward, he climbed out onto the fire escape where he had strung a clothesline. A pair of beige khaki pants hung from the line.

One of these days he would unpack the boxes, and then he'd finally find his other pairs of pants, but for right now, he had to alternate between the two pairs of khakis. Thank goodness he'd accidentally put them in the box with the kitchen implements, the only box he'd actually unpacked since moving to this place eight months ago.

For now, though, all he had were these two and the shorts that he wore over the weekends.

He squeezed himself into the shower stall that he could only turn around in if he pivoted firmly in place and did a quick rinse-down. That was usually enough for the morning grime. For a proper shower, he always used the locker room at headquarters after his shift ended. He found it much easier to get himself clean in a shower that enabled him to lift his arms.

Besides the futon, the only other furniture in the place was a bunch of milk crates Chang had salvaged from the sidewalks. One of them held his clean work shirts, which were all button-downs in either brown or beige, in roughly the same two shades as the khakis. Since he had the beige khakis today, he went with a brown shirt. This was about as complex as he was willing to make his sartorial decisions in the morning.

He grabbed a street snack and bought a fresh pack of cigarettes on his way from the subway station to the office. After eating the former, he stood outside the entry to headquarters smoking a cigarette from the latter.

By the time he reached his desk, his cognitive processes were starting to almost cohere.

Which was more than could be said for the surface of his desk, which was covered in folders, papers, photos, and empty takeout boxes. Maintenance was supposed to take care of the boxes, but the janitorial staff had all taken a collective vow not to touch Chang's desk until he himself cleared it.

His rear end had barely touched the chair when his boss, Superintendent Zhou, walked over.

"Have you checked your e-mail?" he asked, then peered at his desk. "I assume not, since the team of archeologists has yet to unearth your keyboard."

Chang had meant to check his e-mail on his phone, but the lack of food or nicotine at the apartment had kept him from remembering that. At least, that was today's excuse.

"Not yet," was all he muttered in reply.

"You've got plane reservations. You're going to Los Angeles."

"Why would you want me to do that?"

"Overnight we got two hits on murders involving animals and a man wearing a strange mask. One at an aquarium in San Diego, one in the suburbs of Los Angeles."

Quickly, Chang sat up straight in his chair. Immediately, he cleared away the detritus that was covering his keyboard and tapped the space bar so it would come out of sleep mode. Yanking his reading glasses out of the desk drawer, he entered his password after the monitor went live, then checked his e-mail.

Most of his new messages were the usual nonsense, but there were four of note. One was a forwarded e-mail from Zhou with the files on the two cases in California that might have been his masked killer.

Was wondering when you'd strike again.

Chang had built a strong case against the animal-mask killer. He had been less successful in actually identifying him. What little physical evidence had been left behind provided no clue as to his identity, and while there was a smattering of biological evidence, he had yet to match it against anyone in any database.

The other three e-mails included an exchange between Zhou and the chief of the Monrovia Police requesting and receiving permission for Chang to consult on the case, on which Chang had been cc'd, and one from the travel office, who had put him on Vista Atlantic Flight 22 leaving Beijing Capital at nine o'clock that evening. It would arrive at LAX twelve hours later, which would be six in the evening local time. There was also a hotel reservation at a Doubletree.

At that, he looked up with disgust at Zhou. "I'm flying on an American airline?"

Zhou shrugged. "It was the first available flight to Los Angeles."

"What about San Diego?"

Shaking his head, Zhou said, "I've sent a request, but you know how American police are, especially in big cities. Even if the San Diego police accept the request, they will not welcome you with open arms. But the other murder took place in a suburb where they have very few murders and, as you saw, they acceded to our request almost immediately." Zhou put a hand on Chang's shoulder. "It's been more than twenty years, An. Time we got him, don't you think?"

"Past time," Chang said. "I shall need more than two pairs of pants."

———

The chief flight attendant made the announcement in English, Mandarin, and Cantonese that it was safe to use electronic equipment. As soon as she did, Chang pulled out his laptop, put down the tray table in front of his aisle seat, and opened the laptop, plugging his headphones in.

It was probably pointless to go over the files and the footage again. He had it all memorized at this point, and it was an open question whether or not he even registered what he was watching so much as he remembered watching it all the other times.

First things were first, however. He had spent all day trying to find his Travel Document in the mess on his desk. Serving as both passport and visa, it allowed Interpol officers to travel and work freely in all member countries. After he had located it, he had to sign off on several pieces of paperwork that had to get done before he left, go home, pack—which included finally finding the box that had all his other pants—arrange for the neighbors to take care of Xia Xue while he was gone, and get to the airport. As a result, he had not actually had the chance to look at the files that Zhou had e-mailed him.

Among those files was a video that included news reports from CNN, MSNBC, Fox News, and local San Diego television on the murder at SeaLand.

No one had been able to identify the murderer, nor was either the name of the victim or the manner of death released. The killer was dressed as a security guard, with a ballcap obscuring his features, and one person who'd gotten a good look at him saw a mask of a whale covering the man's face.

He picked one of the news reports at random and watched it, seeing a moderately attractive woman in a dark red suit holding a microphone while standing in front of the entrance to an amusement park. "The opening of the new Arjun Keshav Arena at San Diego's SeaLand was marred by rumors of a body part in the mouths of one of the amusement park's prized orcas. Now those rumors have gone into overdrive with the news that a body has been found. Neither SeaLand nor the San Diego Police Department has released a formal statement as of yet, except to confirm that a body was found. A spokeswoman for SeaLand also said that, despite their nickname of 'killer whales,' orcas would not harm a person and are not responsible. We'll have more on this story as it develops."

After watching several other news reports and not finding anything new in any of them, he opened the file on the murders in Monrovia.

That file was much smaller: a PDF of the preliminary report by a detective named Michelle Halls.

Zhou's instincts had been right. The report Chang read was that of someone not accustomed to writing reports on murders. There was a great deal of unnecessary detail, the sign of a neophyte not certain what was important and what was not, and going well beyond what was necessary to include.

For all that, there was precious little by way of detail, because they didn't know very much. Chang hoped that his information with regard to previous like killings would be welcomed by Detective Halls. With luck, they could present a united front to the San Diego detective—J.D. Skolnick, according to the file, was the primary on the case for SDPD.

Once he was done with the new cases, he called up all the other files that he had on his laptop in the folder that he'd simply labeled MASK.

His first stop was the sub-folder labeled ELEPHANT which was full of picture and video files and PDFs of police reports and newspaper articles of the most recent mask killer case, which involved five victims on three continents. First were pictures of the event that had incited the killer's wrath: elephants that had been butchered, their tusks removed. After that, video of three men in Chad who'd been butchered in much the same manner, their teeth all yanked out; a copy of the article from a Sudanese newspaper, the headline of which translated to, "Elephant poachers found de-tusked"; pictures of a Chinese man impaled by an ivory tusk that came from one of those elephants; and a copy of the article from a San Francisco newspaper about an ivory importer found stabbed through the nose by an ivory-handled letter opener.

He was about to open the sub-folder called TIGER when he felt a tap on his left shoulder.

Looking up and behind him, he saw a small American boy, who was standing on the seat directly behind him. "What happened to those elephants, mister?"

For a second, Chang just stared at him.

The boy's mother was in the window seat, and her head popped up next to the boy's. "Arthur, don't be so rude!"

"But Mommy, they—"

While Chang was fluent in English—as well as French, German, Spanish, Japanese, Korean, and Arabic, not to mention his native Cantonese and Mandarin—he decided to simply let out a stream of babble in Cantonese to make it look like he didn't understand the child.

"Arthur, sit *down*," the mother said. Then she added a badly pronounced apology in Mandarin.

Chang grunted in reply and closed the laptop.

There wasn't any point in going over it again anyhow. He knew it all backwards and forwards.

He plugged his headphones into the jack on the arm of his aisle seat and turned on the monitor in the seat back in front of him.

The first channel he checked was CNN. Unsurprisingly, they were doing a story about the SeaLand murder.

Quickly, he changed the channel.

CHAPTER THREE

5 June 2019

Monrovia Police Headquarters
Monrovia, California, United States of America

THE GOOD NEWS was that Halls was approved to take overtime on this case. This was not entirely a guarantee, since there had been an overtime freeze since the end of the first quarter and rumor had it that it would continue through the rest of the year, if not longer.

But this had become a press case, so Halls was granted overtime, as were some of the people in the lab. While this would do wonders for her wallet, if not her ability to sleep, it also meant that every other detective in the house was giving her the hairy eyeball.

Halls had spent most of the last two days interviewing all the people who worked at MCD and the friends and families of Fredi Rodriguez and Alexander Lesnick, coordinating the shutdown of the slaughterhouse so the crime scene techs could go over it, talking further with Agent Franklin about what the FDA found in Sacramento, and giving incredibly bland comments to a press corps that would not leave her alone.

At 8:00 PM on the fifth, she returned to the office to be greeted by Amenguale.

"How'd it go at the slaughterhouse?" the sergeant asked.

Rolling her eyes, Halls said, "Oh, awesome. I got Bronson Quinn bitching for half an hour about the lost business, and then had to listen to him backtracking when I asked him why he didn't notice the extra ground beef that was magically made after hours on Tuesday the twenty-eighth. *Then* I had to let Stankiewicz and the rest of the crime scene nerds loose on the slaughterhouse. It was great, Sarge, they spent *hours* scraping and photographing and swabbing and in the end they're not gonna find a goddamn thing because the crime happened over a week ago, and the place has been at full bore since."

"So it went well, then," Amenguale deadpanned.

"Well, there was one bit of good news. Our guy hung the white coat he wore up in one of the lockers, and nobody's touched it. Stankiewicz bagged it and sent it to the lab, so maybe we'll get lucky."

"Good to hear," the sergeant said.

"So anyhow, I smell like dead cow, I feel like hammered shit, and I'm going to clock out, take the longest shower in the whole history of the whole history, and then try to have a good night's sleep that isn't filled with nightmares about being hung upside down with my tongue being cut out."

Amenguale winced. "That bad?"

Halls nodded. "It'll pass. I hope. So, if you'll excuse me, Sarge—"

"Afraid not," Amenguale said. "You have a visitor from Interpol."

For several seconds, Halls stared at Amenguale, as if he'd suddenly started speaking Sanskrit. "Okay, I must be tired, because for a minute there I thought you said someone from Interpol was here to see me."

"You *are* tired, and that *is* what I said." He pointed at the squad room that contained her desk. "He just got in from Beijing. The chief already okayed his being here, so go talk to him."

"You have *got* to be fucking kidding me."

Amenguale lowered his glasses on his hook nose so that he was peering over the top of them. "Michelle, when have you known me to be funny?"

"Never on duty. At least not on purpose." She rubbed her eyes, which only irritated them more. "I *have* to go to the bathroom and at least try to wash the meat residue off my face and hands. Then I'll talk to Interpol."

She went to the women's room and tried to scour her hands with the shitty pink liquid soap that looked like Pepto Bismol, and was about as effective as a cleaning agent. Every time she used the stuff, it felt like it had ripped the skin off her hands, but somehow left half the dirt behind. Still, at least now her hands smelled like the awful soap, which was an improvement over the slaughterhouse smell that permeated her clothes and hair.

After splashing cold water on her face—which, if nothing else, made her a touch more alert—she went back out to her desk to see an Asian man sitting in her guest chair flipping through a copy of the *Los Angeles Times*. A duffel bag sat at his feet.

At her approach, the man rose. He wore a rumpled button-down brown shirt and beige khakis. "You are Detective Halls," he said in slightly accented English. His struggle with the second consonant sound in her last name indicated that his native tongue was Chinese or Japanese or another language from that region that didn't have an *L* sound.

"Pretty sure I am, yes. I certainly was when I woke up this morning. Which feels like days ago. You are?"

Reaching into the back pocket of his khakis, the man pulled out his identification and credentials. "Inspector An Chang of the International Police. I have some information that may be of use in your case."

Halls blinked. "Seriously? My sergeant said you flew in from Beijing. So you sat on a plane for, what, ten hours?"

"Twelve."

"Twelve hours because you 'may' have information? Try again, Interpol."

Chang bowed his head. "As you say, Detective. I have information about your killer. Or, at the very least, your killer—and the one in San Diego—match the *modus operandi* of a serial killer I am familiar with. I would very much like to see the evidence you have gathered."

"Uh huh. Well, I don't know about the SeaLand thing. I've left about a thousand messages for the primary on that case, and he hasn't called me back yet. All I've got here is some really disgusting video footage and a coat. The coat's in the lab, but if you want to put yourself through it, you're welcome to look at the footage."

"Perhaps later, for now—may we step outside?" He pulled a pack of cigarettes out of his front pants pocket.

Halls stared at the pack for a moment. "Okay, fine, but only if you've got one for me."

"You smoke?"

"This week, I do."

Chang nodded. "I assume I may leave my bag safely here?"

"It *is* a police station," Halls said wryly. She headed toward the rear of the building. "Let's go to the parking lot—the press isn't allowed there."

"Yes, I saw them on the way in," Chang said.

Halls briefly panicked. "Please tell me you didn't talk to them."

"One attempted to query me, but I responded in Cantonese."

"Good." That actually got Halls to smile, a facial expression that the last forty-eight hours had done a decent job of beating out of her. She was grateful that she still remembered how.

When they reached the parking lot, Chang undid the foil on the pack and tapped two cigarettes out against his palm. He handed one to Halls then pulled out a lighter.

"Thanks, Interpol," Halls said after he lit her cigarette. She inhaled the lovely nicotine, and for a brief moment almost felt decent. "God, what a shitty couple of days."

Chang stared at her as he lit his own cigarette. "How many months has it been since last you smoked?"

Halls shot him a glance. "That obvious, huh?"

"To a trained observer, yes."

"I started smoking in high school because everyone was doing it. I quit when I graduated because I got tired of coughing my lungs out. I've taken it back up four times: after my first murder, and after each of my last three breakups, the most recent of which was two months ago, and I went through a pack in one day and then quit again. And now this." She held up the cigarette Chang had given her. "So yeah, two months."

"I came here directly from the airport, and have not had a cigarette since arriving at Beijing Capital." He sighed. "I do miss the days when one could smoke on an airplane."

Halls blinked. "You could smoke on airplanes?"

Chang nodded and took a drag. "Yes. The regulations changed in the late 1990s. And my own government outlawed indoor smoking in public places five years ago. It is to weep."

"Huh." Halls took another drag. Her own smoking habits had only occurred in the twenty-first century. "So what's this information you have, Interpol?"

"Your killer wore a mask. I assume it was in the form of a bull or a cow?"

Halls's eyes went wide. Without a word, she pulled out her smartphone and called up the still of the security footage that she'd saved. It was the best view of the killer's "face."

Staring at it, she nodded. "Okay, now that you've said it out loud, I can definitely see a bull there." She held the phone display-out toward Chang.

He glanced at it. "He always transforms himself into the victim for whom he is seeking retribution."

"Okay, for the record? Everything you just said makes me want about fifty more cigarettes. I'm not sure which is worse, 'always,' 'victim,' or 'retribution.'" She took another drag on the cigarette. "Let's start with 'victim.' Only victims I see here are Rodriguez and Lesnick."

"To him," Chang said quietly, "they are the perpetrators. The victims are the animals they slaughter."

"And who is 'him'?"

Chang shook his head. "I cannot say. Because of the mask, his identity has remained a secret."

"*There* you are," came a voice from behind them.

Turning, Halls saw Amenguale coming out to join them in the parking lot.

"Inspector Chang," the sergeant said as he approached, "I see you and Detective Halls are doing your bit to up the city's smog count."

"I see you've met Sergeant Passive Aggressive," Halls said to Chang. "What's up, Sarge?"

"The chief called SDPD's chief—they're old buddies—and you now have permission to consult on their case."

Halls blinked. "Excuse me? Why would I consult on *their* case? I want to talk to them so they can help with *my* case."

"Right, and our friend the inspector here thinks they're linked. So do both chiefs. At this point, you've talked to everyone you can and you need to wait and see what the lab gives us. So let the techs do their work. Meanwhile, you and Inspector Chang take a nice drive down the 5 to see what the SeaLand murder can tell you about this case under the guise of consulting on theirs."

"I believe this is an excellent course of action," Chang said.

"Yeah, I'm sure you do, Interpol." Halls dragged on the last of her cigarette, dropped it to the asphalt, and stepped on it. "Mind telling me why you came to us first instead of them? We're just a rinky-dink suburban police force with our first double murder in my lifetime. Why come here instead of the big-city cops?"

Chang shrugged. "We learned of this murder first, and by the time we learned of the one in San Diego, my arrangements had already been made."

"Bullshit." Halls shook her head. "You figured we'd be wowed and cowed by your credentials. Lucky for you, you were right. If you're real nice, I'll stop resenting you for that by the time we start driving tomorrow morning."

"Tomorrow morning?" Chang and Amenguale both asked that question in unison, prompting them to glance suspiciously at each other.

"If you think I'm driving to San Diego right now, you're insane. Besides, by the time we get there, it'll be after ten. I need sleep, and Interpol's probably jet-lagged. We'll go first thing in the AM when I don't smell like a butcher shop and I actually trust myself to operate a motor vehicle."

"The autopsy's scheduled for 9:00 AM tomorrow," Amenguale said, "and I told them you'd be there. I assumed that meant you'd drive down tonight."

"Well, you know what happens when you assume," Halls said. "Can you clock me out, Sarge? I'm gonna go do all those things I intended to do before this became an international case. Interpol, meet me here at 6:00 AM."

"Why meet here?" Chang asked.

"I don't trust the tattered remains of my Corolla to make it all the way to San Diego without falling to pieces. Besides, it's official business, I'm taking an official vehicle."

Amenguale pointed an accusatory finger at her. "You can't have the Mercedes."

Halls snapped her fingers. "Damn, thought I'd be able to sneak that one out."

"Oh, I'd be happy to sign it out to you if it was here, but Westphalen already has it for his fugitive pickup in San Jose. Won't be back until day after tomorrow."

"Bastard," Halls muttered good-naturedly. "All right, I'm turning into a pumpkin. Good night."

"Good night, Detective," Chang said. "I will proceed to my hotel and endeavor to sleep."

"You're not jet-lagged?"

"Yes, but my body feels that it is morning." He waved an arm. "It is of no consequence. The nature of working for the International Police is that I travel a great deal. Adjusting to new time zones generally occurs within a day."

"Good for you. Where you staying?"

"The Doubletree on West Huntington Drive."

Halls thought for a moment. "Tell you what, I'll save Interpol some cab fare and give you a lift. Let's go back inside and get your bag, and I'll give you a flash drive with the security footage."

"Thank you, Detective."

———

After Halls dropped him off at his hotel, Chang checked in, showered, and attempted to sleep. He managed to restrain his reaction to the news from the front desk that the hotel was completely non-smoking, and so if he wished to have a cigarette, he would need to exit the premises.

Most of the night was spent staring at the stucco ceiling over the bed, but he did manage to doze for an hour or two. Finally, at 4:00 AM, he got up, put on a beige shirt and brown khakis, and went outside to smoke. Returning to his room, he opened his laptop and inserted the flash drive Halls had given him.

The killer did exactly as Chang expected. He hung his targets upside down in the same manner as the cows and removed their tongues before quartering them and tossing them in with the rest of the bovine grounds.

Whatever doubts Chang may have had were erased by this footage. It was definitely him.

After closing his laptop, Chang went back downstairs and had the front desk call him a taxicab.

By the time the cab arrived, he'd managed to smoke a cigarette, and then another while he waited in the Monrovia Police Department parking lot for Detective Halls.

When she did finally arrive in her poorly maintained vehicle—Chang had feared for his life more than once on the two-mile drive the previous evening, though how much of that was the car and how much was the fatigued state of its driver was an open question—she said, "Sorry I'm late."

To Chang's relief, the detective was practically a different person this morning. There were no bags under her eyes as there had been the previous night, her brown hair was washed, combed, and tied neatly in a ponytail—the previous night it had been badly secured in a poor bun—and she wore a button-down blouse, dress pants, and heeled shoes, which was far more professional-looking than the plain T-shirt, jeans, and sneakers she'd favored yesterday.

Chang figured that at least one of them should look professional, and it was not likely to be him, a thought he had as he rubbed the three-day-old stubble on his chin.

What pleased Chang the most, however, was that Halls no longer carried the odor of fresh meat about her. Given that he was facing at least two hours in the same automobile, this was a legitimate concern.

"Be right back," she said after parking, and one cigarette later, she returned with a set of keys and led him to a high-end sedan that was in far better condition than Halls's.

Chang got into the passenger seat and secured his seatbelt. Halls started up the car, put down both his window and hers— "I assume you're gonna wanna smoke?" she asked as she did so, and Chang nodded in reply—and headed out onto East Lime Avenue.

Halls merged into traffic on Interstate 210. According to the map application Chang had checked on his smartphone earlier, that was the first of several steps that would take them to Interstate 5, which ran down the west coast of the United States from the Canadian border north of Seattle all the way to the Mexican border south of San Diego. As Halls moved into the next lane over, she glanced at Chang.

"So talk to me. What makes you think my meat-packing murderer involves Interpol?"

Chang puffed thoughtfully on a cigarette and stared out at the buildings along the highway. Unlike Hong Kong, Los Angeles had very few skyscrapers. The city's presence on a fault line meant not many structures were more than a few stories tall. It gave the city an openness that Chang found oddly unnerving, especially in the brutal sunshine.

"A year ago," he said, "some elephant poachers received a certain amount of press ..."

CHAPTER FOUR

15 May 2018

Parc National de Zakouma
Barh Signaka, Guera, Chad

THE RAIN WAS COMING down in buckets.

Félix Habré sat in the passenger seat of the jeep, the rain dripping off his brimmed hat and the yellow plastic poncho that covered him from shoulders to knees. The jeep's tires were bouncing as the driver navigated the muddy ridges of the 1200-square mile Zakouma National Park. Félix had always appreciated that the government had gone to the trouble of forming this park back in 1963. Nestled right in the Sahel region of eastern Chad, located handily on the midpoint between the Sahara and the rainforest, the park was a refuge for Africa's dwindling elephant population.

Which made life much easier for Félix. Having them all in one place made it much easier to poach them.

He glanced back at the truck that was pacing the jeep. A third member of his team was driving it, the fourth next to him. Behind them in the truck were the AK-47s, the canvas covering protecting them from the elements.

As they went around a bend, Félix saw a man standing directly in their path. Whoever the man was, he'd chosen his spot well, as the pathway—the ribbon of mud could not truly be dignified with the word "road"—was lined with trees on one side and a muddy pool of water on the other, so there was no way around him.

The man wore a large hat that obscured his face, but as they approached, Félix could see that he was elderly, based on the white wisps of wet hair poking out from under the hat. He could see the man's mouth, though, and it was completely bereft of teeth.

Adoum, the driver, pulled the jeep to a halt even as the old man held up a hand. "Go back!" he cried out in a voice that sounded very peculiar, though Félix figured that to be mostly due to the lack of teeth.

Behind them, the truck also came to a squelching halt on the muddy path.

Félix stood up in the passenger seat of the jeep and shouted to the man over the windshield. "Move aside, old man!"

"Go back! If you harm the elephants, the creature will strike!"

Rolling his eyes, Félix said, "You're insane, old man! Move!"

"What creature?" Adoum asked, suddenly sounding apprehensive.

Whirling on the driver, Félix said, "Nothing." He then chuckled. "A tale told by old fools of a creature of vengeance who harms those who harm the beasts. It's idiocy."

"It's *true!*" the old man cried out. "Listen to me!"

"I am not interested in what you have to say."

The wind shifted a bit, and the brim of the old man's hat was blown back. Félix could now see his entire face.

What was left of it.

His eyes were crazed and haunted. His skin was parched and wrinkled.

That, however, barely registered on Félix, for what drew his attention was between his mad eyes and his toothless mouth.

The old man's nose was *gone*. The barely healed flesh around where it had been was scarred and irritated, surrounding a revolting hole in the middle of the old man's face, leaving the septum and the back of the soft palate exposed.

Félix had always thought of himself as having a strong stomach. He'd seen plenty of exposed innards of both humans and animals in his time, but usually they were already dead or dying. This was a living, talking person, yet he was peering right into his very skull. It took an effort to hold down his breakfast.

For his part, the old man continued to rant. "I was once like you! I once hunted the elephants, but the creature made me pay! He killed my people, but let me live to warn others! Heed my warning, and *go back!*"

From behind him, Hassan, the driver of the truck, cried out, "Should I shoot him?"

Félix swallowed down his nausea, Hassan's bluntness like a welcome bucket of ice water in his face. "No, a dead body would force the park rangers to investigate—or force us to pay prohibitively larger bribes. Just—just move him out of the way."

Nodding, Hassan shifted the truck into park, hopped out, and manhandled the old man until he was off the road.

The entire time, the old man was screaming, "Go back! Go *back!* You won't survive!"

Next to him, Adoum looked as frightened as Félix was starting to feel.

Seeing it in his subordinate helped remove it from himself. Angrily, and as much self-directed as it was at Adoum, Félix cried, "Snap out of it! We have a job to do!"

"What if he's telling the truth? Did you see his nose?"

"He's insane," Félix said quickly, not wanting to think about it, even as Hassan got back into the truck. "Let's move!"

It was always best to go after the elephants early in the rainy season. This soon, the rain hadn't had a chance to accumulate—by the end of June, beginning of July, the region would be better named Zakouma National Lake, there was so much flooding—but the actual downpours were intense enough that most folks stayed away. Especially those tiresome conservationists.

For many years, Félix worked as a guide to the park, usually for insipid tourists or those very same conservationists. The former were irritating, but at least tipped well. The latter were self-righteous and pig-headed, and tipped very poorly. They spoke of the elephant population being endangered, as if the creatures couldn't still reproduce or something. It was madness. They still had calves, which the poachers generally avoided killing, since their tusks weren't developed yet. And they all died eventually in any case. What difference did it make if it was from one of his weapons or from old age?

The heavy rains meant he was likely to be left alone—by everyone except for noseless lunatics, in any event. Not that conservationists wandered around armed or anything, but killing or even injuring one came with difficulties and attention that Félix preferred to avoid. He'd already spent time in Korotoro Prison, an experience he was very much not eager to repeat.

At least he didn't have to worry about the park rangers. He'd adequately bribed all of them to keep their distance and give him and his team free rein of Zakouma. The bribes were considerable, but as nothing compared to what the Chinese were offering for the ivory of the elephants' tusks. Even though it meant bribing pretty much everyone who worked for the park, as well as about a dozen government officials, it was still such a small percentage of what they got from the Chinese that it wasn't much more than a rounding error in terms of profits.

So everybody won. The Chinese got the ivory they craved, Félix and his team got embarrassingly large amounts of money, and a bunch of civil servants got something to actually put into a savings account for once in their miserable lives.

Well, truly not everybody. The conservationists didn't win, but they had plenty of elephants in zoos that were doing fine.

Then there were the crazy people like that old man and his mad stories. Keeping the park rangers away had probably had the unintended consequence of allowing that mad old imbecile to roam free. Félix had, in fact, heard stories about some kind of creature of vengeance before, though never from someone who claimed to have encountered it.

But the old man had likely lost his nose in some accident. He was probably indigent and couldn't afford proper care of it. And no doubt his teeth had fallen out in the natural course of life.

That had to be it.

Checking his GPS, he saw that they were getting closer. Putting a hand on Adoum's soaked shoulder prompted the latter to decelerate, with the truck doing likewise and pulling alongside the jeep as both vehicles stopped.

"We go the rest of the way on foot." Félix then grinned. "Don't wish to spook the herd, now do we?"

The two in the truck chuckled. Adoum said nothing. Hassan went to the back of the truck and started distributing the AK-47s. Each member of the team checked the weapon to make sure it was loaded properly. They also made sure they had spare ammunition.

Félix always felt that he made the right choice in terms of profession, mostly due to how easy it was. He didn't know how poachers who were in it to salvage meat did it. When all you were after were two three-meter ivory protrusions, the fate of the rest of the body was comparatively negligible. If you wanted to bag, say, a pheasant illegally, you had to use buckshot or some other method that left enough of the body intact to serve as a meal or three. Automatic weapons were out of the question.

Not so with elephants. You could keep your distance and pretty much guarantee a kill. Especially with four people doing the shooting.

They moved quickly through the park, their boots squelching in the mud, the rain sluicing off their hats, their arms kept free via slits in the sides of the yellow ponchos. Adoum lagged behind a bit. Apparently the toothless, noseless old man was still distracting him. If he kept it up, Félix was going to dock his pay.

Félix couldn't hear much over the rain, but he felt a mild vibration in the ground that indicated that the elephants were nearby. He raised a fist in the air and stopped moving forward, though Hassan had already stopped.

Moving more slowly now, the quartet eased their way toward the herd, who were under a copse of trees in an attempt to stay, if not dry—that wasn't really possible this time of year—not totally soaked.

"Remember," Félix whispered as he raised his AK-47, "aim high. There's no value in the calves, at least not till they're grown."

Once they got close enough, he yelled, "Fire!"

———

The first break in the rain occurred in the evening. Though he had rented an SUV, Yuvraj Varaich still wasn't entirely comfortable driving into Zakouma while it was actually raining.

He went next door and knocked. "Chanan, you awake?"

His intern opened the door. Yuvraj flinched a bit, as he always seemed to around Chanan Carlisle. It was ridiculous. Over the past three decades working with the Wildlife Conservation Society, Yuvraj had spent time with some of the nastiest predators the Earth had to offer. He'd been proximate to buffalo stampedes, angry bears, and panthers in heat, and never once cowered. Yet every time he was in Chanan's presence, he wanted to throw up his arms and beg for mercy.

Chanan stared at him with his penetrating eyes and shaved head, and said, "I am awake, yes."

"Good. The rain's stopped, and I want to see if I can find out what happened to those GPS transmitters on the elephants. I mean, it could just be that they're not as waterproofed as the manufacturers said."

"That is not what you believe." Chanan did not pose it as a question.

Yuvraj shook his head. "No." Earlier that day, several of the subcutaneous GPS transmitters they'd put in the elephants in Zakouma had lost their signal. One or two would not be noteworthy—the things failed on a regular basis for the most mundane of reasons—but they lost half a dozen. Worse, in the time since then, none of the others had moved.

Long, bitter experience taught Yuvraj to fear the worst.

"You know," he said, as Chanan got his gear together, "I got into this business right around when they passed the international ban on the ivory trade in 1989. It slowed the poachers down for, what, five minutes?" He sighed. "Hey, maybe we'll be lucky, and it really will be the rain."

They were not lucky. A long, difficult drive through the darkened park later, and they arrived at the location from where the GPS trackers indicated the elephants had not moved.

That was, it turned out, for good reason. The headlights of the SUV clearly showed that the elephants had been butchered. Bullet holes riddled what was left of their bodies.

Of course, the tusks had all been removed, dried blood caked around the skin from which the tusks had been violently ripped, meaning it had happened immediately after the elephants had been killed—or, in some cases, no doubt, before they had succumbed to the bullet wounds, but were too injured to defend themselves against the poachers' actions.

"I hear something," Chanan said.

Yuvraj cupped a hand to his ear, and then he heard it too.

Before Yuvraj could even say anything, though, Chanan had sprung into action, running into the sea of elephant corpses.

Following more gingerly, he came across Chanan standing over an elephant calf who had survived. The sound had been the calf keening.

Two drops of rain fell onto Yuvraj's face.

He looked up, and four more drops hit his face. "The skies are about to open. C'mon, let's get the calf back to the SUV before the biblical flood starts. We'll come back in the morning."

As they moved to gently pick up the animal, Chanan said, "The rain will wash away the evidence."

Yuvraj snorted. "Right, because gathering evidence will really matter when park authorities already let this happen in broad daylight." He glanced up at the clouds accumulating in the night sky. "Well, not *broad*, but you know what I mean. I'm sure they were all paid quite handsomely to not give a damn."

"How do you know it was daylight?" Chanan asked as they placed the calf in the back of the SUV.

The infant barely fit, and Yuvraj had to put down the back seats to give the calf enough room. "Because it was midafternoon when the GPS units died." He pointed at the calf. "And because that little guy's alive. They could see their targets. Had to make sure they didn't hit the tusks, and they tried to spare any calves."

"Why would poachers care about sparing a baby?" Chanan asked as he wrapped the calf in one of the blankets they had in the back of the SUV.

Yuvraj opened the driver's side door as the rain started to intensify. "A dead calf's of no use to them. A live calf will grow up to be another source of ivory. Let's go."

"I'll sit in the back with him," Chanan said.

Nodding, Yuvraj got in and put the SUV into gear.

————

Félix held his smartphone to his ear, speaking in Mandarin. "Yes, they will arrive within the month.... No, I cannot send them sooner. Besides, they are already gone.... The ship that I have secured has a guarantee that it will not be searched by any port authorities. Or if it is, those authorities have been paid for.... Well, yes, there's always a chance, but this vessel carries the most minimal risk of such.... It is called the *Flower of Senegal* and it should arrive in Shanghai no later than the thirteenth of June.... Yes.... Thank you, goodbye."

He shook his head and walked across the warehouse floor to Adoum. They had transferred all the tusks to this place in Al Junaynah, right over the border in Sudan. He'd spent the last week cleaning and packing them, and also finalizing the arrangements to ship them to his clients, one of whom he had just had his twelfth reassuring phone call with. For whatever reason, Rao wanted the ivory as fast as possible. If Rao had had his way, Félix would have shipped them via Federal Express. But his shipment was already on the *Flower of Senegal*, where it wasn't likely to be x-rayed by anyone, a state of affairs he would be unable to avoid with commercial shipping carriers.

"How soon until this last batch is all packaged?"

"Excuse me?" Adoum stared at him.

Félix blinked, realized he'd asked the question in Mandarin. In French, he asked the question again.

"Another hour, perhaps ninety minutes," Adoum said.

"Good."

A voice came from behind Félix. "Excuse me."

Whirling around, Félix saw a man wearing a bulky coat and gloves, and a face mask that was in the shape of an elephant.

Unable to help himself, Félix started to laugh.

But that laugh died in his throat when he saw that the masked man was also carrying an AK-47.

Félix pointed at the door through which the masked man had come. "You're trespassing! Get out!"

The masked man's voice was muffled by the elephant mask. "You have committed crimes for which you must pay."

"I've served my time, thank you. Are you familiar with Korotoro?" Félix shuddered at the memory of the lice, the rotten food, the brackish water, the filth, the overcrowding. The place gave snake pits a bad name.

"I'm not interested in arresting you. That has already failed, and I do not have the authority to do so in any case."

Out of the corner of his eye, Félix saw Idriss moving slowly and quietly through the boxes in the warehouse, a Beretta in hand.

Stalling, Félix asked, "Why are you here, then?"

"To make you pay for what you did to forty-three adult elephants in Zakouma last week, as well as one calf."

Adoum said, "We spared the calf."

Félix winced. That was as good as an admission of guilt. Not that that seemed to matter here.

"Elephants have family units very much like humans. The calf saw you murder her parents, and it traumatized her. She would not take any food or water, and she died in my arms. All so you could have your ivory."

"Look—" Félix started, even as Idriss drew in closer, now standing next to one of the boxes.

But before he could continue, the masked man turned toward Idriss and shot the AK-47 on full automatic. It splintered the box and cut Idriss to ribbons.

Félix winced, more concerned with the loss of the goods inside the box than the loss of Idriss. There were always more mercenaries to be hired. Much of central Africa was impoverished, and many nations of the African continent could not afford to pay their military a living wage, which made it easy to recruit them for this kind of more lucrative work.

"As I was saying—" Félix began again, but then the masked man turned to face him with the weapon pointed right at Félix's face.

"I am not interested in what you have to say."

Félix heart skipped a beat as he heard the exact words he'd said to the crazy old man—perhaps not as crazy as he thought—when he warned him about the creature of vengeance.

All at once, Félix realized he should have listened to the old man. Or at least not dismissed him *quite* so readily.

In thirty-two years of life in one of the most violent regions on Earth, Félix Habré had somehow contrived never to be wounded by a bullet. He'd been stabbed a few times, on the streets of N'Djamena growing up, and again in Korotoro, but never once had he been shot.

He had not expected it to be so *hot*. The feel of the bullets as they ripped apart flesh and muscle and bone was almost scorching. That on top of the impact, which he *had* expected, like being hit repeatedly with a hammer.

A red-hot hammer, in fact.

The next thing he knew, he was lying on the floor. His vision was hazy as he stared up at the ceiling. Félix felt no pain—nor much of anything else. Thoughts proved difficult to form, and he couldn't make any of his limbs move. In fact, he couldn't swear to whether or not his limbs still existed.

He supposed he was going into shock.

Dimly, he registered the arrival of the fourth member of his team, Hassan, who started screaming in his native Senegalese. More fire from the AK-47, more screams—all, to Félix's disappointment, from Hassan—more wood being splintered along with flesh.

An elephant mask appeared to block out the view of the ceiling. "That was the first step. Two of your men are dead. You will follow them. But your other employee still lives, and he will remain alive. I have heard that you were warned of me by one of the heralds whom I have left behind. He is obviously no longer effective, so your companion here will take his place as my new herald."

Placing the AK-47 down on the floor, the masked man then reached into the ridiculously bulky coat—why would anyone wear such a thing in this heat?—and pulled out what appeared to be two hooks on long metal handles.

The masked man ushered Adoum over to the two of them. Félix could see the terror in Adoum's eyes, the beads of sweat cascading down his face. The fear the young man had had when they'd encountered the noseless, toothless herald in Zakouma was back tenfold now.

"Sit at the top of his head and hold the forehead still," the masked man said.

With what little energy he had remaining, Félix hoped and prayed that Adoum would fight past his fear and attack this madman.

Instead, the fool did as he was told. Adoum had been a soldier once, and had served Félix well as a mercenary, yet he was completely cowed by this murderer who had killed two of his fellows and was about to do the same to Félix himself.

Félix couldn't move, couldn't speak, could feel the life draining from him as Adoum cupped Félix's jaw with his right hand and held Félix's forehead with his left.

The masked man pulled a small switchblade from his coat pocket next. "I will show you," he said to Adoum, "the fate of those who would rip elephants' tusks from their bodies. You will warn those who come after you of what you are about to see."

"W-what am I—?" Adoum cut himself off and Félix heard him swallow hard.

"I will show you. First, we must cut open his face."

A moment ago, Félix felt nothing.

Then the masked man applied the scalpel to the laugh line on the left side of his face and started to cut.

Suddenly, Félix felt *everything*. The scalpel's slicing through flesh drew him out of shock, as the pain coursed through his body, forcing him to not only feel the blade cutting the flesh of his face, but also bring the gunshot wounds' agony back into sharp relief.

Félix screamed.

Adoum held his head in place, but the rest of his body squirmed and convulsed with agony.

"Hold his head *still*," the masked man said as he gripped the dual-hook device. The rounded bottom part slid easily into Félix's mouth, thanks to his throat-ripping screams. He felt the two straight hooks slide into his nostrils, an action that might have made him shudder with disgust were he not already writhing in brutal agony.

Then he heard the sound.

The dying Félix would probably never be able to articulate what the bone-crunching sound was *like*, exactly. It only added to the pain that simply would *not* stop.

But now, blessedly, he felt himself sliding into oblivion once again, this final assault on his face shutting his mind and body down.

He no longer saw the elephant mask or the ceiling of the warehouse, and the voice he heard seemed so distant: "I have disarticulated his nose and palate from the remainder of his skull. This is the closest one can come to duplicating what you have done to the elephants you've tormented."

The last words Félix heard were Adoum's: "He doesn't look like a person anymore."

His last thoughts were of the old man warning him to go back in a plaintive howl, and wishing to hell he'd listened.

CHAPTER FIVE

7 June 2018

**People's Silk Warehouse
Shanghai, China**

RAO WEI HAD to stop himself from running to the company warehouse when word came in that the crate had been delivered.

He had been ruthlessly keeping track of the progress of the *Flower of Senegal* since Habré had given him the name over the phone, tracking it as it chugged along through the Arabian Sea to Colombo, Sri Lanka; across the Indian Ocean and the Malacca Strait to Singapore, Malaysia; up the South China Sea to Taipei, Taiwan; and finally through the East China Sea to Shanghai, arriving seven days ahead of the vague arrival date Habré had provided.

It took another full day for the shipping container carrying his crate to be placed on the loading dock and his crate sorted out and put on a truck to be delivered to this warehouse.

But as soon he received the text message that it had arrived, he told his secretary to have a car ready to take him to the warehouse.

He did not explain why, and she did not ask, which was why she had remained his secretary for all these years.

Upon arrival, he dismissed the entire warehouse staff for the day.

The foreman—whose name Rao was fairly certain was Hsu—hesitated. "Sir, the accounting department instructed us to have the inventory completed by close of business today."

"Inform the accounting department that it will be completed tomorrow, on my authority. If they question it, have them call my secretary."

Hsu pursed his lips. "Yes, sir."

Rao appreciated Hsu's dedication to duty, but he needed to do this himself.

After Hsu and his workers all left, Rao realized that it might have been easier to keep one or two of them around to open the massive crate. It required physical labor, something Rao detested.

But no. He preferred to keep the company's less legal business affairs to himself. Allowing others to assist him meant also allowing them to participate in the profits. He saw no reason to share in those. Besides, the risk was all his. Additional help would only provide more opportunities for leaks. Rao had done his research. Most illegal operations were shut down by low-level functionaries who were caught doing one thing and then traded a light sentence for information on other illegal activities.

Rao was not about to let that happen to him. Bad enough the number of public officials he had to bribe …

So on his own, he found a crowbar and managed to pry open the crate.

After that, he had to pause for several seconds, winded. Rao was an executive who ate good food and smoked two packs a day. He spent his days sitting at his desk or in meeting rooms, his nights with his family at the dinner table or on the couch. The most exercise he got was when he walked to the elevator that took him to the parking garage, where his car was waiting for him at the elevator bank.

He was not suited to manual labor, and he stood for several seconds, hands on knees, stooped over, coughing, attempting to recover his breath.

Perhaps it might have been worth it to bring *one* manual laborer in on the deal.

Once he recovered, he inspected the interior of the crate and smiled widely. Habré did his work well. The tusks were cleaned and packed carefully, and mostly undamaged. A few dents and scrapes, but that was to be expected from elephants not in captivity. At the very least, Habré's people did a good job of removing the tusks so the cuts on the end were clean.

Rao's smartphone buzzed. With a sigh, he checked it, in case it was a matter of import.

There were two text messages. One was from his wife, which he ignored; the other was from one of his importers in San Francisco, expressing once again his urgent need for a clean tusk. "My clientele is eager for more merchandise," his text said.

"Worry not, Mr. Tsing," Rao muttered at the phone, "you'll have what you need."

Rao hefted one tusk that looked almost perfect out from the crate so he could examine it more closely in better light.

It was indeed unmarred. Somehow, the elephant that this tusk had been attached to had led a sedate life. The tusk was long enough to have come from a full-grown animal, but there were almost no scrapes or other markings.

"Beautiful," he muttered, replacing the heavy tusk back in the crate. "Just beautiful. You'll take this one, Tsing."

From behind him, a muffled voice said, "The creatures you had murdered for those tusks were beautiful."

Whirling around, he saw a man wearing a big coat and with an elephant-shaped mask covering his face.

"Who are you? How did you get in here?"

"Those animals lived in peace in the veldt until your hired thugs destroyed them."

Rao held up his smartphone. "Get out! I'm calling the police—"

"By all means. I am sure the constabulary will be fascinated by all the illegal ivory in this warehouse."

Rao swallowed. The masked man was correct, of course. He couldn't risk the police here, at least not the uniformed officers who would respond to an emergency call. All the high-ranking personnel he'd bribed would not be involved in responding to a break-in.

"What do you want?"

"I want the elephants that were massacred to give you a useless commodity to still be alive."

The masked man started to advance on Rao, who stumbled sideways against the crate of ivory, dropping the tusk he'd earmarked for Tsing to the floor.

The masked man grabbed Rao by his arms.

"Failing that, I want you to pay for their deaths."

Again, Rao swallowed. "And how do you intend to make me do that?"

"Painfully."

———

Hsu Zhung exited the Metro and did the three-block walk to the warehouse the same as he did every morning. While he walked, he played the voicemail on his phone for the twentieth time.

"Mr. Hsu, this is Mr. Lin from accounting. It seems I owe you an apology, Mr. Hsu, as Mr. Rao did indeed authorize your staff's departure for the afternoon today. Obviously, the termination proceedings I threatened you with will not be taking place, and I look forward to the inventory report by the end of business *tomorrow*. Good day."

Hsu intended never to erase that message from Lin. The obnoxious windbag from accounting had been an annoyance for all of Hsu's time with People's Silk, and Hsu took tremendous satisfaction in the obsequious tone that he had been forced to take following his call to Mr. Rao's secretary.

The foreman did wonder what was so important that Mr. Rao had to clear the warehouse for the afternoon, but Hsu hadn't achieved his position by questioning his superiors.

Several of his staff were already waiting by the front door when he arrived. He muttered greetings to all of them, glad to see that they were punctual.

Once he unlocked the warehouse door, though, he was assaulted by a horrible smell.

"What *is* that?" one of the men cried, putting a hand over his face.

Wrinkling his nose, Hsu pulled a handkerchief out of his pocket and covered his nose and mouth with it, entering the warehouse cautiously.

Flies were buzzing about, which combined with the smell made Hsu fear the worst. There'd been a homicide in his apartment building when he was a child growing up. The upstairs flat had carried a similar stench, and there were flies buzzing just like this, too.

Turning a corner, he saw several elephant tusks on the floor, one of which was sticking straight upward. That one was covered in red.

A second later, he registered what the red was, and why it was sticking upward: it was protruding from Mr. Rao's chest. Blood soaked his shirt and chest, with gore and bones and muscle visible surrounding the wound made by the tusk.

Mr. Rao's eyes were wide open, staring blankly at the ceiling, his mouth also wide open, the flies zipping in and out, one landing right on his bloody tongue.

Running quickly back to the door, Hsu tried and failed to swallow down the bile. Before making it more than a meter, he threw up all over the floor and wall, and possibly on one or two of his staff.

One of the women pulled out her phone and called the police.

One of the men pulled out his phone and started taking pictures.

Wiping puke away from his lips with his sleeve, Hsu stammered, "Who—who would do this?"

"What," the woman who called the police said, "kill Mr. Rao or be in possession of all this illegal ivory?"

Hsu had no answer for that.

CHAPTER SIX

6 June 2019

Interstate 5
En route between Los Angeles and San Diego,
United States of America

CHANG FINISHED his tale by telling Halls: "There was another murder a week later of Harold Tsing in San Francisco."

"That one, I remember." She slowed down as she came up upon a car that was only traveling at fifty miles per hour in the left lane. "Got stabbed through the eye with a letter opener?"

"Through the nose. And it was not merely a letter opener, but one that had a handle made from ivory that had been poached from Chad." Chang finished his cigarette and tossed it out the window. He would have preferred not to litter, but Halls had said that they weren't allowed to let cigarette butts collect in the police cars, and then she had added that "it can keep company with all the other dead ciggies on the 5."

"Right, I remember, they couldn't find any prints or DNA or blood that didn't belong to the victim."

"Yes, he was very careful."

"And that was the same guy who killed the poachers and the guy in China?"

"I believe so, yes."

"That's a shit-ton of travel in, what, a week?"

Chang nodded. "The killer obviously has significant resources."

"Yeeeeah." Halls shook her head. "And he wore the elephant mask for each one?"

"Of those three murders, yes. He wishes to complete the circle on behalf of the animals who have been wronged. That is why for your murders, he wore a bovine mask."

Halls gave Chang a sidelong glance. "Look at you with the impressive adjectives. Not bad for someone using his second language."

"In fact, English is the fourth tongue of the nine languages I speak."

"Fancy fancy." Halls blew out a breath. "All these animal masks—it's reminding me of something, but I'm damned if I can remember what. I'm sorry, it's something niggling the back of my head. Could be nothing."

Chang suspected it was very much something. Halls may have been inexperienced with solving murders, but he saw in her the instincts of a detective. If she was reminded of something, then there was something there. But it did no good to fret about it. It would likely migrate to her conscious mind in due course.

"Okay," Halls said, "so what exactly does 'complete the circle' mean in this context?"

"I am fairly certain that the killer was raised as a Buddhist, or at the very least embraces Buddhist teachings."

Halls asked, "And being a Buddhist has what to do with this?"

"Are you familiar with the concept of karma?"

"Sure. So that's what he's doing, goosing karma along? He's making what goes around come around by completing the circle, like you said?"

"Something along those lines, yes. There are other similar cases around the world over the past two decades."

Halls whirled her head toward Chang for a moment, then

flicked her eyes back to the road. "Wait, twenty years? What the fuck, Interpol?"

"Excuse me?"

"Well, don't take this the wrong way, but if it took me twenty years to close a case, they might seriously consider firing me with cause."

Chang allowed himself a small smile. "I *have* had other cases in the ensuing time period, Detective."

"That's a relief."

"In addition, Interpol's policy is to build casework, which requires time and effort."

"Yeah, I get that, but twenty years? That's the time it takes to build a pension, not a case."

"I have exaggerated a touch," Chang admitted. "While I have attempted to solve these murders in my spare time, it did not truly become my most important case until three years ago."

"Bosses didn't take it seriously until then?"

Chang was pleased to see that Halls understood. "Yes, exactly. It has been difficult to convince my superiors that these murders, which go back at least as far as 1997, are a single person."

"At least?"

"The only murders that I have documentation of date to then. And there is little pattern to the duration between the murders, which has made it difficult for authorities to determine that there is a singular presence."

Halls snorted. "You'd think the masks would clue someone in."

"Yes, and no. One reason I have been able to make this case a priority is the improvement in technology. There was a gap of twelve years between killings. Indeed, I had thought—had hoped—that the murders had stopped after 2004. Those deaths were also in several countries, including South Africa, where forensic practices were very much behind the times, shall we say. With the improvements in evidence-gathering and DNA analysis, not to mention more common surveillance, it became a simpler task to gather intelligence. Indeed, were it not for the surveillance footage from

MCD showing the killer in a mask, this would not have obviously been part of my case."

Halls put on her turn signal to pass a sedan on the right that was apparently not going at sufficient speed to suit her. "Slow down, Interpol. I'm not a hundred percent convinced this *is* part of your case. And our surveillance footage sucked big green rocks through a straw."

"Colorful metaphors notwithstanding, when he began his—his crusade, for lack of a better term, forensic science was far more primitive, particularly in parts of the world where many of his targets ply their trade." Chang took out another cigarette and lit it. After inhaling, he mused, "Perhaps that is why he stopped when he did. He feared discovery. At least until 2016, when he could no longer stand idly by."

"That was when you got your bosses to take the case seriously?"

Chang nodded. "Indeed. Since then, I have been able to gather evidence from other cases, but much of it was not catalogued or stored properly. However, I have been able to test some biological residue from previous murders, and the DNA evidence has proven that, for at least some of the cases, it is the same killer."

Halls let out a bitter chuckle that bespoke experience. "No, wait, let me guess—there was no match in the system?"

"Correct. Which simply means he has not been convicted of a crime in a country where they have DNA evidence of criminals, which is an alternate theory to the twelve-year gap."

"So what dragged him out of retirement in 2016?" Halls asked.

"Men in India who were skinning tigers."

"Wait, those four guys who were skinned alive next to a pile of tiger pelts in Kolkata?"

Chang was surprised. Outside of India and Bangladesh, and wildlife conservation circles, he did not believe the case had attracted much attention. "Yes, that's the one."

Halls nodded. "My ex was *seriously* into tigers. Carried on about that case for *weeks*. She kept trying to show me the pictures of the dead bodies and the skinned tigers, but I refused to look. I don't remember anything about a tiger mask, though."

At the use of the feminine pronoun to describe Halls's ex, Chang shot her a glance, but said nothing. In his experience, American police were among the most conservative, and it was rare to find one who was openly homosexual. But then, mores had been changing in that regard in the States with great rapidity, and perhaps Chang's assumptions about US cops were out of date.

Aloud, he said, "Only one witness mentioned an animal mask, and that detail was deliberately withheld from the press."

"Right." As a matter of course, police often withheld one detail from the press as a fact that only the perpetrator would know, making it easier to separate false confessions from real ones.

"There was no surveillance, unfortunately, which was likely a precaution on the killer's part."

"Yeah, that case was revolting." Halls visibly shuddered. "And I guess we're lucky he wasn't so smart about MCD, huh?"

"Or perhaps he is getting sloppier with age."

Halls nodded. "He hasn't been caught for twenty-three years. That makes a guy cocky sometimes." She had been cruising in the center lane for some time, but now signaled and moved back to the left lane. "What was the last case before the break? That was, what, 2004?"

"Yes. There were two, in fact. The first was in the Congo, then another in South Africa."

CHAPTER SEVEN

3 September 2004

Odzala-Kokoua National Park
Republic of the Congo

THE HARD PART for Massimo Scialdone had been convincing Annabella to take a vacation.

She always had the same excuse: she didn't trust the staff of Vino Scialdone—the Tuscan winery that had been in their family for the better part of a century—to do anything right in her absence. However, their sons, Primo and Secondo, were now doing most of the day-to-day of running the place, and Annabella and Massimo were too old to do as much of it as they used to.

Even with that, it had taken Massimo two years—aided by Primo, Secondo, and their daughters-in-law—to finally talk her into it. It helped that their children had jointly given the stay at one of the Odzala Discovery Camps in the Congo to them as an anniversary present. Annabella had spent the day they boarded the train that would take them from the heart of the Tuscan hills to Rome, and thence to the airport, on her phone. Eventually, Primo stopped taking her calls, at which point Annabella sent a stream of texts, which only paused during the period when she wasn't allowed to use her phone on the plane from Rome to the Congo.

After three days, however, Annabella had finally put the phone away, and even admitted that she was glad she'd taken the vacation. For his part, Massimo was grateful for the peace and quiet.

The camp was built into the forest canopy, so it was like living in a treehouse. A luxurious, well-appointed treehouse, but still. It was lovely, from the handwritten note from the staff welcoming them when they checked in to the attentive waitstaff at the bar and restaurant to the expert, and patient, tour guides.

Today, they were doing gorilla tracking, which involved hiking to the locations where gorilla families congregated. Specific families were set aside for people to view, others kept away from people for conservation purposes.

The expedition included only one other couple, two Germans named Helmut and Helga. They each referred to each other as "Hel," which they thought was hilarious, which was more than Massimo was willing to admit. He also wasn't willing to admit that he spoke German—a language that Annabella was not fluent in. Instead, they mostly conversed in French. This worked out nicely for everyone, as their guide, Etienne, was much more comfortable with French than he was with Italian or German.

At one point, Annabella asked, "Etienne, do you have many issues with poachers?"

"Occasionally." Etienne's voice, Massimo noticed, had a tinge of sadness. "More often than we'd like, though less often than we fear."

Helmut said, "I heard there was an incident recently."

"Yes," Etienne said with obvious reluctance. "But the poachers were driven off before they could do any more harm."

"So they did do some," Annabella said.

Etienne simply nodded.

"I saw the most amazing thing in Rwanda last year," Helmut said. "It was a pair of young gorillas actually dismantling one of the snare traps set for them!"

Annabella nodded. "I remember reading about that. I was impressed that they knew the trap for what it was."

"They did it very nimbly, too," Helmut added. "Probably saved a few lives."

"It is a barbaric practice," Etienne said. "Particularly in this case. Most poachers are people who are desperate for money. Bushmeat can be sold for four Euros a pound or more—that is quite a large payday, especially for a three-hundred-pound gorilla."

"Particularly for the poorer people who live here," Helmut added.

"Yes," Etienne said quietly. Massimo noted a bit of resentment at Helmut's tone, but Etienne was too good a tour guide to say anything.

But Massimo was more interested in the reasons for targeting gorillas in particular. "You say people eat the meat of gorillas?"

"Many consider it a great delicacy, unfortunately. Also, their hands are often considered objects of great interest, as ashtrays or other household items. The poachers who attacked recently removed the hands and heads of the gorillas before butchering them. I can only assume they adorned their dwelling places with the latter, while selling the former."

Massimo felt nauseous. "That is appalling," he said, followed by a few curses in Italian.

"That is the word used in polite company, yes," Etienne said dryly, and everyone got a chuckle out of that.

Suddenly, Helga wrinkled her nose. "Do I smell smoke?" she asked her husband in German.

Looking up, Massimo saw the smoke that she smelled about fifty meters ahead, coming from the tree line.

Etienne cursed in French and started running toward the smoke. Massimo did likewise, as did Helga. Annabella and Helmut followed behind, moving more slowly.

As he ran, Massimo saw a man emerge from behind the trees. He was moving quickly and elegantly, like he was trained in how to run.

But that wasn't the odd part. The man was wearing a gorilla mask that covered his entire head.

Massimo knew it was a gorilla mask because the man hesitated in his running just long enough to look at the five of them as they moved toward the smoke.

Then he ran away even faster.

Etienne ignored the man running away, more concerned with the smoke itself. As they got closer, Massimo could smell the fire.

Helga tried to chase down the man in the gorilla mask, but he sped too far ahead, and she was soon out of breath from the exertion. Helmut ran ahead to catch up to her and console her.

Massimo followed Etienne into the forest. He could see the flames now, though they seemed to be in a single, circular area.

Passing several large trees, he came into a small clearing and saw a firepit. Someone had placed several stones on the ground, all about ankle-to-knee height, with a fire inside. Massimo breathed a sigh of relief, seeing that the fire, while surprisingly intense for a firepit, was contained.

Only then did the other smell register: burning flesh.

Peering closely, Massimo Scialdone saw a sight that he feared he would never forget until his dying day: five human bodies being burned.

At first, he didn't believe it. His mind refused to accept what his eyes were seeing.

But though they were quickly being seared beyond recognition, they were definitely human beings.

Massimo heard someone scream.

It took him a few seconds to realize that it was he himself who was screaming at the sight of flesh being boiled and blackened, of body parts becoming so lost in the flames that they were no longer visible, of each burned corpse becoming slowly less recognizable as a person.

Seeing eyes boil away, seeing hands melt, seeing legs shrink and burn.

Massimo didn't stop screaming for a quite a while.

Somewhere he registered that Etienne had taken out his satellite phone—there was no cell service in this part of the park, which was deliberate, but the sat phone was necessary for emergencies—and called the authorities.

———

Much later, Massimo sat with Annabella and Helmut in the bar at the camp. Massimo was on his fifth vodka. Having grown up in a winery, he rarely drank socially, as it was too much like work, but today, he drank. He went with vodka because it was the strongest thing they had. In truth, he would happily have guzzled grain alcohol if it helped get the image of the burned bodies out of his mind.

"Will Helga join us?" Annabella asked Helmut.

He nodded. "Shortly. She said she had to take care of—of something, I don't recall what."

An awkward silence followed.

Annabella had never been one to tolerate silences, awkward or otherwise. "I wonder who that man was."

"He was fast, I'll you that," Helmut said. "Hel ran marathons in her youth. She is not a slow woman. But that—that *person* in the gorilla mask outpaced her easily. Not many can do that, especially when Hel has her dander up."

Massimo threw back more vodka. "I wonder what would drive a man to do that."

"What, kill someone?" Helmut asked.

"Not just kill. To burn people in such a manner—it is despicable. Nothing human could have done that."

"He seemed human to me," Helmut muttered.

Annabella smiled wryly. "Actually, he seemed like a gorilla."

Helmut chuckled. Massimo drank more vodka.

Helga chose that moment to come into the bar. "Schnapps, please," she said to the bartender before kissing her husband. "Hel."

"Hel. We were just talking about the man in the gorilla suit and how he outran even you."

In German, she said, "Of course he outran me, you idiot, I'm fifty-four years old."

Massimo almost choked on his vodka at that. "My apologies," he said quickly between sputters, covering up that he understood German. "I swallowed too quickly."

Helmut added, back in French, "Massimo was wondering how a human being could do what he did to those five people."

Helga said, "I have spoken with Etienne. Apparently, the men in that firepit were among the ones who poached their gorillas. According to the coroner, they were trapped in the same type of snares that the poachers use to trap the gorillas."

"Like the one I saw the young gorillas taking apart in Rwanda last year?" Helmut asked.

Nodding, Helga paused to take the Schnapps from the bartender and take a very long sip of it before continuing. "Not only that, but after they were trapped, they were burned *alive*." She looked at Massimo. "I'd be much more curious what manner of human being could do what *they* did. Cut off gorillas' heads and hands and sell them for meat?"

"We butcher cows," Massimo said quietly. "What is the difference?"

"Cows are imbeciles!" Helga took a breath, realizing she was shouting. "I am sorry. Cows are bred for food. Gorillas are actually intelligent. Remember, Hel saw them *dismantle* a trap! They are not to be eaten, they are to be encouraged! No, my friend, those who did this are monsters, and the world is well to be rid of them forever. Had I caught up to that man in the mask, knowing what I know now, I would have shaken his hand."

Massimo did not respond to Helga's words at first, instead slugging down the rest of his vodka and ordering another.

Once it came, and the uncomfortable silence had gone on long enough that Annabella was on the verge of another attempt to continue the conversation, Massimo finally said, "Perhaps you are right, Helga. Personally, I have always believed that vengeance is the purview of God, not humanity. I also recall a rather tiresome cliché that is nonetheless apt: two wrongs do not make a right. And

I know this as well—until the day I die, I will never ever forget the sight of those human beings being burned alive. And I will never stop thinking of the person who could do such a thing to other people—*any* other people, regardless of what they may have done—as anything but a monster."

The awkward silence that followed Massimo's pronouncement lasted quite some time. Even Annabella found no way to break it.

CHAPTER EIGHT

12 September 2004

Four Seasons Hotel
Miami, Florida, United States of America

AFTER CLIMBING into the backseat of the taxicab that would take him from Miami International Airport to the Four Seasons Hotel, George Moorcroft checked his phone again.

Still there was no new news.

He'd only learned the day before that the reason he hadn't heard anything from Beauvoir's team was that the Congolese authorities finally identified them as the five bodies found in Odzala Park.

Of Beauvoir himself, there had been no sign. He'd been missing since before the bodies were found, and repeated attempts to locate him had failed.

George had spent the past twenty-four hours trying and failing to get more information and to find Beauvoir. All his sources were being unusually tight-lipped. And they sounded scared. George supposed he couldn't blame them, since Beauvoir's people had been burned alive, after being ensnared in the very same traps they had set for the gorillas.

That last was the one detail his sources had been able to provide that was of value. Most of the information he received from his people in the Congo wasn't anything he couldn't get from regular news sources. In fact, he got more from the Congo Planet television program and website than he did from his people.

But the news about the snares made George rather apprehensive. Admittedly, even without the snares, it was a brutal, terrible murder, but making the tools of Beauvoir's trade part of the murder meant that a message was being sent.

George had to figure out what that message was.

As the cab merged onto Route 112, George's phone trilled. Looking down, he saw that it was an international phone call from a number he did not recognize. The prefix was 011-242, which indicated that it was from the Congo.

Hoping it would be something useful regarding Beauvoir's team, he answered it. "'Allo?"

A ragged whisper said, "M'sieu Moorcroft?"

"Who is this?" George said in French.

"B-Beauvoir. In—in hospital," came the reply in the same language.

George winced. It sort of sounded like Beauvoir's voice, but only after his throat had been coated with broken glass and his tongue had been covered in sandpaper. "What happened?"

"Burned. Third-degree b-burns. Will be here for—for some time."

"Who did this?"

"Monster—monster from hell."

Unable to keep the acid from his tone, George said, "Can you be a trifle more specific, please?"

"Punishment, he—he said. For tormenting innocent creatures. Left me alive as warning to—to …"

He trailed off, and George called out his name twice. Then a female voice came on the line, also speaking French, albeit more heavily accented. "This is Nurse Kimbuta. I'm sorry, but Mr. Beauvoir has fallen asleep. He is under heavy sedation, as the burns are covering three-quarters of his body. Who is this?"

"I'm an acquaintance of Mr. Beauvoir's. Thank you, Nurse, please take good care of him."

He ended the call before the nurse could question him further.

At least now he had some idea of what the message was.

The cab pulled into the crowded driveway that led to the hotel's front door. A bellhop opened the door for him and then went to the back of the car to retrieve George's luggage and place it on a cart.

George climbed out of the car into air that felt like a damp sponge. "Careful of the larger valise. It is quite heavy."

"Of course, sir," the bellhop said in an accented voice that sounded Cuban to George's ears.

George tipped the bellhop and then escaped the humidity into the air-conditioned lobby to check in. Once that process was completed with dispatch, he walked to the cart, where a different bellhop was waiting to take him to the two-room suite he had reserved for his stay in Miami.

This second one seemed to be Latino like the one outside had been, but he said, "This way" with an Indian accent. When George looked more closely, he realized that the bellhop's coloration was more central Asian than South or Central American. The latter was the more common ancestry among menial laborers in luxury hotels in Florida.

Having grown up in a South Africa ruled by apartheid, the nuances of skin color were something he had been forced to pay attention to.

Not that he liked it all that much. He had celebrated as much as anyone when apartheid fell and Nelson Mandela went from fugitive agitator to president of the nation. As far as George was concerned, skin color was irrelevant. If you were a person, you should have the same opportunities as everyone else.

As they disembarked from the elevator and entered the suite, he repeated what he'd said outside: "Careful of the larger valise. It is quite heavy."

"Yes," the bellhop said, "so many gorilla hands are quite weighty."

George had been moving to put his laptop case down at the

desk. He froze at the bellhop's words. Suddenly, his apprehension about what happened to Beauvoir and his people had been replaced by a much more immediate concern.

Turning slowly, he saw that the bellhop was holding a nine-millimeter Beretta pistol, a type readily available in this rather violent city. The pistol's muzzle was aimed directly at George's chest, and the room was small enough that the bellhop did not need to have any significant skill with the weapon to inflict mortal harm upon George with but one squeeze of the trigger.

"What is going on here?" George tried to keep his voice even, and mostly succeeded.

The bellhop moved the cart all the way into the suite, allowing the door that had been held open by the cart's weight to fall shut with a resounding click.

"If your objective is to rob me, sir, I'm afraid that you'll find I have no cash."

"What," the bellhop quietly asked, "of the merchandise in your oh-so-heavy valise?"

"Yes, I suppose I should have considered that, given that you already revealed your knowledge of it." Sweat beaded on his high forehead all the way to his widow's peak. The air conditioning in the room was quite robust—it ought to have been, given the room rate—but George found himself suddenly much hotter than he'd even been when he'd gotten out of the cab. "If you wish to take the merchandise, do so and go."

"Your assumption is faulty, Mr. Moorcroft."

"If you are not here to commit robbery, then what do you want of me?"

"For now? To sit."

In truth, George was relieved to be able to take a seat. He planted himself on the chair in front of the desk where he'd intended to place his laptop. Said laptop was instead unceremoniously dropped on the floor. The desk had a box of tissues, and George grabbed one to dab his forehead.

"You have the advantage of me, sir," George said after tossing the tissue in the wastebasket. "You know my name, and you seem to know my business."

"That is not why I have the better of you, Mr. Moorcroft."

"Oh?"

"Learning your name and your business was hardly a difficult task. You provide services for men and women of wealth, and you imagine that protects you. No, Mr. Moorcroft, I have the better of you for one reason and one reason only."

"And that is?"

"You are helpless before me. I have the power of life and death over you. Just as you and your lackeys did over the helpless creatures you butchered in the Congo two weeks ago."

At that, George came very close to breathing a sigh of relief. He had feared that this was a competitor out to take his spoils. But if it was some bleeding-heart conservationist, he knew he'd be okay. The pistol probably wasn't even loaded.

"I am sorry you feel that way, but I'm a businessman first and foremost. Do you mind if I smoke?" Without waiting for a response, George reached into the inner pocket of his white linen suit jacket and pulled out a pack of Morleys. Florida was one of the few civilized states left in the US that allowed indoor smoking, though at this point even they only allowed it in a limited number of designated hotel rooms and in bars. It was one of the reasons why George had chosen Miami as the location of his US business deals.

Even as he opened the pack, though, the bellhop pulled something out of his back pocket.

It was the mask of a gorilla. Somehow, the bellhop managed to pull it over his head without once losing his pistol's aim at George's chest.

"You are first and foremost a murderer. I have already taken vengeance against your lackeys by burning them in the very same park where they committed atrocities on your behalf. In fact, I used the very same traps that you provided for them to do the deed to trap *them*."

George swallowed. It was possible that some random bellhop in

Miami might know about what happened to Beauvoir's team. Not likely, as the press coverage hadn't made it out of east Africa and one or two French newspapers, but still at least possible.

But the detail about the traps hadn't made it to the press. It was something that only the killer could know.

And now he was face to face with the monster from hell Beauvoir had described over the phone.

The sweat returned to George's forehead even as he lit up his cigarette. This wasn't a bleeding-heart conservationist, this was a quintuple murderer who had pursued him halfway around the world for doing his job.

This was a fanatic.

Taking a drag on his cigarette, George regarded his captor, who now looked at once ridiculous and even more frightening with the gorilla mask. "I ask again, sir, what do you want of me?"

"I want you to promise you will never commit such atrocities ever again. I want you to renounce your profession and swear on whatever it is you hold most dear that you will never bring harm to a helpless creature ever again."

"It will not happen again." George spoke with as much sincerity as he could muster. "If you let me live to depart this room, I swear to you on the lives of my mother, father, and grandmother that I will never harm another animal as long as I do live."

As George gave his oath, the bellhop pulled George's valise off the cart and placed it on the couch. His pistol still pointed unerringly at George's heart, the bellhop used his free hand to unlatch the valise. Wisps of condensation from the interior escaped into the suite, and even from several feet away, George could feel the valise's cooling unit do its work, bringing the temperature down in the room even further.

The bellhop removed one of the cloth-wrapped gorilla hands from the refrigerated case, then closed the valise. Slowly, one-handed, he unwrapped the gorilla hand, which was covered in a sheen of crystallized water.

"Tell me, Mr. Moorcroft, do you expect me to believe what you say?"

Taking another drag on his cigarette, George said, "If you were not going to believe me, why did you ask?"

"I wished to hear you say the words."

Then the bellhop put the pistol down and reached behind his back. He removed a Ka-Bar hunting knife from under his uniform jacket.

That actually made George feel less safe.

"What do you want?"

"I want what I asked. I want no harm to come to any animal ever again because of you."

"And I swear to you, it will not happen again!" George cried.

"I know."

The bellhop put the Ka-Bar to George's throat with his right hand, and used his left to pull the cigarette from his mouth. After putting the cigarette down in the ashtray that the hotel had generously provided, he then used his left hand to turn George's arm over so his hand was palm-up.

Then the bellhop took the cigarette and put it out on George's hand.

He screamed as the burning tobacco seared the skin of his palm.

"Ashtrays. That is the principle use of gorilla's hands by your clients. A despicable act to facilitate a filthy habit." Then the bellhop leaned in and whispered into George's ear. "Don't worry, *this* pain will end very shortly."

George did not find that to be especially reassuring.

The bellhop grabbed the gorilla hand he'd unwrapped and put it over George's sweat-drenched face. A shiver spread through him as the cold hand touched his cheeks and nose and forehead, a contrast to the heat of the cigarette burn.

While George felt the bellhop holding down his hand so that it remained face up, he had no idea what the bellhop was doing next.

Then he cried out with a much louder scream that was muffled by the gorilla hand. Pain coursed through his arm, and he didn't even consciously know *why* he was screaming, only that the agony was more than he could bear—and that he could no longer feel the bellhop holding down his hand.

Or feel his hand at all.

Before he passed out, he realized that the bellhop had used the Ka-Bar to slice his hand off.

———

Estrella's feet hurt from being on them all day, her shoulders hurt from hauling around laundry, and her elbows hurt from when she banged them on the sink in 704.

Undaunted, she proceeded to the eighth floor to do the suites on that level. Even though there was as much room space to clean on the eighth floor as the others, there were fewer of the rooms, and that actually made the work go faster.

Most of the time, anyhow. Estrella told herself that so that she could convince herself that she'd be rid of the nails of pain that were being hammered into the soles of her feet that much sooner.

She knocked on the door to 801. According to the run-sheet, this suite was rented to George Moorcroft, a regular. He'd checked in the previous day, so this would be his first time having the room cleaned.

As she approached the door to 801, her nose wrinkled, and she realized that something smelled just *awful* in Moorcroft's room.

Sighing, she knocked on the door. "Housekeeping."

If she was lucky, he was in the room and would refuse service, and it would be Nadia's problem, since her shift started in an hour.

But there was no answer. Which meant that Moorcroft probably wasn't in the room. Which meant that awful stench was something Estrella was going to have to clean up.

Which meant that the nails in her feet were going to be become spikes before too long.

Just in case, she knocked a second time, saying, "Housekeeping!" much louder.

No answer.

They were trained to only try twice, but she went for a third, hoping to avoid the awful stench.

Still no answer.

With a very heavy sigh and a sense of dread, Estrella pulled out her universal key card and opened Moorcroft's suite.

As bad as the smell had been in the hall, that was as nothing compared to the horrible odor that hit her like a slap when she opened the door. She wasn't sure she would be able to get the smell out with what she had in her cart.

First she saw the two hands on the desk, blood pooled at the wrists that had been cut off from the rest of the body. One of the hands had a spent cigarette poking upward from the palm.

Then she saw the body of a man, a very hairy disembodied hand —maybe from an animal?—over his face.

Blood was pooled at the man's feet, some of it still dripping from the two stumps where his hands used to be.

Estrella screamed.

CHAPTER NINE

31 October 2004

**Breytenbach private reserve
Mpumalanga, South Africa**

As DMITRI KONDRATIEV took a drag of his last cigarette, sitting on the dirt, leaning against a tree, having lost all feeling in his legs, blood pooling into the dirt underneath him, a corpse rotting in the midday sun nearby, he wished he'd never answered that damned advertisement.

Dmitri's life had been a good one up until this point. Some would say he'd been blessed, but Dmitri had never felt that his success was due to any sort of providence. He'd worked too hard to give credit to anyone else, least of all a nebulous divine presence whose existence was unprovable.

His brothers and cousins would have said that he was the beneficiary of at least one providential act: receiving all of Uncle Yuri's money when he died of cancer.

Yuri was the only family member to be a financial success in the bleak years following the fall of the Soviet Union. He amassed his fortune by selling drugs and various black-market items and peddling protection and loaning money with back-breaking inter-est. The rest of the family treated Yuri with disgust and disdain. Dmitri, though, made sure to always treat him like any member of the family. As a result of this consideration, Dmitri was the only person named in his uncle's will.

After Yuri's estate was settled, Dmitri proceeded to invest the money he'd inherited, primarily in European and American busi-nesses. In particular, Dmitri put money into various websites that became prominent in the mid-1990s and was sure to divest in the late 1990s before that particular market collapsed. Dmitri saw the latter coming primarily due to so many of those sites not actually *producing* anything, a market correction he was more than happy to avoid.

However, he was able to turn the hundreds of thousands he received from Yuri when he died in 1994 into millions by the turn of the century, at which point, he could pretty much do whatever he wished.

And so he invested most of it, some more successfully than others—his Disney stock had skyrocketed; his Enron stock, not so much—and used the rest to enjoy what life had to offer.

He'd gone scuba diving in Papua, New Guinea. He'd climbed Mt. Kilimanjaro. He'd walked the ice shelves of Antarctica, the volcanoes of Hawai'i, the sands of the Gobi, and the fjords of Norway. He'd seen the Taj Mahal, the Empire State Building, and the Eiffel Tower.

Having done many of the legal things he could do with money, he started to grow bored. Going white-water rafting in Colorado the first time was thrilling. The second time was repetitive. He wanted *new* experiences, not to repeat the old ones, and he was rapidly running through the possibilities.

So he started to look into things that were *not* legal. He had money, after all, and money could buy a great deal of forgiveness and the ability to function outside the confines of law and order. He'd learned that from his uncle.

A trip to India had revealed a heretofore untapped love of hunt-ing, but that legal hunt had provided very little by way of a challenge. However, the gentlemen who'd run that particular hunt had turned him on to more "extralegal" ones.

Dmitri had never had much patience for euphemisms. Yuri always called himself a "businessman" when he was, in fact, a criminal. And the hunt for white rhinos in a private preserve in the northeastern region of South Africa that the Indian hunters had led him to an advertisement for was not "extralegal," it was wholly illegal, especially given the dire state of the white rhinos' survival, as they were very much on the endangered list.

Not that Dmitri cared. He wanted to hunt a white rhino precisely *because* there were so few left. Whatever thrill there was in hunting something of which there were plenty had been drained from him in India.

The advertisement in question said it cost five hundred thousand American dollars, and you got to keep the horns and meat of any white rhino you successfully hunted. Dmitri knew that white rhino horns could be sold for obscene amounts of money, though he didn't care about that so much, as he already *had* obscene amounts of money.

He answered the ad and paid the fee to Byron Breytenbach, the owner of the preserve. Dmitri took his private jet to Skukuzu Airport, where he was met by a vehicle owned by Breytenbach that took him to the wealthy man's preserve.

Initially, it had gone swimmingly. Breytenbach provided a helicopter that flew him over the grasslands in search of the white rhinos. Since the rhinos traveled in packs, it was easiest to spot them from the air.

Eventually, he sighted five of them. The pilot brought the copter within sight of them, and did his best to hover. Dmitri took aim with his Big Horn Armory Model 89 rifle.

In rapid succession, he was able to down all five. It took ten shots, all together—it's very difficult for even the best pilot to keep a helicopter steady in the air—but he did it. And the challenge was a great deal of what made it enjoyable.

Downing the first rhino was a thrill as magnificent as any he'd experienced. But downing the fourth was much less thrilling, and he only killed the fifth out of a sense of completeness.

That was only the first half of the hunt, though. Next was to remove the horns.

The pilot found a clearing to land in, and then headed back to refuel. Breytenbach had provided him with a chainsaw with which to remove the horns, a porter to assist with the packing of the rhino meat and the horns, and a satellite phone with which to call the copter pilot for pickup once he was ready. (Cell phone service was all but nonexistent.)

The rush as he took the chainsaw—provided by Breytenbach— to the rhinos' horns in order to remove them was as powerful as that of his killing the first rhino. He knew that he'd never be able to hunt white rhinos again, because the thrill would never be the same, but that was fine. They were endangered in any case.

He would always have this.

That was what he believed.

He didn't realize how right he was that he would never hunt white rhinos again.

It was when the helicopter came back sooner than expected that it all went to shit.

Dmitri hadn't even taken out the sat phone yet when he heard the rotors of the copter overhead. The porter had packed the meat away, and Dmitri himself had the five rhino horns in a backpack.

Looking up, he saw the copter hovering in the air and then slowly lowering for a landing.

Peering more closely, he saw that the pilot was now, for some inexplicable reason, wearing a rhino mask.

The copter landed, and the pilot got out.

"I was unaware," Dmitri shouted over the sound of the rotors, "that the hunt came with a costume show."

Then the man in the mask held up a nine-millimeter Beretta pistol.

Before Dmitri could say anything, the man shot the porter, who fell to the dirt, his rhino-meat burdens falling next to him.

For his part, Dmitri stood very still, his hands raised, the back-pack filled with rhino horns suddenly very heavy on his shoulders.

"Please don't kill me," Dmitri said.

He had, of course, been speaking Russian, but the man in the mask spoke in another language, one Dmitri did not know.

Dmitri attempted Afrikaans. "Please, I have no wish to be dying today."

In the same language, the masked man said, "No doubt the rhinos you massacred could say the same. I had endeavored to arrive before the latest hunt, but I see that I have failed. I regret that a great deal."

"I do as well," Dmitri said. "Perhaps we can come to some manner of arrangement."

"Unless you have a method of resurrecting the herd of rhinos you have killed, I doubt that any arrangement is possible."

"That is beyond my power I am afraid. Would it matter if I told you I had no intention of hunting these animals again?"

"Does this promise extend to all other animals?"

"No."

"Then I am afraid that *no* arrangement can be made between the two of us."

Dmitri nodded. He recalled Uncle Yuri on his deathbed. "For a long time," Yuri had said, "I was angry. But then I realized that was a waste of energy. I am dying, but I have been dying from the moment I was born. I'm simply fortunate enough to know the method by which it will occur. So I accept and I do what I may with my remaining time."

As he faced the man with the Beretta, Dmitri found that he wished he had a bit more lead time, the way Yuri had.

The masked man lowered the Beretta a bit, and then shot Dmitri in the hip.

Screaming out in pain, Dmitri collapsed to the ground.

At some point, he passed out, which was embarrassing, but when he woke up, he was leaning against a tree.

The masked man was now wearing his backpack, and had also collected the sacks that the porter had been carrying.

"You know, if you were going to take those to sell," Dmitri said, "I would understand. But you aren't, are you?"

Shaking his head, the masked man said, "No, I will give them a proper burial, which is the least that they deserve. And more than you deserve."

With that, the masked man boarded the helicopter and flew away.

Dmitri shifted position against the tree, and that was when he felt the squelchy ground beneath him that indicated that it was soaked. Glancing down, he saw that it was his own blood.

It seemed he was as close to death as Yuri had been the day he died.

Reaching into his shirt pocket, Dmitri took out his cigarette case and lighter. He preferred to roll his own cigarettes—the preservatives the companies put in their cigarettes were noxious—but he was down to the last one in the case. He had more in his luggage, but that was back at Breytenbach's mansion, a location Dmitri doubted he would live to see.

Nonetheless, he removed the final cigarette from the case, lit it, then dropped both case and lighter to the ground, seeing no reason to go to the trouble of replacing them in his shirt pocket.

Then Dmitri heard the sound of footfalls. Someone was running very quickly through the grasslands.

A moment later, he heard the sound of the helicopter once again.

Within a few moments, he saw a familiar-looking man running toward the tree. It was Byron Breytenbach. Dressed in the same white linen suit he'd been wearing when he saw Dmitri off on his hunt, he looked haggard and sweat-drenched as he stumbled his way through the grasslands.

Above them, the man in the rhinoceros mask flew the copter toward them.

As soon as Breytenbach was within about ten meters of Dmitri, several reports from the masked man's Beretta echoed. The moment the shots started, the copter bucked and weaved, as the masked man had trouble keeping the copter steady with a one-handed grip. His accuracy with the Beretta was also diminished by firing it one-handed.

Dmitri watched as one of the bullets ripped through Breytenbach's left thigh, blood splattering outward along with torn linen. Breytenbach stumbled to the ground, his hand clenching his wounded thigh.

Having brought his prey down, the masked man landed the copter and exited it.

In Afrikaans, Breytenbach cried out, "Who are you? Why are you doing this?"

Walking toward him from the copter, the masked man continued to point his Beretta at Breytenbach. "You take money from people like this man"—he pointed at Dmitri with his gun —"and allow them to murder innocent animals. That will not continue."

The masked man then holstered the Beretta and unshouldered a pack. Only then did Dmitri realize that it wasn't the same one that he'd taken from Dmitri himself. Dmitri had used a large tan pack that he'd obtained from an online dealer. What the masked man dropped to the dirt was a smaller black one. Reaching inside it, the man pulled out a machete.

Dmitri swallowed. He had several notions as to what the man in the mask might do with such a weapon, and he wasn't keen on any of them.

Breytenbach tried to crabwalk away from the masked man, but his thigh—which was gushing blood now—made it impossible for him to gain any headway. The masked man closed the distance in an instant.

He knelt down, pressing his left knee into Breytenbach's chest.

Then he pressed the machete to the bridge of Breytenbach's nose.

Even though Dmitri watched it as it happened, he found he couldn't quite believe it.

Slowly, the masked man sawed the machete downward, slicing into Breytenbach's nose.

When he'd been shot, Breytenbach hadn't screamed, he hadn't

even cried out. His breathing had been heavy and labored, but that had been true before he'd been shot thanks to all the running he'd been doing. Dmitri had, in fact, been impressed with his stoicism.

Now, though, Breytenbach's screams echoed off the trees in the grasslands, a shrill, violent cry that Dmitri felt in his ribcage.

By the time the machete reached the end and finished slicing off the nose, Breytenbach's scream had become a gurgle. Blood was gushing out of Breytenbach's face.

The masked man stood up. Breytenbach lay flat on the ground, his noseless face and left thigh both completely blood-soaked. The killer himself was also covered in blood from head to waist.

"Do you think this matters?" Dmitri asked in Russian. Then, recalling that the masked man didn't speak his language, he asked the question again in Afrikaans.

"Of course it does."

"You're a fool." Dmitri shook his head. "So I die. So Breytenbach dies. There are dozens of others who will take our place. The animals will still be hunted. At best you've saved one, maybe two herds. If that."

The masked man shrugged. "That is one or two herds that will survive, then. Better that they live and you die than the other way around."

With that, the masked man turned and walked back to the copter.

Dmitri took a final drag on his final cigarette as the copter took off. The smell of the porter's body decaying and of the blood of both himself and Breytenbach permeated his nostrils. He wondered if Breytenbach would have been able to smell it, were he conscious.

He also wondered how long it would take him to finally die.

And so he sat, leaning against the tree, watching the sun slowly go down over the horizon in the west, wishing he could have one more damn cigarette.

CHAPTER TEN

6 June 2019

Interstate 5
En route between Los Angeles and San Diego,
United States of America

HALLS RODE the brake as the traffic slowed to a crawl on the 5 as they neared San Diego. She had chosen her departure time in order to minimize traffic and still allow herself to get a sufficient night's sleep.

Unfortunately, while you could minimize traffic on the 5, it was damn near impossible to completely avoid it.

Between the stop-and-go cars all around her and the stories Chang had been telling, she seriously considered asking the Interpol cop for one of his cigarettes.

She only didn't because she would have to drive one-handed. Not a big deal in this kind of traffic, but she always held her cigarettes with her dominant hand, her left, and that would mean driving with her less functional right hand. If it was her own piece-of-shit Corolla, she wouldn't care, but this was an official vehicle of the Monrovia Police Department. It wouldn't do to let it get damaged because she was driving one-handed with her weaker hand.

"Listening to all this shit," she said to Chang, "is making me nostalgic for the time in my life when the only awful images in my head were two guys hanging upside down in a slaughterhouse having their tongues cut out. That was yesterday, by the way." She sighed. "So the rhino thing in South Africa, that was the last time your guy hit anyone until the tiger thing three years ago?"

"Yes."

Halls shuddered. "Cutting body parts off is pretty hardcore."

"He seems to particularly dislike when animals are used for sport or other frivolous purposes."

"Sport!" Halls blurted out suddenly.

Chang actually jumped a bit in his seat. "Excuse me?"

She herself wasn't entirely sure why she even said it, at first— and then it all came back. "Jesus."

"What is it?"

"What's been bugging me since last night. Okay, back when I was around twelve or thirteen, the summer camp I was supposed to go to suddenly went out of business a week before I was supposed to go. The couple who ran it fled the country or something, so my parents were stuck, since they'd paid a lot of money for the camp— and that money was gone. My grandparents were retired, though, and they lived in Atlanta, so I spent the summer there."

"That was generous of them."

Halls snorted. "Yeah, well, let's just say I prefer the drier heat you get in SoCal. The humidity in Georgia was horrible. It started out okay—I got to go to the Coke Museum and Dr. King's grave and the aquarium and the natural history museum and the park they held the Olympics in …"

"So this was after 1996?" Chang prompted.

"Hm?" Halls stared at him for a second. She'd actually been lost in the memories, briefly. "Uh, yeah. I think it was '98."

Chang nodded, but he looked disappointed.

"What's the problem?"

"Finish your story, please."

Frowning, Halls went on. She recognized the interrogation technique—don't interrupt a perfectly good confession—but she didn't appreciate it being used on her.

Then again, she was the one who started blurting out the memory.

"Anyhow, after the first couple of weeks, I was bored shitless. I didn't have any friends, the humidity was horrible, there were no beaches, and my grandparents kinda got worn out taking me to all the tourist places pretty quick. Their idea of a big day was to spend the morning watching game shows and the afternoon watching soap operas. They both died within six months of each other in '03."

"I am sorry."

"It's okay, they were both past ninety at that point. They really didn't have the energy to deal with a bored teenager who was still trying to figure out her sexuality."

Halls noticed Chang shift a bit uncomfortably, but she ignored that. If Mr. Tight-Ass Interpol Cop had an issue with her being a lesbian, he could go fuck himself.

"So one day, I went out on my own. I said I was going to check out Emory University, but I really wanted to see what else the city had to offer. I just went wandering, went to restaurants, went to clubs, went to bars."

"At that young an age?"

Halls smiled. "I hit my growth spurt early—I was already the height I am now, and I'd hit puberty, so most people thought I was at least eighteen. I almost never got carded." She sighed. "Didn't take long for me to find the gay clubs. This one girl, her name was Lori, she was hitting all over me—and buying me beers, so I let her, even though she wasn't really my type. She was your classic biker chick, and I figured, what the hell, the attention was nice, and it's not like I could afford to buy my own beer. I had, maybe, three bucks to my name."

Halls hesitated, and Chang had to prompt her to continue. "Go on."

"We wound up back at her place. I—I don't remember agreeing

to it. Honestly, I don't remember a lot of that night, just laughing and drinking in the bar, I remember being on a MARTA train, and then I'm walking up this rickety flight of stairs to a beat-up old house with a squeaky front door. We get inside, and I'm really woozy, and I collapse on the couch. Except it hurt when I did that because the couch was a mess. It was covered in VHS tapes. Store-bought blank ones, labeled in magic marker. I pulled the one I'd sat on out from under my butt, and it said something like 'DF' and then some numbers, I don't remember. Probably a date. I remember 'DF' though. So I asked her what it was, and she told me it was video her brother had taken of a dog fight. Naïve me didn't even know there was such a thing as a dog fight, but she explained that there was a place in College Park where they had pit bulls fighting against each other." Halls chuckled bitterly and shook her head. "I remember thinking that that was weird, since our neighbors had a pittie, and she was the sweetest dog." She shrugged. "I was young and stupid."

"Actually, pit bulls are generally quite a pleasant breed."

"Oh, I know, I meant I was young and stupid for not knowing about dog fights." She blew out a breath, really wanting one of Chang's cigarettes. "Anyhow, she asked me if I wanted to watch one, and because I was awestruck and drunk and spectacularly idiotic, I said yes."

She blew out a long breath. "There was a ring with a wood barricade that was only about chest-high. You can see over it, but it's high enough, I guess, to keep the dogs from getting out. I don't remember the details of the fights, just a lot of growling and barking from the dogs and a lot of whooping and cheering from the people." She snorted. "I also remember feeling *really* nauseous from the combination of too much beer and her brother's shitty camerawork. Finally, I asked her to turn it off because I thought it was gross."

Dryly, Chang said, "I would have expected you to use a stronger word to describe that."

Halls snorted. "I was a teenage girl in the 1990s, 'gross' was as bad as anything could *possibly* get. Anyhow, Lori said that if it made me feel any better, that dog fight didn't exist anymore after what happened last month. And I, of course, asked her what happened last month. And she pulled out another tape, and it was labelled 'LAST DF.'"

The traffic was starting to speed up, so she let up off the brake and gently accelerated.

"The video started with screams and a lot of people in a big-ass cargo elevator. The other video had started in the arena, but her brother apparently started his camcorder while he was riding down in an elevator, because he turned it on in the middle of people screaming from a distance—and the people in the elevator panicking." She swallowed and then coughed, the taste of the second-hand smoke she'd been breathing for the past hour-plus welling up her throat. "Then the elevator doors open, and the screams are getting louder, and now I'm hearing more growling like I heard in the first video. I'd never heard anybody scream like that in real life before. The camera moved into the arena—and then I saw it."

Halls paused to get over into the center lane, which was now moving faster than the left was. She needed the temporary distraction to gather her thoughts.

"Fuck, I haven't thought about this in *so* long." She exhaled slowly. "It's the same ring, and there were two dogs in it like usual, but there were also two men in it, who were chained up."

Softly, Chang asked, "The dogs were attacking the men?"

Halls nodded. "They were ripping these two guys apart. One dog was biting into one guy's leg, and the other one was going for the other guy's throat. I was a teenager, I'd seen plenty of horror movies, but this—it wasn't anything like the movies. The blood was *everywhere*, particularly when the dog went for the guy's throat." She let out a very dry, very bitter chuckle. "It's funny, we took a class in blood spatter when I made detective, and the professor was impressed with my aptitude for it. Didn't even remember that then, but I guess I got a real hardcore lesson in it back in Atlanta, huh?"

"Indeed," Chang said.

"The funny thing is, the screams got quieter when the dog went for the guy's throat. Once that happened, it was just a gurgle, not a scream. The one having his leg chewed had plenty of lung power, believe me, but that gurgle from throat guy was even scarier, especially with all the blood splurting all over everywhere. But it wasn't only the blood, it was all the other stuff. The bits of bone, the muscle, the gore ..."

After Halls trailed off, the car was silent for several seconds.

Chang broke the silence. "Then what?"

"I ran. I got up off that messy couch, threw open that squeaky door, ran down those rickety stairs, and I ran like hell. I was in a strange city in a strange house with a strange woman who thought it was cool to have videotapes of dog fights and murders lying around on her couch, and it *finally* occurred to me that I should be safe with my grandparents instead of there. Somehow, I found my way back to the MARTA station near her house—took me about twenty minutes, but I found it. I went back to Grams and Gramps's place and I told them I was sorry and I got lost and I was sorry and I'd never do that again and I was sorry."

"That must have been very traumatic," Chang said quietly.

"You think?" Halls palmed a tear from her cheek. She really hadn't even thought about this in years. "The worst part was the next day. I asked Grams if she knew anything about dog fights. Grams started making clicking noises with her tongue and said they were illegal and awful, and those two men deserved what they got. Trying to play dumb, I asked her what two men, and she explained that it was all over the news a month earlier, right before I got to Atlanta. Two guys who ran a dog fight in College Park were killed by their own dogs. Grams said she saw on the news that there was someone standing outside the ring wearing a dog mask." She glanced over at Chang. "I was going to ask if that sounded familiar, but since you obviously know about it ..."

"Yes." Chang pulled out a cigarette and lit it. "That was one of the first instances. I did not get to see the file on that particular case until several years later, once I began to piece the pattern together. The murders used to be more spaced out, which is part of why it has taken so long, as I said earlier."

"And two of them were twelve years apart."

Chang nodded. "But I fear the frequency is increasing. In the past, when murders have been close together, they have been directly related. But the slaughterhouse murder and this one in SeaLand do not appear to be connected except in the most general sense of his usual *modus operandi*. There was another earlier this year in Las Vegas that may have been him as well."

"What case was that?"

"An elephant trainer for a circus was found impaled on a bull hook, which is the item used to train elephants to do tricks."

"I remember hearing about that, but how was that part of your case?"

"An elephant mask was found at the scene. That detail was also not revealed to the press."

Halls nodded.

Silence again reigned in the car as she merged into the right lane. They were coming up on the exit to Interstate 805, which would take them toward the San Diego County Medical Examiner's in Kearny Mesa.

"I know you know this," Halls said as she put on her right turn signal and moved into the exit lane, "but big-city cops hate four things: suburban cops, Feds, Interpol, and being told by their bosses that they have to work with one or more of the first three. Whoever's in charge is probably going to bust our balls from jump."

Chang's lips actually turned upward at that. "Worry not, Detective, over the years, my balls have turned to iron."

"Whoa," she said with mock gravity. "Is that the possibility of a smile I see?"

"I have had very little cause for amusement these past two decades, Detective." Chang's gravity sounded quite real.

"I get that, believe me." She merged onto the 805. "So let's capture this fucker so we can both smile again."

CHAPTER ELEVEN

1 June 2019

SeaLand Water Park
San Diego, California, United States of America

AMELIA KORN really hadn't figured that the longest-running role on the resumé on the back of her headshot would be "host of orca show at SeaLand."

She'd come to Hollywood hoping to be a star. Every review of every theatre production she'd been in back home in Saginaw, Michigan described her "movie-star beauty," and when she turned twenty, she decided to put her money where her looks were.

Unfortunately, Amelia was blonde, blue-eyed, and white, a physical type that the casting-agency waiting rooms of Los Angeles were *really* well stocked with. She went to thousands of auditions, but the only roles she even got called back for turned out to be porn, and there was no way she was doing that.

Then she heard from a friend about SeaLand looking for actors to MC their animal shows, and she figured why not? She'd always loved animals.

Her interview with the CEO, Jim Atkinson, was pretty straight-forward. He gave her a script to read, she read it, and he said, "Perfect. I like the enthusiasm. As far as the families in the bleachers are concerned, you're the one who trained the animals and worked with them and they love you all to pieces."

"Why not use the actual trainers?" she'd asked.

"Yeah, we tried that. As MCs they make great trainers. No stage presence, plus they kept going off the script. Most people don't care about the scientific details on how they live, they only want the simple stuff. And honestly? The animals don't give a good goddamn who's throwing fish at them, as long as you throw the fish. Doesn't have to be whoever trained them, just a warm body tossing seafood down their gullets. So it may as well be someone who has more charisma than a college professor teaching an intro course to bored freshmen."

On the one hand, it involved a two-hour (at least) commute to San Diego. On the other, she was rapidly burning through her savings (really the money her parents gave her to get her started), and it was getting to the point where it was this or live the cliché and get a job at a restaurant or bar.

So Amelia took the job. The rehearsing was pretty easy. For starters, the script was way simpler than most of the audition lines she had had to run (though more complex than the porn had been). And she got the killer whales, or orcas, the subject of the newest exhibit at SeaLand, and Amelia had always thought orcas were adorable.

SeaLand had two new orcas, to go with the three they already had. The older orcas, which had been obtained by the aquarium two decades ago, were named Sid and Nancy. Nancy had given birth to Pixie six years ago, and Pixie had rapidly become SeaLand's most popular attraction, as she was tremendously playful and loved people.

According to the head orca trainer—a very sour woman named Lucy Zakarian—they didn't think Nancy was still fertile. "We kept trying, but nothing worked. We were about to give up when she became pregnant with the twins. President Obama and his family were visiting when they were born, so we named them Sasha and Malia. We got a donation to open a new facility to show them off, and the grand opening's in June, so you need to be ready."

Amelia practiced under Lucy's watchful eye for several months before the grand opening. In the meantime, she went to auditions and got no callbacks. By April, she was doing the orca shows, mostly showing off Pixie's friendliness. She responded to simple gestures—which Amelia had learned much faster than Lucy had expected—and to rewards of fish.

For the first couple of months, Amelia did her thing in the small arena with the uncomfortable bleachers and no shade. They always got decent crowds, as a lot of other aquariums had discontinued their orca shows, so Atkinson had started a major ad campaign pushing SeaLand as the only place to see an orca show.

Of course, he didn't mention the part about how the other aquariums had done so due to pressure from conservationists, as orcas in captivity had significantly shorter life spans and other major health issues, not to mention the horrible means by which they were captured. Amelia had gotten several earfuls on the subject from the protestors who congregated outside SeaLand's doors periodically—and occasionally from one of the security guards, a cantankerous old ex-hippie who went by "Yogi" because he looked like some old baseball player or other. Yogi had always been careful to not say anything around Atkinson or even around Lucy, but he loved ranting and raving about how the animals were treated to Amelia.

Finally, the first day of June rolled around and the new arena—which had more comfortable seats, an overhang so you could sit in the shade, and better sight-lines—had its grand opening.

Amelia arrived Saturday morning ten minutes early. On weekdays, she was always late, but there was less traffic on the 5 on the weekends, so leaving at the same time from LA got her to work on time on Saturday and Sunday, at least.

A security guard she didn't recognize looked up from the tablet he was reading and checked her ID when she came in. "What happened to Yogi?" she asked, worried that the old man had mouthed off to the wrong person.

The guard, who had a slight Indian accent, said, "I don't know. I only started this week." He frowned. "You weren't at the party last night."

Amelia swallowed, suddenly nervous at the guard's strangely accusatory tone. "I—I couldn't make it." Last night had been the staff shindig to celebrate today's grand opening to the general public.

Nodding, the guard went back to reading his tablet.

Moving quickly away from the creepy guard, she went to the locker room to change into her neoprene suit. Lucy was there, of course, and insisted on going over the routine with Amelia *again*.

However, Amelia noticed that Lucy was quieter and more subdued than usual.

"You okay, Loos?"

Lucy put a hand to her forehead and looked up at Amelia with bloodshot eyes. "Nothing an IV of Earl Gray won't cure. And don't call me that."

Amelia couldn't help but grin. *Everyone* called her "Loos," even though she despised the nickname. "Good party, huh?"

"God, no, it was dreadful. Jim got drunk, his date left early—and his date wasn't Britney, by the way, and I bet there's a story there—Alfredo kept hitting on every woman in the place, and Teresa threw up over the railing right into the sea lion enclosure."

"Sorry I missed it," Amelia said sardonically.

"I wish I could have." Lucy frowned. "How did you get away with telling Jim you couldn't make it?"

More willing to discuss the particulars with Lucy than with the weird guard, Amelia said, "I didn't tell him. I just didn't show. My roommate's in a play at the Geffen and last night was opening night. It's the first big role either of us has gotten, and when we moved into the apartment together, we pledged to be there for each others' opening nights." She shrugged. "Can't go back on a pledge."

"Especially when you go behind your boss's back."

Amelia shrugged. "My mom always said it's easier to get forgiveness than permission."

"Your mother never met Jim." Lucy glanced around. "Not that it matters much—for all that he was carrying on about this opening, I haven't seen hide nor hair of him today." She snorted. "He's probably even more hung over than I am."

The first show was at noon, and from backstage, Amelia peeked out to see that the fancy new arena was filling up fast. She hadn't performed for this big a crowd since opening night of the Broadway Holiday Show at the Heritage Theatre back home in Saginaw.

Not that she was complaining. They'd been doing an old-time Broadway theme that year, and opening night was when she got a standing ovation for her performance of "(I'm Just a Girl Who) Can't Say No" from *Oklahoma!*

Lucy was giving her unnecessary last-minute instructions. "Don't forget to mention that Nancy having two healthy babies at her age shows how well taken care of she is."

"Right," Amelia said automatically. Then she went over to the barrel to pull out enough fish to put in her satchel. After three months, she didn't even notice the smell anymore.

Lucy went off to make sure that Sid, Nancy, Pixie, Sasha, and Malia were all ready to go. That was actually the job of several other trainers, but Lucy was always looking over their shoulders to make sure they didn't do anything wrong. Amelia was grateful that Lucy was annoying them now instead of her.

Tim, the PA announcer, started his spiel warning people that they might get splashed, especially if they're in the first ten rows, and to make sure electronic devices were protected (taking a moment to plug the waterproof cases sold in the gift shop, of course), and all the other safety stuff. While he did so, one of the tech guys clipped on her lavalier microphone and tested it.

"And now," he finally said, "here's Amelia to tell you all about our happy family of orcas!"

On that, she switched on her lav and ran out onto the platform near the interaction area. For the first part of the show, she talked to the audience a bit from the platform, then went over to a shallow part of the tank where the animals would interact more directly. Only one of the orcas could fit in the space, though Sasha and Malia were still small enough to double up in it. For the sea lion show they could get two or three of them prancing about in there.

"How's everyone doing today?"

Cheers from the crowd.

"Hey, how about this new arena, huh? The Arjun Keshav Arena is a state-of-the-art facility that has been made possible thanks to the very generous donations from the Keshav family over the years. And you all are the first to see a show in it! So give yourselves a hand!"

More cheers and applause.

"Now, as you all know, SeaLand prides itself on our happy family of orcas. We've got the best orca show in the country, and the *only* one in California!"

That got some cheers and applause, but not as many. There were protestors out front today, after all. Atkinson had been able to clear them out every once in a while, but for the grand opening, the protestors had the foresight to get a court order allowing them to assemble. While Atkinson was an asshole, he wasn't stupid, and he wasn't about to violate a judge's order. At a staff meeting, he'd said that it would be better if the story was about the huge crowds going to see adorable aquatic creatures, not about Atkinson and his lawyers going to the courthouse.

Amelia continued her spiel. "Orcas used to be known as killer whales because of their teeth, and because they're near the top of the food chain. But honestly, they're no more or less dangerous to humans than any other cetacean, and a lot more playful and friendly. Let's hear it for the matriarch and patriarch of our orca family!"

On that cue, Shari, one of the trainers, opened the gate from the large tank to the arena, and Sid and Nancy swam out. It was right around their feeding time, so they swam straight toward Amelia. She tossed fish at both of them from the satchel, and they both leapt into the air to catch the food in their mouths.

As expected, the crowd responded to that.

Amelia gestured in a circle, and the pair of them proceeded to swim around in circles in the water, after which she rewarded them with more fish.

For the next several minutes, she gestured for a trick, the orcas did the tricks unerringly (they'd had a great deal of practice), and Amelia tossed fish at them.

However, they were also both old by orca standards, and didn't have the stamina for a long show, so Amelia quickly said, "SeaLand acquired Sid in 1989 and Nancy in 1991, with the object of breeding them. It's been a hugely successful breeding program, most recently when Nancy gave birth to twins!"

That prompted Shari to release the baby orcas.

"Let's put our hands together for our one-year-old orcas, Sasha and Malia!"

They weren't as well trained yet, though the crowd responded to them anyhow, because they were so small and cute. While the two of them frolicked in the tank, Amelia told the story of how the former President was visiting SeaLand with his family right after the twins were born, and how they were named for the Obamas' daughters in honor of their visit. The twins didn't do the complex tricks that Sid and Nancy did, but they were able to gad about in a cute enough manner that was good enough. With time, they'd be trained to be as good as Pixie.

Amelia also noticed that, while Sasha was going for the fish she tossed and yumming it right up, Malia was a bit more subdued and less hungry. Given their ages, that was odd—they both devoured food in obscene quantities—but Amelia knew better than to draw attention to it.

However, she did gesture for the twins to come to the interaction area. Sasha came right away, with Malia following more slowly afterward.

As she'd hoped, even this more lethargic version of Malia was very playful once she got to the interaction area, rolling around in the shallower water and looking adorable as all get-out. As Amelia rubbed their heads, and as they cavorted, she could hear "awwww" and "eeeee" from the crowd, especially the kids.

"Of course, Sasha and Malia are still new to the world and still learning. But in Sid, Nancy, and their older sister Pixie, they've got the best possible guides."

That line was the cue to Shari to let Pixie out. She said it about a minute sooner than she was supposed to, but it was obvious that if she did more with the twins out in the tank, people might notice Malia. Best not to risk it.

She hoped that Atkinson appreciated what she was doing. Lucy, she wasn't worried about—in fact, she probably would compliment Amelia for noticing, although she'd be very reluctant to give that compliment. But Atkinson always got cranky when something messed up the show and rarely gave a damn about the welfare of the animals except insofar as it related to the show.

In this case, though, Amelia was looking out for both the animals—Malia wasn't in any shape to go on much longer—and the show—her lethargy would spoil the fun.

Amelia glanced out at the larger tank and saw a black shape zipping through the water just beneath the surface.

"Speaking of which, here comes our lovely leading lady now. Let's all give a warm welcome to our six-year-old orca, Pixie!"

After a half-second, Pixie burst forth through the surface of the tank and straight up into the air. The crowd gasped and applauded and cheered. Sid and Nancy were too old for this trick, and Malia and Sasha hadn't learned it yet, but Pixie was easily able to jump upward, going about fifteen feet into the air.

Pixie hit the apogee of her jump and turned and flopped back down toward the water, and as she did so, Amelia swore she saw something in Pixie's mouth.

She frowned. The trainers were supposed to check them to make sure they didn't have anything in their mouths—or stuck anywhere else—before they went out. Atkinson had gone on at some length once about the time a sea lion had a very visible turd dangling from its bottom. The trainer responsible for checking the sea lion had been fired.

Now Amelia was worried. She had signaled for Pixie to come out sooner than expected—it was completely possible that Shari hadn't had time to check her over.

Whatever it was in her mouth, it didn't seem to be that big. Still, Amelia figured it was best to get it out as soon as possible. Malia and Sasha had swum back into the tank, so Amelia gestured to Pixie to come to the interaction area.

Pixie swam quickly over to Amelia, and now she could see that the orca definitely had something in her mouth. She was moving too fast for Amelia to make it out, but Pixie looked like a dog with a stick, bouncing her head back and forth.

Once she got into the interaction area, she flopped down in front of Amelia, exactly like she was supposed to, her head up a bit out of the water.

Amelia then got a good look at the human leg she had between her teeth.

Behind her were the special new VIP seats. For an extra twenty dollars, you could sit right by the interaction area, and get a nice close look at the animals.

Unfortunately, that meant that the couple in the front row got a very clear view of the leg that Pixie was displaying between her incisors.

"Is that a leg?"

"What is that?"

"Oh my God!"

Amelia froze. She'd undergone quite a bit of training, endured endless lectures from Lucy on the subject of how to handle things going wrong, but at no point did anyone instruct her on what to do if the animal showed up with a human limb in its mouth.

Instead, she found herself staring at the leg. It was a right leg, based on what was left of the foot. The little toes were all missing, but the big toe was on the left-hand side, so it had to be a right leg. It went up to the knee, and at the other end it was obviously cut raggedly, with bits of bone and muscle jutting out from the end. The leg itself was hairy, and also streaked with dirt and bits of debris amidst the wet leg hair.

Thankfully, Lucy came running out. She was wearing her SeaLand polo shirt and khakis, and both got pretty much instantly soaked as soon as she came out. But she immediately went to Pixie, gestured to her, and she dropped the leg into the tank. The water was just shallow enough that the leg was completely underwater, so only the people in the front row could make out what it was, and they'd already seen it.

Lucy whispered, "Keep going." She also continued to gesture and pet Pixie, and the orca happily cavorted about, enjoying the attention. For a moment, Amelia noticed that Pixie seemed confused regarding the leg, but playing with Lucy got her attention.

It wasn't so much Lucy's admonition as watching Pixie gad about that snapped Amelia out of it. She swallowed, blew out a quick breath, and then started talking again.

"Sorry about that, folks, but Pixie got something caught in her mouth. This is another one of our trainers, Lucy Zakarian. Give her a big hand! She's done a lot of work with Pixie."

There was applause, but it was far more subdued, and most of it came from the seats farthest from the interaction area. Amelia could hear lots of outraged mutters and grumbles from the VIP seats.

"Orcas are also sometimes called killer whales, but we here at SeaLand prefer the term orca. For one thing, Pixie and her family are much closer to dolphins than whales. And also? Look at that face. Is that the face of a killer, ladies and gentlemen?"

Pixie's mouth had widened into what looked like a smile, thanks to Lucy's signals, and then Lucy sent her back into the tank. At Lucy's signal, Pixie did another jump into the air, including a twirl. Amelia tossed her some fish as a reward, and the crowd was slowly starting to get back into it.

But Amelia could still hear the people grumbling in the VIP seats.

After the show, the applause was stronger, but nowhere near what it was before Pixie showed up with a leg in her mouth.

As the crowd filed out following the show, Amelia could hear bits and pieces of what people were saying, and most were speculating.

"I think that was an arm."

"Nah, it was definitely a leg. I saw a foot."

"You're imagining things, dude, it was totally a stick."

"Some kind of tree, maybe?"

"Probably some unlucky fish."

"I'm pretty sure it was a foot."

Helplessly, Amelia looked at Lucy, but she was already heading into the back area.

Amelia followed, and Lucy was immediately barking out orders. "Someone find Jim! And get me a change of clothes!"

Shari came running up to Lucy. "I'm sorry, I didn't have time to check Pixie's mouth, Amelia jumped the gun!" Shari was giving Amelia a nasty look.

"It's okay," Lucy said quickly before Amelia could try to defend herself. "Malia's looking poorly, I don't blame Amelia for cutting the twins short. I'd have done the same."

Relief washed over Amelia, and she let out a breath she hadn't even realized she'd been holding. "Thank you."

"Shari, I want you to take a look at Malia, see what's wrong."

"Okay." Shari shot Amelia another venomous look and then dashed off.

Amelia was about to go change out of her neoprene suit, when Lucy grabbed her arm.

"You may have done the right thing, but don't expect Jim to be all forgiving. What just happened was a PR disaster, and it'll probably cost you your job."

Swallowing, Amelia nodded.

Another one of the trainers came into the back area. "Um, what are we supposed to do with the leg?"

Lucy stared at him. "I don't know!"

"Don't they store dead bodies in freezers?" Amelia asked. God knew she'd watched enough procedurals on TV, usually right before auditioning for them. In fact, she'd been up for the part of a woman who was killed in an episode of *The Rookie* last month.

After shooting Amelia a grateful look, Lucy said, "Good idea—put the leg in the freezer."

"Then what?"

"I have no idea, I'm just tap-dancing until someone finds Jim. *He's* the damn CEO!"

CHAPTER TWELVE

6 June 2019

San Diego County Medical Examiner's Office
San Diego, California, United States of America

DETECTIVE J.D. SKOLNICK had woken up to a half-empty bed and a text message from his shift commander, Lieutenant Reinaldo Iturralde.

Both initially confused him. He was not used to being alone in the expansive king-sized bed that took up most of the floor space in the bedroom of the house Skolnick owned with his wife. Then he recalled that today was Emanuela's day to do a shift at the Palomar Medical Center. Skolnick had never understood why Em bothered, but she loved doing it, and her private practice managed without her one day a month.

As for the text, reading it didn't really clear things up much: "LA Detective Halls, Interpol Inspector Chang to be at autopsy today."

Sitting up, Skolnick immediately hit the icon on the text conversation that would call the lieutenant's number.

After two rings, he heard his boss's voice say, "Iturralde. What is it, J.D.?"

"Hi, Rey. So Detective Halls and Inspector Chang are meeting me at the autopsy."

"That's what I sent in the text message." Iturralde sounded impatient. Skolnick knew that the lieutenant preferred to communicate by text or e-mail and hated talking on the phone.

Which was why he'd called. "That's great. It'll be wonderful to see them. There's one question I have to ask, though, if you don't mind?"

"Sure, J.D.," the lieutenant said with exaggerated patience.

"Who, exactly, are Detective Halls and Inspector Chang?"

"Halls caught a case in Monrovia—"

"I thought you said she was from LA."

"Monrovia's a suburb."

"Yes, I *know* that, but that's a pretty salient detail you left out."

"I didn't leave it out, I simplified." Iturralde let out the long-suffering sigh he always let out when he talked to Skolnick. "Anyhow, she caught a double murder at MCD Meats up there, and Chang thinks it and our SeaLand disaster are all part of a bigger serial case. So they'll be consulting on it."

"Consulting? That seems vague. What does that mean, exactly?"

Another sigh. "It means they'll be *consulting* with you on the case, adding their insights."

"Well, I can certainly see that a detective from Monrovia would have a *ton* of insight about homicide, what with the one murder per century they've had there. Certainly I can see how you'd think I'd need her help, since I only have five years in the Homicide Unit of a major city's police force."

"You finished being a sarcastic asshole? I haven't had my tea yet."

"Evidence to date suggests I'll never be finished with that, but never mind. What's Interpol's interest?"

"I already told you, this may be an international serial killer."

"You realize that 'consult' has become the most meaningless word in the English language, right? Well, second most meaningless after 'literally,' which everyone now uses as 'figuratively.'"

"J.D., if you start a lecture on the evolution of language, I will hang up on you."

"Does it count as 'hanging up' if all you do is touch a screen? 'Hang up' is a phrase that's only meaningful with a phone that actually gets hung on a hook, and nobody really does that anymore."

One more instance of the sigh. "Autopsy's with Dr. Bhatt at nine." And with that, Iturralde made good on his promise and ended the call.

Skolnick smiled at the phone as he put it back on the end table. Iturralde really should have known better than to ask him not to start a lecture. That was the best way to get him going.

He'd never been able to help it. For his entire life, Skolnick had thought about things. Important things, dumb things, weird things, esoteric things. It served him both well and poorly in school growing up—the former because he was able to learn things quickly, the latter because he had a tendency to get so far ahead on his schoolwork that he got bored and disregarded it. Once he almost failed an algebra class, even though he knew the subject as well as the teacher.

Swinging his legs around, he hopped off the huge bed and headed to the shower stall. The master bathroom in the house that had been built with the money his wife Emanuela had made in her private practice had a large bathtub that doubled as a jacuzzi, and also a stall. The tub had been put in at Em's request, but Skolnick was the one who used it the most, usually at the end of a long shift of wrangling the murdered bodies of San Diego.

Iturralde had used the word "disaster" to refer to the SeaLand case, and the word fit. SDPD hadn't even been informed of the details until Monday, two days after the incident. Knowing that it was possibly part of a serial case …

This wasn't the first time Skolnick had had to take on a consultant from another jurisdiction, nor would it be his first serial case. The last one, however, was purely domestic, and the case wound up being taken over by the FBI. Skolnick's contributions were limited to the San Diego portions of the investigation, as the Feds were parsimonious with cooperation.

As he toweled off, he wondered why Interpol went to Monrovia first. He'd heard about the MCD Meats thing—it was mentioned by Iturralde at roll call, Em had talked about it after the recall made the news, and he'd gotten some voicemails about it that he'd ignored—but Skolnick didn't see how this could possibly connect to his murder. Thinking about it, he realized that those voicemails he'd ignored were probably from Halls.

He supposed he would find out at the ME's office.

It was morning rush hour, so while the office of the San Diego County Medical Examiner was about a twenty-minute drive normally, he left at 8:00 AM for the 9:00 AM autopsy, and with that, he didn't arrive until Dr. Pooja Bhatt was all ready to start.

Entering the large room with the sterile-feeling metals and plastics, he found, not just the very perky form of the excitable Indian woman who was the ME assigned to the case, but also a white woman about his age wearing a light blue blouse, dark blue slacks, and shoes that were knockoffs of a more expensive brand of footwear, and a middle-aged Asian man wearing a beige shirt and brown khakis.

"There you are, Skol," Dr. Bhatt said. "Another minute and I was going to start without you."

Bhatt had always felt that nobody's last name should be more than one syllable, so anyone with a multisyllabic name like his only got the first one. (The lieutenant was referred to as "It.")

"Sorry, Pooja, there was construction on the 52. You must be Detective Halls and Inspector Chang." He looked at the woman and deadpanned, "I'm guessing you're Chang."

She smirked and held out her hand. "Michelle Halls, Monrovia Police. This is An Chang of Interpol."

Skolnick accepted the handshake. "And you think the MCD thing up your way connects to this?"

Chang said, "Among many others dating back two decades."

"Twenty years?"

Halls snorted. "Two decades usually means twenty years, yeah."

Before Skolnick could respond to Halls's smartassery—which

he actually kind of admired—Bhatt said, "If you cops are all done with the witty banter, I have an autopsy to perform."

She walked to the large metal bed and pulled the sheet back with surprising caution. It revealed a torso, a leg, and three fingers. The head was still attached to the torso, but it had been mangled beyond recognition. Most of the face was bitten, chewed, or ripped off.

The reason for being so gentle with the sheet removal became clear instantly: the torso was wrapped with barbed wire, which would have caught on the sheet if she'd pulled it off quickly like usual.

"That's all there is?" Halls asked.

Bhatt nodded. "Unfortunately, one of the orcas ate some of our victim's remains—made her sick, too. Divers have searched SeaLand, but all they found were a few fingers and this torso—in addition to the leg that was in another orca's mouth."

Halls looked at Skolnick. "Have you ID'd him yet?"

Shaking his head, Skolnick said, "We *think* it's the CEO, Jim Atkinson. We found an ID badge wrapped around what's left of his neck. The badge was for a staff-only party that SeaLand held Friday night, and it had Atkinson's name and picture on it, but that doesn't mean this is him. Although we haven't been able to *find* the man, either. Unless Pooja has news from the lab?" he finished with a glance at Bhatt.

She smiled, showing perfect teeth. "Pooja does have news. The young orca who chewed up our victim's remains passed a pin in her stool. It's the type they use to help mend compound fractures. This one had a serial number, and it belongs to the one used on James Atkinson when he broke his arm as a teenager."

With a smirk, Halls said, "Well, I guess we know why you haven't been able to find him, then."

"That would go a long way toward explaining it, yeah," Skolnick said dryly.

Halls was studying the torso. The arms, legs, and head had very obviously been removed sloppily, probably by the same orca teeth that messed up the face. Skolnick saw her eyes fall on the scar that ran across his abdomen under the barbed wire. She pointed at it and asked Bhatt, "What's that, a surgical scar?"

The ME laughed. "If the surgeon was unlicensed and incompetent and operating with her eyes closed, then yes, it's a surgical scar. For what it's worth, it appears to be post-mortem."

"After he died?" Halls asked, her eyes wide.

"Post-mortem usually means after he died, yeah," Skolnick said with a small grin.

Halls shot him a look that Skolnick couldn't quite read—he wasn't sure if it was appreciation or annoyance.

Dropping the grin, Skolnick continued: "For what it's worth, now that we know for sure it's Atkinson, we might be able to get more cooperation from SeaLand."

"They've been recalcitrant?" Chang asked.

"Yes. In their defense, it's been because most of the stuff we've asked for—like surveillance footage—has to be authorized by the CEO, and we couldn't find him. Now that we know he's dead, maybe they'll be more amenable to helping." He took out his smartphone and texted Detective Guerra, the secondary on the case, telling him to ask for the footage again, and that Atkinson was in no position to deny it. "Anything else you want to tell us, Pooja, or can you cut him open?"

"One thing," Bhatt said. "This torso weighs too much. I got Atkinson's medical records to try to identify him—that's how we verified the pin was his—and at his last physical, he weighed two hundred and seven pounds."

"So?" Skolnick asked.

"So this torso alone weighs almost three hundred pounds. That physical was a month ago. And he ain't *that* fat."

Within a few minutes, Bhatt had dictated some notes into a digital recorder—mostly paperwork stuff, her name, the case file number, the name of the victim (while saying "previously John Doe," as the file still had that generic name on it and would until later today), the ligature marks on the neck combined with the ID badge lanyard found around the neck that indicated strangulation as the likely cause of death, and so on.

As she did so, Skolnick observed his two new consultants. Both of them had a look that Skolnick had seen on the best detectives he'd worked with—truly only about three people, two of whom had retired, and the other of whom was now wasting his talents as an administrator in the chief's office. These were people who saw *everything*. Even if they didn't know what it all meant at first, they took it all in, including the things that normal people never cottoned to. Halls's was diluted a bit by her obvious discomfort with being in a morgue, but Chang was utterly unperturbed, and instead seemed to be checking everything out.

Bhatt pulled over the X-ray machine and set it up on the torso. She took shots from a few different angles, with the results slowly scrolling as high-res images onto the computer monitor that was on a far wall.

"That is peculiar," Chang said, looking up at that monitor.

Only then did Skolnick actually take a gander at the X-rays. There were various spherical shapes inside the abdominal cavity.

"I've seen an X-ray like that before," Halls said. "Teenager who was working as a drug mule. He'd swallowed about a dozen condoms filled with heroin, and one of them broke open and he OD'd instantly."

Shaking her head, Bhatt said, "Heroin in condoms wouldn't account for the extra weight."

"Rocks would," Chang said.

Skolnick whirled to face him. "Why did you jump straight to rocks?"

"It fits alongside the barbed wire."

After a second, Skolnick nodded. "Yeah, okay, I can see that."

"I can't," Halls said.

"Whales," said Skolnick. "Some of the nastier forms of whale training involve barbed wire, using it to punish the whales when they do something wrong. You don't see it much anymore—hell, you don't see orcas in amusement parks hardly at all anymore."

"And what, they throw rocks at the whales if they don't have barbed wire?"

"Cute, but no—way worse, actually. Back in the 80s, SeaLand

commissioned fishermen to capture whales for them. The captains of the boats corralled the baby whales from their mothers. A lot of the adults died trying to rescue their pods, and a lot of the baby orcas died from the stress of being hunted. Mind you, the captains weren't stupid, and they knew that finding dead baby whales was bad for business, so they cut open the stomachs and filled them with rocks to weigh them down. Of course, that didn't work—rocks don't weigh as much as people think they do, and the gasses that build up in a fresh corpse make it pretty buoyant, so the baby orcas would wash ashore with rocks in their abdominal cavity."

While Skolnick had been talking, Bhatt had put a second pair of gloves on over the pair she was already wearing, gone over to the torso, and had unwrapped the barbed wire. The points shredded the outer glove, and she gingerly placed the wire in a large metal tub. It would get sent off to the lab for a more detailed examination.

Doing so caused the skin from the incision to come apart. Bhatt reached into the abdominal cavity with gloved hands and started pulling out blood-and-gore-covered rocks.

Halls shook her head. "Rocks in the abdominal cavity. And it fits the MO." She looked at Skolnick. "You knew all that stuff off the top of your head?"

He smirked. "Yeah, I'm the guy everyone wants on their bar trivia team." Then he dropped the smirk, as it was his turn to get information from them. "So how does this connect to MCD Meats and your other cases?"

Chang ran a hand through his thinning and uncombed hair. "As Detective Halls said, the *modus operandi* tracks with the other instances. The news reports also mentioned that the person who did this was wearing a mask of a whale?"

"Yeah, one witness said that, but we haven't verified it," Skolnick said. "Still waiting on the—"

His smartphone buzzed. Yanking it out of his pocket, he saw a text from Guerra saying that SeaLand Security had the footage from Friday night all ready for him.

"—security footage. Tell you what, we can all look at it together and make our conclusions, how's that? You guys come in one car?"

Halls nodded. "We'll follow you."

"If you want. It's listed as an attraction on most GPSes, so I'm sure you can find your way there if we get separated on the freeway. According to my partner, we're to see the head of security, Frank Lake. Pooja, anything else you can tell us right now before we go?"

She pointed at another X-ray she'd taken that was up on the monitor. This focused on the neck area. "Hyoid bone looks broken. My COD of strangulation is looking more likely. Also, the liver's been removed. That may be something else the orca ate, since the divers didn't turn it up. Or maybe the murderer kept it as a trophy."

"I doubt that," Chang said. "That is not the type of trophy he prefers. It may have been removed to make room for more rocks, however."

Skolnick shot Chang a look. He seemed to know a lot about a guy he hadn't caught for twenty years. "All right, Pooja, keep me posted if there's anything weird."

"Weirder, you mean," Bhatt said with a snort. "Nice meeting you two."

"Likewise," Halls said with a smile. Chang just nodded.

Indicating the door with his head, Skolnick said, "Let's go see SeaLand."

CHAPTER THIRTEEN

31 May 2019

SeaLand Water Park
San Diego, California, United States of America

JIM ATKINSON WAS PRETTY sure he was drunk.

But that was okay. You were supposed to drink when you celebrated.

And it was a party, goddammit!

Ostensibly, the party was to celebrate the grand opening of the new arena tomorrow morning.

That was kind of why Atkinson was celebrating, too.

The others were all drinking and eating and laughing because there'd be this awesome new attraction at SeaLand.

Atkinson was drinking and drinking and drinking because his nightmare was finally over.

For Atkinson the nightmare had begun when he took the call from someone in the Keshav family—Atkinson couldn't remember who it was, they all sounded alike over the phone—bitching and moaning about how uncomfortable the old arena was and that their donations would cease unless they built a new one.

Being blackmailed into providing a new arena wasn't actually that bad, especially since getting publicity for building a new state-of-the-art arena was better than getting publicity for being the only water park who didn't cave in to conservationists and their whining about the treatment of orcas.

Still, the time since they'd cordoned off the area where the new Keshav Arena would be built with a sign reading OPENING IN JANUARY 2019 had been one headache after another.

Cost overruns. Incompetent contractors who had to be fired and replaced. Trying to get the new contractors to rush their work to make the January date. A support strut collapsing due to that very rushing and injuring three workers. Changing the sign to OPENING IN SUMMER 2019. More cost overruns.

But now it was over and done with.

And Atkinson threw a party for his staff mostly so he wouldn't get drunk alone.

He stumbled around the new arena's lobby, where the open bar was set up, clinging to Britney's arm.

No, wait, Britney had split up with him the week before. Something about him being too grumpy lately. Like that wasn't for a *reason*, and if she'd only waited a week ...

This was—shit, who the hell was that on his arm?

Whoever she was, she seemed to be having a good time.

They were talking to a group of people. Atkinson probably knew who they were when he was sober, but he was fucked if he could remember their names right now. They were all wearing party badges, of course, as Atkinson was, but he couldn't really focus his eyes enough to read them.

Besides, it looked bad when you looked at people's badges to get their names when they were people you knew who worked for you.

Clutching whatever-her-name-was's arm with his right hand, he put his whiskey glass to his lips with his left—only to find it empty.

"Fuck."

Not-Britney turned away from the group and asked, "Is something wrong, Jim?"

He held up his glass. "M'whiskey's broken. Gotta go fix it."

Extricating himself from his nameless date, he stumbled over to the bar.

"Yes, Mr. Atkinson?" the bartender said.

"I like 'at. R'spect. Callin' me 'mister.' Good job." Atkinson placed the glass on the bar. "'Nother one."

"Maker's Mark?"

Was that what he was drinking? He couldn't recall now.

Not that it mattered. It was all paid for anyhow, it would've been a waste not to drink it.

The bartender handed him a fresh glass that had a generous pour of Maker's. "Than's."

Atkinson stumbled away, pointedly ignoring the shot glass with bills in it. He knew exactly how much the bartender was being overpaid, and he saw no reason to add to it. For all he knew, it was the wrong drink!

When he got back to The Eternally Nameless Date, she was talking only to one person. Atkinson knew it was somebody who worked at the souvenir shop, but that was as far as his alcohol-addled memory could recall.

The souvenir guy noticed him first. "Oh hey, Jim! Great party! I was just telling Sarabeth here what a great party it was, in fact."

Sarabeth! Why hadn't he remembered that?

Immediately Sarabeth grabbed his arm. "Now that you've got your drink, darling, maybe you could take us to see the whales like you promised?"

Souvenir Shop Person's face fell. "Oh, crap, you're his *date*? Uh, 'scuse me."

As he beat feet, Sarabeth shook her head. "Thank *God*. He was *impossible*. Soon as he came over, he was hitting all over me, and everyone else walked away."

A name burbled to the forefront of Atkinson's conscious mind. "Alfredo. He runs'a souvenir shop. Good man'ger, but 'e's a harass-ment suit waitin'a happen." He looked down at Sarabeth. "So you wanna see the whales?"

"We don't have to, I just wanted to get rid of Alfredo."

"Nah, c'mon, le's see 'em. S'why I built this fuckin' thing, f'the whales an' orcas an' sea lions an' stuff. Well, that, an' 'cause'a Keshavs're fuckin' extortionists. C'mon, le's go."

"Um…"

He led her toward the restricted area that had the orca enclosures. Only the animal caretakers and scientists were allowed back here. Even the actors they hired to MC the shows weren't permitted past this point.

There was a security guard at the entrance. Atkinson didn't recognize him, but he was probably somebody he knew. Unless he wasn't. He seemed to recall a new hire or two lately. Or maybe not. It was hard to focus.

The guard had a ballcap on that was about a size too big, and he seemed to have some kind of neck problem—Atkinson couldn't see his face.

"Excuse me, but no one is allowed back here." The guard had some kind of accent that Atkinson couldn't place. He was also talking in a whisper. "The animals are very touchy and still adjusting to their new surroundings, and it could be danger—"

Atkinson couldn't believe he was hearing this. Well, he could believe it, because he was there when Lucy Zakarian told the security guards what to say to anyone who tried to go back there, but fuck that.

"You see 'is badge?" He held up the party badge that had his picture on it and the words JAMES ATKINSON, CHIEF EXECUTIVE OFFICER, 2019 KESHAV ARENA OPENING STAFF PARTY. "I run this fuckin' place, an' I'll go whe'ver I wan'!"

He barreled past the guard.

"Jim," Sarabeth said, "maybe we shouldn't—"

"Fuck that," he said. "I wanna see 'em."

"I'm going back to the party, Jim."

"Yeah, fine, Britney."

Too late, Atkinson realized that he got the name wrong. Sarabeth made a "hmph!" noise and stomped off.

Well, fine. She was probably annoying anyhow. Or was that Britney?

Dammit.

He wandered through the corridor, heading to the large pool where the orcas Sid and Nancy frolicked. Standing at the top of the tank, he saw one of them—he honestly couldn't tell Sid from Nancy, that was what he paid scientists for—swim toward the surface. The spray from their breaking through the surface misted across his face, and it actually felt pretty good.

Probably wasn't good for his suit, but fuck it. He had a good dry cleaner. He certainly paid the bastards enough.

This close, he could see the scarring from the barbed wire they used to use in training. They'd stopped that a year ago to shut the protestors up.

It didn't work, of course. *Nothing* shut the protestors up. They always found *something*.

Watching the orca spew water made Atkinson painfully aware of his full bladder.

So he unzipped his suit pants, yanked out his manhood through the folds of his boxer briefs, and peed in the tank.

"Hell," he muttered as relief washed over him even as his urine washed over the tank, "y'r used t'swimmin' in piss."

Just as he finished and zipped up his pants, he felt someone come up behind him.

"Sarabeth, 'at you? Look, I—"

Something tugged at the lanyard of his party badge and wrapped it quickly around his neck.

A strangled "Wha—" was all Atkinson was able to get out before the lanyard started crushing his windpipe.

After a moment, he fell to the floor, darkness spotting his eyes.

As he passed out, he found that he was oddly grateful.

CHAPTER FOURTEEN

6 June 2019

SeaLand Water Park
San Diego, California, United States of America

ON THE ONE HAND, the experience of having watched two people be brutally tortured and murdered in the MCD Meats security footage made it far easier for Detective Halls to stomach watching Jim Atkinson be brutally tortured and murdered in the SeaLand security footage.

On the other hand, Fredi Rodriguez and Alexander Lesnick's deaths were chronicled on a cheap-shit security camera that Lesnick probably bought on sale at a local mall. Halls was being treated to Atkinson's death on video taken from a state-of-the-art high-definition security camera that had been purchased to keep an eye on his shiny new arena.

She was standing behind a SeaLand security guard whom nobody had bothered to introduce, who was operating the video playback. Next to him was Frank Lake, the head of SeaLand's security. They were seated in the only two chairs in the tiny security room, so Halls was left to stand between Chang and Skolnick.

The security guard who'd strangled Atkinson after the latter peed in the tank was the same one who'd tried to stop him entering. Halls noticed that he'd carefully kept his face from view of any of the cameras.

She noticed something else, too. "He's got a long-sleeved shirt on."

Lake shrugged. "Happens sometimes. Usually if people have a sunburn or something."

"That matters for a night-time party?" she said.

Again, Lake shrugged. "Maybe he likes long-sleeved shirts."

"Probably trying to let as little of himself be seen as possible," Halls said. "He's kept away from the cameras. Did Atkinson's date see anything?"

Skolnick shook his head. "No, she didn't get a good look. She was pretty messed up about Atkinson dying, though, so we'll take another run at her once she's had a little time." He looked at Lake. "Who is that guard, anyhow?"

"No fucking clue," Lake said angrily. "He stole someone else's ID to get the job. Used a social security number belonging to some old guy in Oklahoma. Ain't seen him since the opening, and trust me, we've *looked*."

"When did you hire him?" Halls asked.

"Right before the party. One of my guys quit out of the blue, and I needed all hands on deck for the party and the opening."

Once the mystery security guard dragged Atkinson's passed-out body out of the field of range, the video operator said, "Okay, after that, we pick him up in the training area about a minute and a half later."

The main screen switched to a view of a tank that was smaller than the one Atkinson had urinated in, but still pretty large.

"That's right next door," Lake said. "What took him so long?"

As the guard dragged Atkinson into the frame, Halls saw that he was letting his face be seen—because it was now covered by a whale mask. "I'd say he had to pause to put on his face," she said dryly.

Skolnick was standing with his arms folded. "That doesn't make sense. He's been subtle up to this point. Why would he suddenly go all goofy with a silly mask?"

Quietly, Chang said, "It is part of his ritual. He is avenging the spirit of the abused animal by taking on its ego via the mask."

"That's—" Skolnick hesitated. "That's weird."

While they watched, the security guard started trussing Atkinson up, using thick ropes to bind his hands and feet to the upper bar of the safety railing on the top of the rectangular tank. His hands were tied to the vertical railing, and his feet to the horizontal railing, so his body formed the hypotenuse of a right triangle with the corner of the railing. Atkinson's body was face down, so he was looking down at the water just beneath him. The guard also tied a gag over the CEO's mouth.

The water in the tank was mostly still, but as Atkinson was secured, it started to roil a tiny bit, gently slapping him in the face and body.

Eventually it woke him up. "Mmmrrrrrmmmm?" was about all he could manage through the gag.

The guard moved off camera for a second, then came back with a satchel. From it, he removed a thick pair of work gloves and a coiled length of barbed wire.

Halls watched in disgust as he uncoiled the barbed wire and then started using it like a whip on Atkinson's back.

With each strike came a gurgled scream from Atkinson, muffled though it was by the gag.

With each strike, Atkinson's suit shredded and blood spurted out and into the training tank.

As they watched, Skolnick looked over Halls's head—both men were taller than her—and asked, "Has this guy really been doing this for twenty years?"

"Not consistently, but yes," Chang said. "This is, however, the most detailed I have seen him."

Halls shot him a look. "What do you mean?"

"He has not been captured by surveillance often, and when it has, it has been of quality commensurate with that of the video taken at MCD Meats. This is the first time he has been filmed in high definition."

"Yeah," Halls said, turning back to watch as the last bits of Atkinson's dress shirt shredded and fell into the tank, leaving his bare back to be whipped by the barbed wire. "Not that it's helping much. I mean, the only thing we know is that he's a toned man, and we kinda already knew that. He kept his voice too low to make out on the video."

Lake said, "If it matters, he has a funny accent."

"What kind of accent?" Skolnick asked.

"I dunno—foreign?"

"If that's as specific as you can get, then it doesn't matter."

"Whoa!" Halls let out that exclamation as she watched the barbed wire get caught on the knot of the gag against the back of Atkinson's head. The whale-masked man tugged on it, and it came loose—but so did the gag.

The barbed wire itself rebounded straight onto the killer's left arm, tearing into the long sleeve Halls had commented on as readily as it had torn through Atkinson's suit and flesh.

A snarl came from the killer's lips as he bent over, dropping the barbed wire so he could hold his left arm with his right.

"The fuck're you doin'?" Atkinson, now free of the gag, cried out. "Gonna fuckin' kill you you fuckin' sumbitch! Y'hear me, I—"

Even as Atkinson ranted and raved, the killer walked over to the tank and grabbed the lanyard that was still around Atkinson's neck. Once again he strangled the CEO, but this time, he finished the job, not loosening the lanyard's grip until Atkinson had stopped breathing.

Halls shook her head. Atkinson was obviously a complete asshole. Bethany had bitched and moaned about SeaLand once or twice because they still had orca shows when everyone else was discontinuing them due to the cruel practices.

But he didn't deserve that. No one did. And even if he *did* deserve it, it was against the law.

And then she saw it.

The killer was kneeling down by his satchel and removing rocks from it—the same rocks that Pooja Bhatt had pulled out of Atkinson's torso earlier—and she caught a glimpse of something on his left arm.

"Stop the recording," she said. "Knock it back a second."

The video operator did so and hit rewind.

"Pause it there," Halls said when the video went back to it. She pointed at the killer's arm. "Enlarge that."

A moment later, she could clearly see a tattoo on his inner arm. It looked like a pair of cat's eyes, albeit without pupils, with what looked like a candle flicker or maybe a Christmas light over it, the latter with three lines sticking out of either side of it.

"That, my fellow detectives, is what we in the business call a distinguishing mark."

"Specifically the mark of Shiva," Skolnick said.

Halls shot him a look. "You recognize it?"

Skolnick nodded. "Indian god, Shiva, sometimes called the Destroyer, sometimes the Transformer. That particular symbol represents the opening of Shiva's third eye, which is when he'll destroy the world."

"Charming." She turned to Chang. "So Interpol, you think maybe …"

She trailed off when she saw the ashen expression on Chang's face.

"You recognize it?" she asked.

Chang blew out a long breath. "Indeed I do." He looked around. "This room is rather cramped. And I could use a cigarette."

Skolnick looked at Lake. "I think we get the gist here. Can you send a copy of all the footage to Detective Guerra at SDPD?"

"Yeah, sure," Lake said.

In silence, the three detectives went to the SeaLand parking lot. The water park itself was closed, and had been all week, so the lot only had a few cars in it, belonging to employees—plus, of course, Halls's department-issue Chevy and the Ford that Skolnick had been driving.

The moment they hit the asphalt of the parking lot, Chang

pulled out a pack of cigarettes. He offered one each to the others. Skolnick declined politely, but Halls grabbed for one.

As she lit up, Skolnick said, "Nice job spotting the tat, Monrovia."

"Yeah, us suburban cops have brains occasionally, too, y'know."

Holding up both hands, Skolnick said, "Hey, easy. Look, I admit, I didn't think you guys were gonna have much to contribute. I was wrong. This is some serious stuff going on."

"Very serious," Chang said as he exhaled nicotine.

Skolnick leaned against his Ford. "So obviously you recognize the tattoo."

"And its location." Chang looked at Halls. "I last saw that tattoo many years ago on a young man who carried considerable anger toward any who might harm animals."

"That's probably not a coincidence," Halls said slowly.

"The owner of that tattoo fits the profile in many other ways. He is a skilled martial artist, so he is capable of the physical feats the mask killer has performed. And he is a child of wealth. His father was an American diplomat and his mother the heir to a great fortune."

Skolnick blinked. "Holy shit."

Halls, however, found her fists clenching almost involuntarily. This was a helluva time to be hearing about this for the first time. "Mind telling me why you haven't brought this perfect suspect up before?"

"Detective, I have not seen him in thirty years. I saw his sister socially shortly after I joined the Shanghai Municipal Police, and later met him through her. Their father was the US ambassador to China, but his post was revoked after a new president was elected in 1988 and I never saw her—or any other members of her family —again."

Halls blew out a breath. She supposed she could buy that. Kind of. Either way, she could yell at him for being an idiot later. "So who is this lunatic?"

"He is not a lunatic, for starters," Chang said quietly. "That word has connotations of chaos and insanity. Neither of those words apply to our mask killer. He is gifted, and clever, and principled."

"A principled serial killer?" Halls couldn't believe what she was hearing. "That's an oxymoron. Jesus, we just watched him whip a guy with barbed wire right before he strangled him, cut him open, and stuffed rocks in his gut so he could be dropped into a tank and have his corpus eaten by orcas. Four days ago, I watched him cut out two people's tongues before feeding them into a shredder so they could become literal hamburger. He's burned people alive, cut off their noses, stabbed them, shot them, beaten them, tortured them, cut off their hands—and you're gonna tell me he's principled?"

"Actually, it makes sense," Skolnick said.

Halls regarded him with the same skepticism that she'd been giving Chang. "Your threshold for sense-making is obviously different from mine."

"It's not unheard of." Skolnick stopped leaning on the Ford and started pacing, gesturing as he spoke. "Sure, some serial killers are nuts, but some of them really think what they're doing makes sense. Peter Sutcliffe said he heard voices that told him to kill the women he killed. Some theories of Jack the Ripper are that he had a serious issue with prostitutes. For that matter, there's Aileen Wuornos—she killed men who tried to rape her. It may not be *our* principles, but still ..."

"Uh huh." Halls was not convinced.

Chang said quietly, "He believes that he has been given the task of protecting animals from torture or exploitation."

"Let me guess, given to him by the same voices that spoke to Peter Sutcliffe?" Halls glanced at Skolnick. "That's bullshit, by the way, Sutcliffe was yet another misogynist who tried to use schizo-phrenia as an excuse to justify it."

"Not voices," Chang said, "but learned from his time in a monastery in China."

"A Buddhist monastery?" Halls asked, recalling their earlier conversation about karma. If the answer was yes, it was another way this guy fit the profile.

"Not entirely. The Hé Ping Monastery is not of any particular faith. There are elements of Buddhism, but also of Hindu, and even a few Western notions."

"How modern," Halls deadpanned. "Mind explaining how the fuck being raised in a monastery leads to becoming a serial killer?"

"The monastery didn't form the killer within him. It was something else that happened when he was much younger ..."

CHAPTER FIFTEEN

21 April 1979

Bhatnagar family estate
Shanghai, People's Republic of China

KAI NEVER GOT to see Daddy very much.

Mommy had explained it once. Daddy's job was in Peking. But Mommy's house was in Shanghai.

So they lived in Shanghai. Kai didn't understand why they couldn't have a house in Peking or why Daddy couldn't have a job in Shanghai, but Mommy said that that was the way it was and then she got that look on her face that she got when she was upset, and Kai didn't say anything else.

But he thought it was stupid. Because he barely ever got to see Daddy.

At least he had Nandita. Daddy was always in Peking working, and Mommy was always doing things with other grown-ups.

Nandita, though, was always there for him. Kai couldn't remember a time when the dog wasn't there. Mommy wasn't always around, and the governess wasn't always around, but Nandita? Every time Kai wanted to play with someone, she would galumph up to him and play with him and lick his face and run with him and let Kai ride her—though Mommy didn't let him do that anymore, she said he was too big—and all that.

Nandita was the best. As long as Kai had Nandita, he was happy.

This Saturday morning, though, he wasn't happy because the governess was making him do schoolwork. Kai was apparently very smart, whatever that meant, and because of that, he had to go to school and go to classes with a bunch of six-year-olds. The five-year-old Kai thought that six-year-olds were dumb, but nobody asked him.

It was bad enough that he had to go to school for five straight days, but here it was Saturday, and he *still* had to do stuff for school!

So he sat in his room writing words on a piece of paper, making sure they were between the dotted lines. Kai didn't understand what he would need penmanship for anyhow, and it was a stupid word anyway. It was just writing.

The door to his bedroom opened, and the governess, Miss Lim, stuck her head inside. "How is it coming, Chanan?"

Kai hated that name. Kiara, his older sister, always called him Kai, which was short for Kayaan, his middle name, and he liked that better than Chanan. Chanan sounded stupid.

So he didn't answer, because he didn't like that name. He just kept writing.

"Chanan!" Miss Lim barked, and this time he did look up, because her voice got all scary.

"I'm doing it!" he whined.

"Good. When you're finished, you may go outside and ride your tricycle in the yard."

Kai sat up in bed and bounced on it. "Can Nandita come with me?"

Miss Lim frowned. "Well, I don't know …"

"Please?"

"I suppose she could use a good run."

"Yay!"

"But you must finish your schoolwork first!"

"I will."

Kai lay back down on the bed and hurried through the rest of his penmanship homework.

He wrote a bunch of things outside the lines, but he didn't care. The teacher would probably tell him he did it wrong, but so what? Writing between the lines was stupid.

Once he was done, he ran out of his bedroom, only to run directly into his older sister Kiara.

"What are you doing running about, Kai?" Kiara was twelve years old, which made her old, but not as old as Mommy and the governess.

"I finished my homework so now I can go outside and ride my trike with Nandita!"

"Oh, you can, can you?"

"The mean old lady said so!"

"What mean old lady? There aren't any mean old ladies in this house."

"Yes, there are!"

"Really? You're not talking about Mommy, are you?"

"Nooooo!" Kai couldn't believe that Kiara was being so dumb.

"You mean Miss Dalyn?"

Miss Dalyn was the Hawai'ian woman who cooked their food. "Noooooo!"

She stared at him with squinty eyes. "You don't mean *me*, do you?"

"Noooooooo! I mean Miss Lim!"

"Miss Lim isn't mean or old!"

"Yes, she is! She's always making me do stuff!"

"That's what she's supposed to do, silly Kai."

"I am *not* silly." Kai folded his arms.

"Did she say you could go outside with Nandita?"

"Yes!"

"Then let's go find them."

Together, they walked through the big house with all the funny-looking paintings on the walls and the red and gold curtains on the windows and the red and black carpets on the floor, all in search of either the dog or the governess.

They weren't in any of the rooms upstairs, so they went down the big wooden staircase that led to the foyer.

Walking back to the kitchen, they found both there. Miss Lim was reading a newspaper while sitting on a stool at the breakfast bar while Nandita was munching her food from the metal bowl on the floor.

As soon as they came into the kitchen, though, Nandita looked up from her food, saw Kai, and ran right at him.

Kai caught the dog in his arms and laughed as Nandita licked his face, tickling his cheeks. "Hiya Nandita! You wanna go outside?"

Miss Lim looked up from her paper. "Did you finish your schoolwo—"

"*Yes*, I finished it!"

Then Miss Lim looked at Kiara. "Did he really?"

Kiara shrugged. "He said he did. I trust him."

"He's five years old."

"That doesn't make him untrustworthy."

"Obviously, you haven't known many five-year-olds." Then she smiled. "All right, go ahead."

"Yay! Let's go, Nandita!"

"But Chanan!"

Kai looked at her. "What?"

"Stay in the back of the house. Remember when she got out through the front gate last week?"

"Yeah, I remember," Kai said, even though he didn't. Though now that Miss Lim mentioned it, he recalled that Nandita had gotten out onto the street, but it was right when Mommy was coming home from something, so Nandita ran straight to her car.

"Promise you'll stay in the back and away from the front gate."

"I promise." Kai ran toward the front door, then, Nandita zooming ahead of him and then skidding to a stop on the hard-wood floor and slamming into the front door, like she always did.

She scrambled to her paws as Kai got to the front door.

Stretching his legs, he reached up for the doorknob, but the tips of his fingers barely brushed it.

"I got it," Kiara said from behind him.

"Thank you!" Kai said as his sister, who was *so much* taller, grabbed the knob and turned it, letting the big wooden door fall open.

The tricycle that Daddy had gotten him for Christmas last year was sitting in the midst of the front yard, untouched, of course. Their house was surrounded by a gate, so Kai could leave his toys outside without having to worry about thieves. He heard about other kids who had to lock their things up in their houses, but their parents weren't as important as his Mommy and Daddy, obviously.

He climbed into the big tricycle, resting his little feet on the pedals.

"I'll race you, Nandita!" and then he started pedaling as hard as his little legs would go, moving the tricycle forward as fast as he could.

Of course, Nandita outran him. She always did, the big dumb dog.

So Kai pedaled faster.

Nandita shot ahead of him, running to the side of the house and all the way around it.

As Kai followed, he thought that maybe he should stop Nandita, since they weren't supposed to go to the front.

Not that it mattered. She only left that other time because of Mommy's car.

Nandita would never leave him. Daddy was away all the time, Mommy left the house all the time, Kiara went to school all the time, and Miss Dalyn and Miss Lim went back to wherever they lived when they weren't at Kai's house.

But Nandita *never* left Kai. Every night, she slept with Kai in his bed, and every morning she licked his face to wake Kai up and every day they played together except when Kai was at the stupid school. (He tried to get Mommy to let him bring Nandita to school, but Mommy said no. She said the school wouldn't allow it.)

He would always have Nandita. Nandita was the only one who really loved Kai.

The dog went running around to the front of the house where Kai couldn't see her. He pedaled with all his might, though, and he got to the front, to see Nandita standing there staring at him, her tongue lolling out of her mouth.

Then, as soon as Kai got close to her, she started running again, back around to the back of the house.

Laughing, Kai kept pedaling.

They kept that going for a while. Kai chased her around the house, Nandita would go out of sight, Kai would catch up to find Nandita waiting for him, then she would galumph off as soon as Kai got close.

The third time they came around to the front of the house, though, Nandita wasn't standing there waiting for him.

Scared, Kai looked around and saw the dog dashing toward the front gate, barking her dumb head off.

He heard more barking too, and looking through the thick metal poles that made up their gate, he saw a big truck with a bunch of other dogs in it!

Nandita kept running straight for the gate, and Kai called out her name.

But Nandita didn't even stop running, she jumped right up to the top of the gate, wrapped her front paws around the top of the gate, used her back legs to scramble over it, and jumped to the sidewalk.

"Nandita!" Kai tried to get out of his tricycle and fell onto the grass. He pushed himself up and got to his feet, and didn't even brush off his pants like Miss Lim always told him to. "Nandita!"

The dog had run up to the truck that had the barking dogs. She was sitting next to one of the tires, still barking like crazy.

Kai could see the other dogs in the truck now, and they were barking right back.

A man came to the truck, holding some kind of bag with mesh that Kai could see a dog through. It was just lying there, though, not barking. Nandita ran toward him, barking up at the bag with the dog in it.

"Nandita, cut it out! C'mon, girl, come back!"

Now Kai was at the gate, but it was locked of course. He pulled on it, but it didn't budge.

"Nandita!!!!" He was screaming the dog's name at the top of his lungs now, but the stupid dog kept barking at the dog in the man's bag!

The man went to open the back of the truck, and Kai could see that the dogs were all in cages, which was a terrible thing to do to them. They'd never kenneled Nandita, just let her roam free like dogs were supposed to.

Now she was yipping at the man's feet, and then the man grabbed Nandita by the neck and put her in the truck! Nandita whimpered—the man grabbed so meanly!

"Noooooo! That's my dog! Nandita! Nandita!!!!!"

Nandita kept whimpering as the man put Nandita in one of the cages and slammed it shut.

Kai hadn't noticed that Mommy had come outside until she said, "Kai, what's going on?"

"Nandita got over the fence and that man is *taking* her!" He pointed at the truck, which was now driving away.

Mommy stared down at him for a moment, then grabbed his little hand in her big one. "Come."

She practically dragged Kai to one of their cars, and put him in the front seat. She fastened his seatbelt, and then got into the driver's side.

"Look for the truck, Kai," she said as they pulled out of the garage and onto the busy street.

It seemed like forever that they drove around, but Kai couldn't find the truck.

And then he saw it! "Mommy, there, there's the truck, I see it!"

At this point, they were on a street that was almost entirely all other cars. They weren't moving very fast, but neither was the truck. It was turning into an alley.

Mommy pulled the car over to the side and got out. Kai didn't wait for her, he undid his own seatbelt—he was five now, he could do it himself!—and threw the door open.

He was about to run, but Mommy grabbed him right before someone almost stepped on him. Which was good, because he couldn't actually see the alley, there were too many people around, but he knew it was in front of him somewhere.

Mommy picked him up and held him so his face was as tall as she was and he could see more. He saw the alley, but he couldn't see the truck anymore.

"Come, Kai, we'll find Nandita."

Kai smiled at Mommy. "Uh huh. She's a good dog, she just likes everybody. She probably liked the man who drove the truck."

"No doubt." Mommy carried him to the alley.

The place was big and crowded and stinky, and Kai didn't like it. He bet Nandita wouldn't like it, either. Kai knew that as soon as Nandita saw him and Mommy, she'd run to them and want to come home.

Mommy pushed her way through the crowd, but it was really, really slow. Kai was starting to get worried, because he knew that Nandita wouldn't like this place.

Kai didn't like it much either. It was smoky and smelly and loud. He heard animals making all kinds of noises—it was like going to the zoo only much worse.

He had to get Nandita out of here.

"I'm sorry, Mommy," Kai said, "I didn't think she'd jump over the gate again."

"We shall discuss it later, Kai. For now, let us find her in and take her home."

Kai didn't like how Mommy sounded. That was her angry voice. But Miss Lim had said he could play!

Of course, Miss Lim also said to stay in the back of the house. But Nandita wanted to run!

It didn't matter. They were here now and they'd get Nandita and take her home.

But they were almost at the end of the alley, and there wasn't anywhere to go, it was a dead end.

Where was Nandita?

Suddenly, right outside a small shop, Mommy stopped.

She put her hand on Kai's head. "We have to go."

"What?" Kai tried to see where Mommy was looking, but she held his head against her chest.

Again she said, "We have to go."

"We can't, we haven't found Nandita yet!" Kai struggled and squirmed and pushed and jumped out of Mommy's arms and ran down the alley.

"Kai!"

He barely heard Mommy's voice as he ran toward where she'd been looking.

And then he saw Nandita!

But why was she hanging in the window like that?

And why wasn't she moving?

"Nandita!"

It didn't make sense. Nandita should have been running toward him.

But she wasn't moving. At all.

"Nandita?"

"Come on, Kai." Mommy had caught up to him and tried to pick him up.

"Why won't she move, Mommy? She's not moving at all!"

Nandita was dangling in the window, not moving even a little bit. Nandita was *always* moving constantly, barking or panting or running or laying down or *something*. It didn't make sense that she would be *so* still.

A large man with a crew cut was standing near the door.

"Don't worry," the man said, "Mr. Hongzhou's is the best. They'll make good food, you'll see. And I should know, because *I'm* Mr. Hongzhou!" He laughed, but Kai didn't think he was funny even a little bit.

"Let's *go*, Kai." Mommy was pulling at his arm now.

Food? That didn't make sense.

"Nandita?"

She picked Kai up and took him to the car.

Why would that man do that? Why would he take his dog away and turn him into food? What kind of person would steal Nandita's life like that?

He was supposed to take Nandita home. They were supposed to be running and playing.

Mommy put him back in the car after they made their way through the crowded, stinky alley. Tears streaked down his cheeks.

He didn't say another word except for the dog's name one last time.

CHAPTER SIXTEEN

31 August 1979

Hé Ping Monastery, Yandang Mountains
People's Republic of China

ONE OF THE things Abhaya Bhatnagar Carlisle liked about having a personal fortune was that you had various aircraft at your disposal, including a private jet to fly you from Shanghai to Wongyan, and the means to hire a helicopter to take you from Wongyan to the remote monastery buried amidst the Yandang Mountains.

Not that money could buy everything, but that was where her husband came in. As the US Ambassador to China, Albert Carlisle was able to get permission to land the Bhatnagar private jet at the Lugyow Airport, which was a military facility.

As a result, she found herself standing at a large stone gateway on a plateau in the Yandangs, her fur overcoat barely impeding the wind. She had spent an hour putting barrettes and pins in her hair, but the mountain wind made a mockery of her efforts.

The gateway itself had two posts with what appeared to be crude symbols carved into them, though a closer look revealed that they were simply weather-beaten. The one on the left was a Buddha, and the one on the right was another symbol that she vaguely recognized as a Hindu religious symbol of some sort, but she couldn't recall what it was, though she had the feeling it related to Ganesha, or perhaps Kali.

Raj Bhatnagar had little time for traditional religions, busy as he'd been worshipping the accumulation of profit, and he'd passed that on to his daughter. Still, she knew that it was odd for a monastery to embrace both Hindu and Buddhist symbology. But then, everyone was experimenting with religions these days, it seemed.

Next to her were Albert, shivering in a coat that wasn't warm enough; Kiara, looking miserable in her own fur coat; and Kai, who simply stared straight ahead.

He had done little else since Nandita had been taken.

Abhaya had initially thought the punishment to be fitting. After all, Nandita was only allowed to roam untethered in the back of the house. Kai had chosen to disobey that order by letting the dog run to the front of the house, and Nandita had paid the price.

What Abhaya had not reckoned with was Kai's response.

They stood outside the gate waiting for one of the acolytes to arrive. As instructed, they had rung the giant bell next to the gate, but they had been told it would take several minutes to come down the many stairs that led to the monastery proper further up the mountain.

Albert rolled his eyes and made a show of checking his watch as they awaited the acolyte's arrival. "Are we sure this is a good idea?"

With a long-suffering sigh, Abhaya said, "What choice do we have? The finest therapists in the Orient have had no success. He has not spoken a word since Nandita was taken, he's only taken sustenance that is put directly in front of him, and even then he barely eats and drinks enough to survive."

"Those therapists would've had success," Albert said tightly, "if you'd allowed them to prescribe Tofranil like they wanted."

"I will *not* turn my son into an addict!" Abhaya shuddered. The tendency of Americans to leap to pharmaceutical solutions was one of the many things that appalled her about her husband's people. "The acolytes we spoke to in Shanghai said they can help him, and nothing else has worked. At least here he will learn discipline and meditation."

"If you say so. I never really went for this Bruce Lee stuff." Albert looked at his watch again. "How long will this *take?*"

As if in answer to Albert's question, Abhaya saw a tiny figure emerge from the distance onto the staircase that seemed to extend to the very heavens. As the figure grew closer, she saw that it was a man with a shaved head wearing simple brown robes, tied shut with a white sash. His feet were bare, yet he showed no sign of being affected by the cold.

He passed through the threshold, put his fists against each other, and bowed. "I bear greetings from Sifu. He hopes your journey to our sanctuary has been a safe one and that you will return in a like state."

"Well, it's about time," Albert said. "We've been—"

Abhaya interrupted her husband with a quick glare. "Thank you for coming, and for your greeting."

"What's that tattoo?" Albert asked.

It was only when the acolyte held up his arm that Abhaya even noticed that he had a tattoo. It was some kind of writing.

"It is the one I was given."

"So everyone up there has to get a tattoo?"

The acolyte almost smiled. "Only if he reaches the appropriate stage."

"What stage is that?" Albert was, to Abhaya's mind, sounding belligerent.

To his credit, the acolyte did not sound as if he took offense. "Sifu will inform him when he has reached it." He then looked at Kai and then at Abhaya. "Is this the boy?"

For the first time since they'd landed in Wongyan, Kiara spoke. "His full name is Chanan Kayaan Carlisle."

Kneeling down in front of Kai, the acolyte held Kai's shoulders and looked into his eyes for ten full seconds.

Then he stood back up.

"He is lost. Sifu will help him be found."

Again Albert rolled his eyes. "What does that even mean?"

"It means they can help him," Abhaya said. "Is it possible for us to visit him?"

"Not for the first year," the acolyte said. "If and when he may see outsiders, we will convey a message to you through the acolytes you spoke to in Shanghai."

"I understand."

"I don't—but whatever," Albert added quickly at another glare from Abhaya. "If you can help my son *talk* again, that'd be great."

Again the acolyte knelt before Kai.

"You are about to embark on a grand journey, Chanan Kayaan Carlisle. It will be a very difficult road, and it is one you may not succeed in traversing. But the journey will be the most worthwhile one imaginable."

Albert muttered, "Maybe *he* can imagine it, I sure as hell can't."

"You must say goodbye to your family. It will be some time before you see them or anyone else."

Kai still didn't move or talk or do anything but breathe and blink.

The acolyte rose. "Please say your goodbyes to him." He then walked back to the gate and stood at the threshold to the stairs. Abhaya appreciated the gesture of privacy.

Albert went first, standing in front of Kai and saying, "I really hope you find what you need here, Colin. God knows, it's costing enough."

Abhaya let out the latest in a series of sighs related to her husband. It wasn't even *his* money they'd used for the donation to the monastery. She had pulled the funds from the rather large trust Abhaya's parents had set up for Kai when he was born. Intended to pay for college, Abhaya had lost a fortune in interest and fees in order to remove some money early, but as far as she was concerned, it was well spent if it would finally bring peace to her son.

Plus, of course, Albert did insist on continuing to call their son

"Colin," even though that had never been his name, and never was going to be his name, no matter how many times they argued about it during the pregnancy.

Abhaya put her hands on Kai's shoulders. "Be well, Kai. I love you."

Then Kiara knelt down before him. Tears were streaming out of her eyes and down her cheeks.

"This sucks, Kai. It sucks that Nandita's gone, and it sucks that you won't talk to me, and it sucks that we can't see you for a year, and it all *sucks*. I miss that big silly pooch, too, y'know?" She shook her head. "I love you. I always will, no matter what happens, okay?" She pulled him into a hug.

As usual, Kai didn't respond. He no more responded to affection than he did to conversation. Abhaya had given up trying. Kiara had not.

"I love you, Kai." Then Kiara got up and ran toward the helicopter.

Abhaya couldn't blame her daughter for not wanting to watch Kai leave them. Albert, for his part, moved to join Kiara at the helicopter, while Abhaya took Kai by the shoulders and led him to the threshold of the gate.

The acolyte said, "Only Sifu and his students may pass this threshold."

"Of course." Finally she felt tears well up in her eyes. She had been sad since they saw Nandita hanging dead in the shop window, but she had not cried at any point in the weeks since.

Now, it was as if a faucet had been turned on. Shudders wracked her body as the acolyte led Kai up the seemingly endless flight of stairs that took him up to the heavens.

She tried very hard not to carry that metaphor through in her mind. Kai was *not* dead, even if Nandita was. He'd acted like it, but maybe this Sifu person could resurrect her little boy.

The coughing noise of the helicopter rotors starting up startled her out of her reverie, and she realized that Kai was now out of sight, having moved too far up the mountain for her to be able to make out his tiny form amidst the stairs.

She turned and joined her husband and daughter, wondering if she would ever see her son again.

CHAPTER SEVENTEEN

11 November 1985

Hé Ping Temple
Taichow, People's Republic of China

KIARA's favorite time of the year was when she flew to Taichow to visit Kai.

They'd first been allowed to visit him in 1980, and the whole family had flown to Taichow to meet at the temple that Kai's Sifu maintained in that city. Kai was talking, which everyone was grateful for, though he didn't say much, and his head was shaved.

Since then, Mother and Father had cut down their visits to once a year. Father was busy with his ambassador job—he was constantly flying all over the place, not just to Peking, but all over China and regularly back to the States as well—and Mother found that she couldn't deal with Kai being covered in bruises. Intellectually, she knew that they were the result of training, but she couldn't look at him like that. And the bruising had subsided as the years had gone on.

But Kiara made sure to come see him as often as possible. She wasn't allowed in the mountain retreat, but she really didn't want to take that trip anyhow. Luckily, Kai went to the temple in Taichow four times a year as part of the group that did supply runs for the monastery. As long as the timing didn't conflict with her class schedule, she went when he came to Taichow. Even when it did, she usually skipped class. The only time she wasn't able to come was when his supply trip was in the middle of finals.

This time around, she was bringing someone else along as a surprise for Kai.

An looked nervous as they approached the temple. It was located on an out-of-the-way back street of the city, and from the outside, it looked like a warehouse.

"You sure you're okay with this?" she asked.

Quickly, An nodded. "Of course."

"You don't look okay," she said with a smile.

"Perhaps I do not. But it is irrelevant. You asked me to accompany you and I have never been able to resist the wishes of those who love me."

"Good. Because I do love you, and I do wish you to meet my brother." She put her arm in his and they both entered the temple.

Inside was an open space filled with wooden practice dummies, punching bags, staffs, nunchuks, and a few other weapons. In addition, there was a shrine in the back of the space.

"What is that?" An asked as they entered. Unlike the monastery, the temple was open to anyone. They simply walked in the front door, their nostrils assaulted by the incense that permeated the space. He was pointing at the shrine.

"It's a shrine. I told you, they both train in martial arts and become more spiritual. I always think of them as monks, honestly, but they're not, really."

"That looks like no Buddhist shrine I'm familiar with."

A voice from the back of the temple said, "Because it is not. Sifu's teachings are his own."

Kiara turned, and thought it was Kai for a second, before realizing that he was too tall, and it was Ajay. He had the same coloring as Kai—who, like Kiara, took more after their mother than their father in that regard—and proportionately the same build. Though, truly, a lot of the acolytes had the same build, since they all ate the same grain-heavy diet and all had similar physical regimens.

"Is that your brother?" An asked. "He's grown."

Laughing, Kiara said, "No, this is Ajay. He does look like Kai if he grew a foot, doesn't he?"

An nodded. He had only seen pictures of Kai.

Ajay gave a small bow. "It is good to see you again, Kiara. Your brother is downstairs with Yong."

Kiara smiled. "That figures." She turned to An. "Yong is one of the children that the Sifu has taken in. He was just left here at the temple one day as a boy. He has a cleft lip."

"That's horrible." Quickly, he added, "I mean that he was left here, not that he has a cleft lip."

Ajay nodded. "It is tragic, but it is good that Sifu is willing to take such outcasts in when no one else will. Many have made their home here—including your brother. With each passing day, he grows stronger—and wiser." He turned to An. "And who is your friend?"

"Oh, I'm sorry! I have horrible manners. Ajay, this is An Chang. He was just recruited by the Shanghai Municipal Police. We've been dating for about six months now."

"Congratulations—on both your recruitment and on your taste in girlfriends." Ajay approached An and offered his hand.

Blushing, Kiara said, "You're very sweet, Ajay."

As he returned the handshake, An said, "That's an interesting tattoo."

"We all get one when the time is right," Ajay said. "Mine is of Shiva opening his third eye. Some say that is when the world will be destroyed."

An blinked. "That's—very pessimistic."

"The world often gives us reason to be pessimistic, my friend," Ajay said sadly. "Many nations of this world possess the ability to do Shiva's destructive work, including the one we inhabit. Perhaps the image on my arm serves as a symbol to ward off that destruction. Or perhaps it predicts the future. We shall see. Excuse me, I have some duties to attend to."

Ajay went off to perform those duties.

"What do you think?" Kiara asked eagerly.

"It's an interesting place. Not what I expected from the way you described it." As he spoke, he reached into his pocket for a pack of cigarettes.

Before he could say anything, a voice with a pronounced lisp came from the staircase in the back: "Please do not smoke in the temple."

Kiara recognized the voice, and turned to smile at the two figures emerging from the staircase landing. One was a little boy whose upper lip was bisected by a cleft. This was Yong, and Kiara recalled with shame that she had been unable to stop staring at his mouth when she first met him a year ago.

But now she barely even registered it. She did notice that An was staring at him, though whether it was due to the deformity or to being rebuked about smoking by a six-year-old was unclear.

"This must be Yong," An said blandly as he put the cigarette pack back in his shirt pocket.

Behind Yong was Kai. "Yes. Who are you?"

"Kai," Kiara said, "this is An. We've been going out for a few months now. He's a policeman in Shanghai."

Kai stared at An for several seconds as he entered the main part of the temple. As always, despite his short stature—he was still only eleven years old, and he hadn't yet hit his growth spurt—he moved like a coiled spring. Kiara expected her brother to attack them all any moment.

"I've heard a lot about you, Kai," An said.

"My name is Chanan. Only my sister calls me Kai."

"That's my fault," Kiara said quickly. "That's what I always call you, and I really have told him all about you."

"I see," Kai said blandly.

"That's a great deal of bruising you have," An said after a moment.

Kiara didn't even notice the bruises anymore. "This is nothing, it used to be a lot worse."

"If you say so." An shook his head. "I'm sorry, Kai, but my first call on the job last month was to a domestic violence case. A man beat his wife and children and pets."

"What kind of pets?" Kai asked. It was the first time his voice changed from the odd monotone that had been the only way he'd talked since they left him at the monastery six years ago.

Kiara winced. An should have known better than to bring that up. After all, this whole thing had started because of the incident with poor Nandita.

"It was a couple of birds. They can no longer fly. They both died at the veterinarian." An sighed. "But the wife was covered in bruises a lot like what you have. Except for that one inside your arm."

Kai held up his left arm. "That is not a bruise."

Eyes widening, Kiara said, "You're getting your tattoo!"

Nodding, Kai said, "Work has begun on it. It will be finished when I return to the monastery."

"Can't wait to see it."

Ajay walked back in at that point. "You already have. Sifu is giving him the same tattoo he gave me."

An frowned. "You didn't choose it?"

"No." Ajay shook his head. "Sifu chooses it for us."

For the first time since they'd arrived, An smiled. Kiara had been getting worried, as An was usually relaxed and happy, but he'd been out of sorts since walking into the temple.

He said, "Is that why you have two possible interpretations for it? Because you didn't choose it yourself?"

"Possibly, though I might have chosen it for myself in any event. One of the lessons Sifu has taught us is that there is never a single right answer, nor a single wrong answer, and that contradictions are the very nature of life."

"Interesting. Do you—"

Kiara caught sight of a rat scurrying across the wooden floor, and screamed at the top of her lungs upon spying the filthy creature, interrupting An.

She *hated* rats.

The vermin scampered right toward An, who picked up a foot to step on the little beast.

Kiara didn't entirely *see* what happened next. One moment, An was picking up his foot to step on the rat, the next Kai was standing over An, who was flat on his back, Kai kneeling on his chest with a hand near An's throat.

"There will be no abuse of animals here."

Kai said the words with his usual monotone, but the intensity behind the words was scarier than anything Kiara had ever heard before.

An swallowed audibly. "My—my apologies. I was simply—"

"You were behaving as a predator would." Kai got to his feet and then offered a hand out.

An stared at it for a second before accepting it and being pulled to his feet.

For her part, Kiara wondered how the hell Kai was strong enough to help a grown man to his feet.

Or how he was quick enough to sweep out An's leg so fast she didn't even notice it.

"What makes us human," Kai continued after An had gotten to his feet and started brushing off his clothes with his palms, "is that we can rise above our predator instincts. We have intelligence. We can make choices. We are not slaves to our instincts. We do not need to harm those who are helpless to mentally or verbally defend themselves. And to do so betrays a savagery that we should be above."

Kiara blinked.

"You raise an excellent point," An said quietly. "My apologies for violating the sanctity of the temple with my attempted actions."

"It is not the sanctity of the temple I was defending. It is merely a structure to which we give significance because we use it as a way station and for training and meditating. It is the sanctity of life that I defend."

Kiara walked up to her brother. "Kai, that's the most you've said in—in years."

Kai stared up at her with eyes that seemed as dead as the ones he stared blankly ahead with right after Nandita died. "It is the most I have had to say." With that, he turned and walked away, saying, "Yong, Ajay, and I have chores. We will meet for lunch in half an hour."

He and Yong went back downstairs. Ajay looked at Kiara almost apologetically. "We will likely be done sooner than that. And then we shall retire to the noodle shop for lunch." He smiled and then followed Yong and Kai downstairs.

"That," An said slowly, "was not what I expected."

Kiara shivered even though she wasn't actually cold. "That rant after you almost stepped on the rat? That was twice the number of words we've gotten out of him since Nandita died."

"It seems the training is working, then."

"I guess." Kiara stared at the staircase.

An walked over to the wooden dummy. "They have one of these at the training facility as well."

He tried to hit each of the protruding poles in succession, and abjectly failed to do so, crying, "Ow!" and rubbing his wrist after two seconds of flailing about.

Unable to help herself, Kiara burst out laughing.

An smiled. "It seemed much easier when Sergeant Li was doing it."

Kiara chuckled, and kissed An on the cheek. "C'mon, let me show you the rest of the place before we go to lunch."

CHAPTER EIGHTEEN

4 January 1989

Bhatnagar family estate
Shanghai, People's Republic of China

"Understood. I'll be on the next plane to Peking. Goodbye."

Albert Carlisle untangled the phone cord before placing it back on the hook. He'd been expecting this phone call since November. He'd been appointed ambassador to the People's Republic by President Carter back in '77, and his knowledge of the region had allowed him to remain in the position after President Reagan's inauguration four years later. Albert had always prided himself on his ability to work both sides of the aisle. But Reagan's erstwhile vice president was about to take office, and President Bush wanted someone more in his inner circle to be his official eyes and ears in China. Besides, he and George had never gotten along since the latter's days running the CIA.

Leaving his study, Albert went out to the living room. Abhaya was there, of course, reading the latest Danielle Steel hardcover, and their son was sitting on the floor in that cross-legged meditation position that he'd been favoring since they had finally brought him home from that ridiculous monastery in the mountains last year.

Albert had never liked the idea of leaving his son Colin with those fanatics, but it seemed to have worked. At least now he took an interest in the world around him, though he still hardly spoke a word.

And he'd gotten a tattoo like some kind of sailor. His wasn't the same as that of the acolyte they'd met that first time a decade ago. Colin's looked like two blank eyes with a candle over it.

"It's finally happening," he said without preamble. "My tenure as ambassador is coming to an end. George—or, I guess, President-Elect Bush—wants his own man. I have to fly to Peking tonight." He gave Abhaya a significant look. "And then we're going home."

Steeling himself for an argument, he was surprised to hear his wife say, "Of course."

Albert blinked. "You're sure?"

"I have no wish to subject Chanan to this misbegotten country any longer than necessary."

"Very well, but Kiara's heart will be broken. She has grown quite fond of her young man."

Abhaya made a *tch* noise. "He's a policeman. He's beneath her, she'll realize that soon enough."

"Oh, so you'll tell her, then?" Albert asked with obvious relief. That was not a conversation he wanted to have with his twenty-one-year-old daughter.

Besides, if he told her, and she announced that she was staying behind to be with her cop boyfriend, he'd have let her. Abhaya would not tolerate such nonsense. Better that she have the confrontation. After all, this house in Shanghai belonged to her family. It was through marrying her that Albert had gained many of the connections in both the People's Republic and in Taiwan that had led to his diplomatic appointment. Abhaya, Kiara, and Colin—or, rather, Chanan—had continued to live here while Albert went back and forth between here and the embassy in Peking, as he didn't wish to subject his wife and children to the nonsense of politics.

Without a word, his son unfolded himself from his meditation pose with great speed, gave his mother a significant look, and then left the room.

Albert stared at Abhaya, who said, "He's going to take one final bike ride around the city before we have to start packing."

He shook his head. "How do you even know that?" he snapped. "All the boy does is *sit* there with that damned shaved head, he looks like a demented pool ball. He still doesn't talk."

"He talks. Just not to you."

Albert winced.

"Perhaps," Abhaya added, "if you called him by his *name* ..."

"Colin is a respectable name, one that's been in my family—"

Abhaya rolled her eyes. "—for generations, yes, I know."

Albert closed his eyes and exhaled slowly. "Why are we still having this argument fourteen years later?"

Standing up and setting her book down on the end table, Abhaya said, "Because you refuse to admit that you lost it. Colin is not his name."

And with that, she left the living room, presumably to have someone on the staff fetch Kiara from the university in order to give her the news.

Albert watched her go. He could have sworn he loved her once. Though perhaps that was simply what he told himself because her family connections were useful. Certainly being married to Raj Bhatnagar's only daughter had proven *incredibly* useful ...

With a sigh, he went to the bedroom to pack a suitcase for what would likely be his last flight to Peking.

———

Chanan pedaled his bicycle through the crowded streets of Shanghai. Most of the people ignored him, or cursed at him as he rode too close to them, but he imagined that those who did look didn't see a fourteen-year-old boy. His lithe sinewy form was hidden by the brown robes he continued to wear even outside the monastery, but his powerful legs took him quickly through the smoggy streets.

Since achieving puberty a year and a half ago, he had grown considerably in a very short time, currently sitting at six feet. Both the Carlisles and the Bhatnagars had a genetic disposition toward great height.

It was after he'd adjusted to his new height in training that Sifu told him it was time to leave Hé Ping. "I have nothing left to teach you that you will hear," he had said.

Chanan knew better than to argue, even though he would have preferred to stay with Sifu forever. But he could hardly go against Sifu's wishes. One did not do that—at least not twice.

The sun was beginning to set, painting the sky a flaming orange, muted by the miasma of pollution that hovered over Shanghai.

He'd heard Mother tell Father that he was going to take his bicycle for a final ride around the city. That was almost true. Certainly that was what he would say if asked by someone he deemed worthy of being spoken to.

But he had a very specific goal in mind. If Father was being recalled to the States, then he had one last errand to take care of before departing Shanghai.

The smells of slaughtered fish and rotting vegetables assaulted his nostrils as he turned the bike down the Wufu alley where Mr. Hongzhou's shop lay.

He pedaled more slowly, as the people were much more crowded together here. The alley assaulted his senses as much now as it had when he'd first come here with his mother as a five-year-old. Now, though, his training allowed him to keep those sensations from overwhelming him.

Instead, he took those sensations into him, channeling them into his grand purpose.

He saw the shopkeepers slaughtering animals and preparing them. He heard the goats bleating and the dogs barking. He smelled the stale cooking oil. He tasted the sweat and death and blood all intermingling with the smog in the air.

And he felt his grip on the handlebars tighten as he wended his way through the alley to Mr. Hongzhou's stall at the end of it.

Though he hadn't set foot in this alley in almost a decade, he still remembered it with perfect clarity.

About ten yards from the stall, he stopped the bike, placing it near a lamppost, pulling the bike backward to allow the kickstand to fall and stabilize the vehicle. His left hand moved to his left hip to make sure the satchel was still tied securely to his side.

The smell of fried meat that permeated the alley revolted him. His reverence for all life had been reinforced and tempered by Sifu's teachings. Today, though, his focus was on the dogs who lost their lives for food.

Like Nandita.

When he closed his eyes, Chanan still heard Nandita's whimpering as she was taken by the truck, still saw Nandita hanging from Mr. Hongzhou's meat hook, dead, waiting to be skinned.

When he opened his eyes, he saw more corpses hanging from hooks in the front window of Mr. Hongzhou's shop. His sandaled feet making not a sound on the sawdust-covered floor, Chanan entered to see that the front of the shop was empty. The counter was quiet, the cash register closed, the large fryer that took up the entire side wall switched off. He slowly walked over to the fryer and turned the gas on, knowing that the detritus-filled oil would be sizzling hot before too long.

Chanan heard the yelping of dogs in the back. They sounded exactly like the dogs in the truck that Nandita had leapt the gate to be near.

Still walking quietly, Chanan moved to the entryway to the back room, separated from the front by a battered, grease-stained curtain, which he pushed aside.

He saw a pen in one corner of the back room filled with dogs. There were at least twenty of them in the tiny pen, with no room to move. Animals who loved running and wide-open spaces more than anything, and Mr. Hongzhou had trapped them in a place where they couldn't even move without stepping on each other—or in their own waste. Urine and fecal matter overcame the cooking oil in Chanan's nose.

Opposite the dog pen sat a large man on a small stool. Though he saw only the broad shoulders, salt-and-pepper crew cut, wide belly, stunted legs, and the rolls of fat on his neck from behind, and couldn't see his face, and though it had been more than nine years, Chanan recognized Mr. Hongzhou immediately. He was eating peanuts, and dropping the shells to the floor, mixed in with the sawdust that was dampened from absorbing dog urine.

Chanan continued to move silently. The only sounds in the back room were the crunch of peanuts and the pathetic whimpering of the imprisoned dogs. He reached into his satchel and pulled out two of the three items it contained. The first was a rubber mask of a dog that he'd purchased back in October. He'd told Mother that it was for Hallowe'en, which led to Mother sadly informing him that they would not be flying to Peking for the embassy Hallowe'en party. Chanan had managed to, he thought, feign disappointment competently.

The second was the dragon's-head knife that Ajay had given him as a going-away present following Sifu's pronouncement that Chanan would depart Hé Ping.

After placing the mask over his face, he gripped the knife's ornate hilt in his right hand, the elegantly sculpted contours of the dragon's head cutting into his fingers and palm.

Walking soundlessly up behind Mr. Hongzhou, he raised the knife and slid it directly between the third and fourth cervical vertebrae.

Mr. Hongzhou let out a throaty gasp and his entire body went rigid. Chanan cupped his back with his right arm and guided him to the floor with his left. Mr. Hongzhou could say nothing, as spinal shock had started to set in, his breathing growing labored from the paralysis of his diaphragmatic muscles.

Chanan only had limited time now. Or, rather, Mr. Hongzhou had limited time in this world, and Chanan needed him to experience a great deal in that short duration.

He knelt down near Mr. Hongzhou's head and whispered to him through the mask: "Before you beat a dog, find out who his master is."

Mr. Hongzhou's eyes went wide at the old proverb, sweat now beading on his fat forehead.

Reaching into the satchel, Chanan pulled out the third item: the Wüsthof carving knife he'd removed from the kitchen in the house. Miss Dalyn—still Mother's cook after all these years—kept the blades sharpened and well cared for at all times, so Chanan knew it would be up to the task.

He placed the point of the knife underneath Mr. Hongzhou's left ear and started to slice around on the jawline.

Once he'd reached the right ear, he cut around it, up along the edge of his hairline, and down and around to alongside the left ear, meeting his start point beneath that ear. He cut a small circle around the nose, which would leave it intact when he pulled the skin upward, away from the facial muscles and bones.

Paralyzed, unable to scream, the only sign of the overwhelming pain that Chanan was inflicting on Nandita's murderer were his dilating pupils and the increased sweat. By leaving his nose and ears intact, he knew that even as Mr. Hongzhou died, he would still smell his own blood and sweat and fear, and also hear the barking and yelping of his victims, excited by the smell of that selfsame blood.

Chanan stood up and walked behind Mr. Hongzhou's head. Crouching, he slid his hands under the large man's shoulders and picked his head and shoulders upward. The blood from his flensing soaked into the sawdust and drenched the floor beneath it, as well as Mr. Hongzhou's butcher's apron, as Chanan dragged the dying body. Chanan brought him to the front room. He heard the crackling sound of boiling oil as he entered, dragging his burden toward the fryer he'd turned on. Hefting him up higher, Chanan turned the body over and dropped the butcher's exposed face, blood pouring into the oil and sizzling, the face doing likewise a second later.

Leaving Mr. Hongzhou's face to be fried, Chanan went into the back and freed the dogs from their pen. Some stayed in place, confused, not having known anything but the confines of this pen for days on end. Others scampered immediately, barking their glee at attaining freedom once more.

Calmly, Chanan walked out of the shop, his dog mask still covering his face.

Voices cried out.

"Those are Mr. Hongzhou's dogs!"

"What happened?"

"Mr. Hongzhou, are you all right?"

As several of the other shopkeepers ran into Mr. Hongzhou's place to find out what had happened, and others tried to catch the errant dogs, Chanan went to his bike, pushed it forward so the kickstand would lever back up into the standby position, and then he hopped onto it. A few people did a double take at the sight of a tall man in brown robes wearing a dog mask, but nobody spoke to him or tried to stop him.

Pedaling away, the last thing he heard from the Wufu alley were the screams of the shopkeepers who discovered Mr. Hongzhou's body face-first in the fryer.

CHAPTER NINETEEN

7 June 2019

The Beverly Hills Hotel
Los Angeles, California, United States of America

Hélène Caspari always hated coming to the Beverly Hills Hotel.

She often thought that her husband insisted on staying there when they came to southern California for precisely that reason.

The hotel had a storied history, constructed when Beverly Hills was merely a collection of bean fields, quickly becoming the go-to hotel for the stars of Hollywood. The first time Jean-Pierre announced that they would be going to Los Angeles and staying there, Hélène did some research, and found old pictures of Fred Astaire and Cesar Romero and Carole Lombard lounging by the pool. She thought it would be delightful.

Then she realized that her least favorite movie was filmed there. She had seen *California Suite* as a child, which was about four different sets of people who stayed at the Beverly Hills Hotel. She had no real memory of three of the plots, except that one had the woman who played McGonagall in the *Harry Potter* films and another had the star of *M*A*S*H*, but the fourth was seared on her memory as simply horrid. It had Bill Cosby and Richard Pryor playing two very competitive doctors who had a series of mishaps that were supposed to be slapstick, but were painful to watch, closing with a scene of them and their wives hobbling out of the hotel in bandages and casts. It was supposed to be funny, but Hélène didn't understand how anyone could find that level of pain to be amusing.

On top of that, the Sultan of Brunei had a stake in the hotel's ownership, and he had adopted the repressive Sharia law in his country. Several important people had decided to boycott the hotel as long as the Sultan was part-owner, and Hélène had wished to respect that boycott.

She had begged Jean-Pierre not to stay there. They could just as easily go to the Hollywood Hills home of her film producer brother. Michel maintained the palatial home, but only actually lived there when he was in town. It was at least as luxurious as the hotel, more private, and didn't remind Hélène of her least favorite movie.

He ignored her and booked the room.

"I'm the head of a large corporation," he had said the first time. "That means that when we go to London we stay at the Connaught, when we go to New York we stay at the Waldorf Astoria, when we go to Tokyo we stay at the Ritz-Carlton, and when we go to Los Angeles we stay at the Beverly Hills Hotel. That is simply how it must be done."

That was the last time Jean-Pierre was even willing to discuss it.

On this particular occasion, they were met—first at Bob Hope Airport in Burbank and then at the hotel itself—by both press and protestors.

Jean-Pierre ignored them at the airport, muttering a quick "no comment" before getting into the limousine they had hired, but at the hotel, he decided for some reason to speak to them. He made that announcement to her inside the limo in French as they approached the phalanx of people on Sunset Boulevard, after telling the driver in English to let them off on the street instead of at the front entrance to the hotel.

Hélène sighed as she stroked the heavily groomed white fur on the back of her Bichon Frise, Précieux, who sat quietly in her lap. She also spoke in their native French when she replied, as she could understand English, but couldn't speak it worth a damn. "Must you? There would be no press if we were at Michel's home."

"I will not hide at your brother's house, and besides, it would be unwise to avoid public speaking. That leads to speculation, and speculation is always rigged against the company. Better to put a personal face on it. If I cry 'no comment' constantly, they view me as a corporate monster. If I speak to them as a person, with a wife and a dog, they might file more compassionate—or at least balanced—stories."

Shaking her head, and patting the dog in her lap on the head, Hélène said, "I was wondering why you allowed me to bring Pré this time."

"Well," Jean-Pierre said with a smile as he reached for the door handle, "that and I grew weary of listening to you speak of how much you miss the dog when we travel."

Hélène rolled her eyes as he got out of the limo.

She followed him, and about a half-dozen people with microphones approached, trailed by half as many video cameras. In addition, there were a ton of protestors on the sidewalk of Sunset Boulevard, though they were kept from coming any closer by sawhorses and members of the Beverly Hills Police Department.

One of the women with microphones spoke as soon as he exited the vehicle. "M'sieu Caspari, Luisa Sotomayor, KCAL-9. Is it true you're here to lobby the state government to repeal the ban on *foie gras*?"

In his lightly accented English, Jean-Pierre said, "My purpose in coming here, Luisa, is to *discuss* the ban on *foie gras*. I am meeting this week with several lobbyists and activists and politicians on *both* sides of the issue to discuss strategies. Next week, I shall fly to Sacramento, where I will testify before the California State Senate on the subject."

"But given that d'Artagnan Foods is one of the leading exporters of *foie gras*, I think it's safe to assume that you're for repealing California's ban?"

"Absolutely. Mind you, I do understand the reasons for the ban, and I am appalled by the horrid force-feeding of ducks and geese to fatten them up that some suppliers indulge in, but d'Artagnan has always carefully sourced our *foie gras* from waterfowl who are fed humanely and kindly."

Still seated in the limo, Hélène tried not to roll her eyes. That last sentence had been provided by d'Artagnan's publicity people, and Jean-Pierre had said it in the dullest of monotones.

Sotomayor had another question. "There are reports that you are still, in fact, force-feeding the animals, and that the farms you've shown to the public are a smokescreen."

Jean-Pierre hit the woman with the disarming smile that had first charmed Hélène twenty years ago. "I have found the process of debunking conspiracy theories to be exhausting, and rather akin to attempting to teach ballroom dancing to a hyena. The result is frustration for you, and the hyena still cannot dance."

Several people laughed at that.

Then Jean-Pierre reached into the limo and offered his hand to Hélène. She took it with her right hand, cradling Pré with her left.

"Now then, my lovely wife, our delightful dog, and I have had a very long flight. We would like to check into our hotel and relax."

Belatedly, as she clambered out of the car, Hélène realized that simply cradling Pré in the crook of her arm would be insufficient. Had they gone to the front door of the hotel as planned, a porter would have been present to aid in bringing the little Bichon Frise inside.

But out here, surrounded by unfamiliar people, Pré started squirming and barking, and then suddenly jumped out of her grasp and ran down Sunset.

"Pré!"

To his credit, the limo driver immediately ran after the dog, but Pré was small and fast, and he darted around the legs of the camera operators and reporters and toward the police officers and protestors.

Hélène tried to follow as best as she could, but the Jimmy Choos she wore were not conducive to running. And Pré kept dashing back and forth, so that even the driver—whose own footwear was also chosen more for fashion than practicality, though they at least didn't have four-inch heels—was having difficulty getting to him.

If only the dog whistle wasn't in the luggage, Hélène thought dolefully. If she had that, she'd be able to get Pré's attention.

Then she heard a dog whistle! It wasn't quite the same as hers—this one was scratchier, probably an inferior, cheaper model than the custom one she'd had made at the shop in Chartres—but it was close enough to get Pré to stop running.

Another toot of the whistle and Pré ran straight across Sunset to a man wearing a hoodie.

The driver immediately ran after the dog, even as the man in the hoodie started to gently pet Pré and rub his ears. He gave the happy whimper he always gave when you rubbed his ears, and Hélène breathed a sigh of relief. This was likely someone who cared about dogs.

As she approached, she noticed that the man had a tattoo on his inner arm, which was an odd place for a tattoo. Usually people had them on the outer arm, away from close-to-the-skin veins, and where they could be more readily seen.

In French, she said to the man, "Please, may I have my dog back?"

The driver translated her words into English.

However, the man picked up Pré and stroked his back for a second, before handing him to Hélène.

She was able to see him more clearly now, though the hoodie and the large plastic sunglasses he wore obscured his face. He had very hard, weather-beaten features, and no smile lines that she could see, even though he was obviously in his thirties at least.

As she took Pré back, she said, *"Merci."*

He responded in kind, speaking French with very little accent: "This being should be treated with the same responsibility as your husband treats you."

Snorting, Hélène said, "I would say that he should be treated a good deal better than that."

The man quickly walked away, disappearing into the crowd of protestors.

Luisa Sotomayor was on her in a moment, asking, "Who was that?"

"*Je n'ai aucune idée.*"

Jean-Pierre was right behind the reporter. "My wife does not speak English, I'm afraid, Luisa. That man is obviously a good Samaritan, and we thank him for rescuing little Précieux."

In French, Hélène muttered, "If you had not insisted on speaking to the reporters, this would *not* have happened."

"We will discuss it later," he said in the same language, though she knew that they would not. In English he said, "I'm sorry, but obviously this is too much for our beloved pet to handle, so we must take no more questions."

As they approached the front door, they were passed by a porter who was wheeling a luggage cart to their limousine. Hélène was grateful that the hotel staff had the wherewithal to adjust to Jean-Pierre's absurdity by working to take care of their baggage.

And then right behind the porter was a frighteningly gaunt man who stepped right in front of Jean-Pierre.

The man was wearing pants with an over-large waist, a shirt that was a size too large for him, suspenders—likely because no belt would be sufficient to hold up the pants—and moccasins. His legs were sufficiently skinny that they looked like poles that had been inserted into the moccasins. Hélène could clearly discern the bones in his neck and the line of his skull behind his sallow cheeks.

He looked like someone who had not eaten in months.

To Hélène's shock, the man spoke in French even as he put a tiny hand on Jean-Pierre's large chest.

"You must go back," the man said.

In the same language, Jean-Pierre asked, "Go back where, sir?"

"Home. Do not pursue this course. Havoc will be wreaked upon you if you continue. If you go home, you may avoid this terrible fate—as I did not."

"If I am to meet your fate, so be it." Jean-Pierre smirked. "I could afford to lose a few pounds."

Hélène rolled her eyes in disgust. She stepped forward and said, "Sir, you should go to a hospital."

"Thank you, ma'am, but we are far past the point of that. I am serving my penance."

The reporters had noticed this *tête-à-tête* and some were starting to move toward the entrance.

Jean-Pierre saw this and grabbed Hélène's elbow, guiding her past the thin man and toward the hotel entrance. "Come, my dear."

But even as they entered the hotel, Hélène looked over her shoulder to see the reporters approaching the man. They tried to ask him questions, but he simply walked away on his bony legs.

She wondered what he had done that required him to starve himself to serve penance. More importantly, she wondered what that had to do with Jean-Pierre's work that he had to do here in America.

CHAPTER TWENTY

7 June 2019

Nelson's Motel
Van Nuys, California, United States of America

CHANAN INSERTED the key into the motel room lock and turned it. It didn't open at first, and he had to jiggle the key twice before it finally did so.

Nelson's Motel was very cheap, and was worth every penny. The neon was broken in the motel sign, so from a distance, it looked as if it was called "NEL N M TEL." The air conditioning didn't work, the fan in the ceiling spun slowly, and the windows were welded shut. The rooms had no televisions or telephones, and were only cleaned between clients, and then only occasionally.

But they took cash, which was the part that mattered. Even cheap chain hotels insisted on credit cards these days, and Chanan needed to stay off the proverbial grid. As an added bonus, Nelson's did not have video surveillance. (They kept a camera at the front desk, but it wasn't actually functional, something Chanan determined in fairly short order. They used it to create the illusion of security.) And they still used keys and locks rather than plastic key cards with magnetic stripes. Those stripes made it possible to ascertain their users' movements, but tumbler locks and metal keys had no such traceability.

It was getting harder and harder to maintain his secrecy. Kiara's former boyfriend was on his trail, and detection techniques had improved considerably since he began his campaign. He had to be much more careful.

Even if it meant staying in squalor for his work here on the west coast of the United States.

He had planned it out very carefully. Getting the security job at SeaLand. Kidnapping the floor manager and CEO of MCD Meats. Obtaining Jean-Pierre Caspari's itinerary. Renting the unoccupied warehouse in Vernon. Renting the limousine and renting a driver's uniform and hat. And directing one of his heralds toward Caspari to warn him off, as his other heralds had warned Félix Habré and George Moorcroft and many of his other targets. Not a single one of them had heeded his herald's warning, and not a single one of them survived their subsequent encounter with Chanan himself.

Once, he had talked himself into believing that things were improving. He had done good work, the world was becoming a better place, and it was getting harder to do what he did without attracting the attention of the constabulary.

Besides, he had made a promise. Mother had lain there on the huge poster bed in the family mansion in the Vasant Vihar neighborhood of Delhi, wasting away from the cancer, her voice papery and fragile, begging him to stop. The last words he spoke to her before she died were a promise that he would.

For a time, he'd been able to keep that promise.

Yet for every law passed against poaching, there were still poachers. For every species saved from extinction, more were endangered. For every amusement park that banned animals who were mistreated there were places like SeaLand that still abused the creatures they forced to perform for people's amusement.

No, his work was not yet done. And though he had promised Mother he would stop, the fact of the matter was that she was dead and dust. Sifu may have believed in reincarnation, but Chanan had known better. Besides, if the people he killed were going to come back as something else, what was the point of killing them? True, their behavior dictated that karma would not be kind to their next life, but Chanan couldn't find a way to believe that. The world was simply too capricious for him to believe that it would act in a sufficiently just manner to guarantee that, for example, Jim Atkinson would come back as a sloth or that Byron Breytenbach would come back as a destitute beggar.

No, it was best that he take matters into his own hands and kill them himself. That was the only way to achieve redemption for the defenseless creatures they had tormented and killed.

After entering the wretched little room, he removed the hoodie and sunglasses he'd used to hide his face from the cameras at the Beverly Hills Hotel. He hadn't intended to get that close to those cameras, but then Caspari's wife's dog got loose, and he *had* to act. While Caspari was a pig, his wife very obviously cared for her Bichon Frise, so he took the risk. He had only gone to the hotel in the first place to make sure that his latest herald—whom he had force-fed to the point that he couldn't bear to eat anymore—did his job.

Chanan moved to the small shrine he had set up on the cracked wooden dresser. It was like the shrines at Hé Ping, with a small replica of a circular garden gateway, a pestle with the words HÉ PING written in Chinese, and an incense stick-holder engraved with the yin-yang symbol.

Next to the shrine was a box of incense sticks and a lighter, and he removed one stick and placed it in the yin-yang holder. Once it achieved balance, Chanan used the lighter to ignite it.

As the room's stale air filled with the sweet smell of the incense, Chanan knelt before it in *zazen* and meditated.

He stayed there for over an hour, the only sounds in the room the labored whirring of the ceiling fan and the slow inhalations and exhalations of the *Ujjayi* breathing of Chanan.

Eventually, the incense stick started to lose its potency. Getting to his feet, Chanan put out the incense completely and then turned his gaze on the wall adjoining the uncomfortable, unmade bed.

He had taped photographs, printouts of pictures and websites, and newspaper and magazine clippings to the wall with Scotch tape.

There was a photograph of several tiger carcasses that had been cut into quarters.

A picture of several malnourished deer.

Two screengrabs from a video of a whale being whipped with barbed wire at a water park in Europe.

A picture of cows hanging from slaughterhouse hooks.

Several newspaper clippings from around the world that reported the death of Ian Gibson, trampled to death by an elephant he was hunting in Zimbabwe.

A French newspaper clipping of an article about the force-feeding of ducks and geese in a plant in France whose biggest client was d'Artagnan Foods.

The Facebook page belonging to a teenager named Deena King who posted pictures of herself holding a dead cheetah and kneeling next to a dead rhinoceros, both of which she claimed to have killed single-handedly.

A website story about pigs being gutted and left to bleed to death.

The Wikipedia page about the death of Cecil, a lion in Africa killed by Walter Palmer, a big-game hunter.

A photograph of an elephant's scars from being chained and beaten.

An illustrated website article about a perfectly healthy racehorse being euthanized by his owner because he could no longer run as fast as he used to.

Another newspaper clipping, this a recent one, about the death of Jim Atkinson, the CEO of SeaLand.

A web page about the MCD Meats recall.

On top of all these, close to the molding for the ceiling, he kept the three most important pictures. One was the picture taken at the Taizhou temple of Sifu along with Chanan, Ajay, Yong, and a few other students. One was of Kiara from when she was a teenager.

And the third was of Mr. Hongzhou's place in Wufu alley in Shanghai, where Nandita met her doom.

She had just wanted to play with the other dogs.

Chanan reached for the French newspaper clipping about the force-feeding of ducks and geese. It detached from the tape on the wall with a snap.

Placing the clipping on the bed, he rooted through one of his two bags. One contained his clothes and toiletries. The other, that he was going through now, held his other equipment.

Including the masks.

He found the goose mask and put it next to the clipping.

As he turned, he saw himself in the mirror. His hard face was tanned, but not wrinkled, still. Thanks to that lack of wrinkles, as well as his broad shoulders, athletic build, and crew cut, no one would look at him and assume he was in his forties.

In truth, he hoped that no one would look at him at all. Merely another human amidst the others.

Secrecy was the key to his campaign's efficiency and success.

One of the ways he kept from being noticed was to take on the roles of people who were never really looked at—bellhops, security guards, drivers. He went to the closet where he'd hung the limo driver's outfit he'd rented.

He was not sure how much longer he would be able to continue his work. But continue it he would, for as long as he drew breath, and as long as animals were mistreated by humans who should have known better.

The human race had no need to be predatory, and only continued to be so out of cruelty.

It was Chanan's task to revisit that cruelty on those who perpetuated it.

He quickly removed the garment bag holding the uniform from the closet and placed it on the bed. Shrugging back into his hoodie, he retrieved his burner cell phone from its pocket and called a cab company to pick him up at the motel.

Then he flung the garment bag over his shoulder, shoved the

French clipping and the goose mask into his pockets, and left the room.

Some day he would renew the promise he'd made to Mother on her deathbed and he would again stop. Either he would be caught or killed or he would be forced for some other reason to give up his crusade.

But today was not that day.

As Jean-Pierre Caspari was going to find out to his eternal regret.

CHAPTER TWENTY-ONE

7 June 2019

Roney Warehouse
Vernon, California, United States of America

"I CANNOT BELIEVE that you hauled my motherfuckin' ass out to motherfuckin' *Vernon* just so you could lay hands on some motherfuckin' *books*."

Anwan Jones chuckled. "I told you, Cheese, county jail ain't got shit worth readin' in the library."

"Since when does your ass read?" Greg "Cheese" Wilson asked.

"Since *always*, motherfucker!" Anwan chuckled again. "And you *know* that shit, 'cause you was always gettin' up in my face about it."

"An' you *still* readin' anyhow, so I guess *that* shit ain't worked too good."

"Nope," Anwan said, patting the canvas bag that now held his prized first editions of Ursula K. Le Guin's *The Left Hand of Darkness*, Samuel R. Delany's *Dhalgren*, and James Tiptree Jr.'s *Ten Thousand Light-Years from Home*. County didn't have any of them in the library, and he was jonesing to reread them.

"Then let's get our asses to the damn train so I can pretend I don't know you and shit."

They continued down the empty street toward the Vernon Metro station that would take them back to Cheese's apartment in Compton. Anwan had been staying with his childhood friend since he made parole.

"Yo yo," Cheese said suddenly, hitting him on the arm with the back of his hand, "you remember when Ms. Perez took that book right outta your hand back in fifth grade?"

Anwan smiled. "Yeah, she said, 'You'll get this back at the end of the semester.'"

"An' your ass said, 'Why, it take you that long to read it?'" Cheese was giggling now at the memory. "Motherfucker, you were in detention for *life* after that shit."

Shaking his head, Anwan said, "I should go by the school, say hi. Tell her I been in the joint, she'd fuckin' *love* that shit. She'd be all 'I told you so' up in here."

But Cheese had stopped laughing, and was shaking his head. "Nah, man, bitch died 'a cancer last year."

"Shit." Anwan sighed. Aside from Cheese, everyone he ran with back in the day wasn't around no more. Cake-Man and De'Andre both got their asses shot in a drive-by, Booger was doing time for killing a motherfucker, Jeets was paralyzed and up in some hospital somewhere, and Yo-Yo was still in County, since he didn't make parole 'cause he was a stupid motherfucker.

Cheese stopped suddenly when they were across the street from some warehouse and grabbed Anwan's arm. "Yo yo yo, look at *that*."

Anwan followed where Cheese was looking and saw a limousine parked outside the warehouse.

"Gotta be done," Cheese said.

"Nah," Anwan said quickly. "I'm on *parole*, I can't be—"

"*Look* at it!" Cheese pointed at the limo. "It's just *sittin'* there!"

"I—"

"We gotta *look*, at least."

Before Anwan could say anything else, Cheese ran across the street.

For a second Anwan stared after him. Cheese was *always* pulling this shit, ever since they were kids.

He ran after him saying, "Y'all remember that I was up for grand theft fuckin' auto, right?"

Cheese was bent over at the driver's door, and then stood up and grinned. "I ain't sayin' we should be stealin' it, but I'm seein' a fine-lookin' sound system, a bar with the good shit, an' a hot-shit wireless router." Then he reached for the handle.

"*Fuck*, Cheese, don't—"

He pulled on the handle and the door opened. "And the mother-fucker's unlocked."

Anwan closed his eyes and sighed. "A'ight, motherfuckers *that* stupid deserve to get their shit took."

But before they could even consider violating Anwan's parole by taking stuff from the inside the limo, Anwan heard a scream.

He'd heard lots of people scream in his life. Him and his people were always getting beat and shot and stabbed and shit. Pain was always there, and there was always screaming. There was all kinds of screams, too. Broken bones, gunshot wounds, stab wounds, they all had different screams.

Even with all that, though, Anwan had *never* heard a scream like what was coming from the warehouse.

"The fuck was *that?*" Cheese asked.

The screaming continued, though it was mixed in with coughs and other weird noises.

Cheese and Anwan looked at each other, then they both made a beeline for the warehouse. Anwan was a felon, and even before that he had *no* use for the police, but hearing that scream, he instinctively wanted to call 911 and get po-po down here.

The warehouse had two big double doors that a truck could fit through and one small metal door right near where the limo was parked. But none of them had windows. Down closer to the corner, there was one tiny window, so Anwan and Cheese went there and peered in.

Anwan had been wondering what that scream could've been, and lots of ideas kept popping into his head. "A fat white guy having a tube shoved in his mouth that came from a funnel" was not one of them.

But that was what he and Cheese saw. The white guy was zip-tied to a folding chair, and there was a guy in a limo driver's outfit and some kind of mask holding the hose.

"Is that a motherfuckin' *goose* on his face?" Cheese asked.

"Could be a duck," Anwan said.

"Seriously, what the *fuck* is that?"

Anwan glanced around. There were pillars blocking a lot of his view, but it looked like the funnel that fed the hose that was in the white guy's mouth was attached to a machine.

Goose Mask put the hose down on the floor and then walked over to the machine.

The white guy wasn't screaming no more, but now that Goose Mask had moved away, Anwan got a better look at him.

He wasn't wearing a shirt, and his stomach looked like it had been blown up like a balloon. Even from this far away, Anwan could see the veins of his stomach sticking out. That shit wasn't natural.

Then Goose Mask grabbed some cans of food that had already been opened, and dumped them into the machine. A minute later, he grabbed the hose, which started spurting ground-up brown stuff. Goose Mask put the hose back in the white guy's mouth.

"Fuck this shit," Anwan said, "I'm callin' po-po."

Cheese looked at him like he was nuts. "You on parole, moth-erfucker!"

"All's I'm doin' is gettin' my books outta my storage unit. Shit's in my name and everything. And *look* at that shit!"

For a second Cheese stared at him, then he shook his head. "Motherfuck. Call their asses."

Anwan pulled his cell phone out of his pocket. It was a Trac-Phone he'd picked up at a store near Cheese's apartment after he made parole. His smartphone had been taken as evidence when he got arrested.

"Nine one one, what is your emergency?"

"There's some motherfucker got a man tied to a chair at a warehouse in Vernon." He gave the cross streets and then added, "Look like he bein' tortured and shit! He wearin' some kinda mask, too, looks like a goose."

"Or a duck," Cheese added.

"Yeah, or a duck. Crazy shit."

"A unit is on its way. Are you in any immediate danger?"

"Nah, motherfucker don't even know we here."

"Please be mindful of your own safety. A unit will be by shortly."

At first, Anwan thought there was no way somebody would be here that fast, but then he remembered he was in Vernon. The town only had a couple hundred people, and the Vernon Police was only about fifty cops. Vernon was mostly businesses, and this warehouse was a business, and that was what they'd be protecting.

Sure enough, he heard sirens less than thirty seconds after he ended the 911 call.

"Shit," Cheese said. "We better get outta here before—"

Before Cheese could finish the sentence, Goose Mask looked up and then moved quickly toward the door, dropping the funnel and the hose on the floor of the warehouse.

A few seconds later, the small door opened. Goose Mask came running out and got right into the limo. If he noticed that Cheese and Anwan had left the door open, he didn't seem to care. He started the ignition and drove off.

"Fuck." Anwan ran toward the door and went in.

"The fuck you doing?" Cheese yelled. "You crazy motherfucker, don't go *in* there!"

But Anwan didn't care. He didn't know this guy, but Goose Mask was obviously trying to kill him, or at least make him suffer a helluva lot. That shit wasn't *right*.

Running inside, he saw that the white guy was muttering something in a language Anwan didn't know. It wasn't Spanish, though he recognized a few words. Maybe French or Italian or some other shit that was close.

The white guy's belly was fucking huge. It was all shiny—kind of like he was sweaty, but not really—and the veins were even more obvious now.

Anwan stood helplessly. He wanted to do something, but he didn't have nothing on him that could cut through a zip-tie, and the hose wasn't in the dude's mouth no more, so he couldn't fix that.

The sirens got louder. Then he heard voices. He couldn't make out specifics, but he heard Cheese shouting, "Fuck you, mother-fucker, we fuckin' called 911 and shit!"

More voices and then the two cops came in, holding their Berettas out and pointing them.

Throwing his hands up, Anwan said, "I ain't armed! I called 911! This guy got force-fed!"

One of the cops said something weird: "This one ain't wearing a mask, either, and the ink on his arm's wrong. And the hot sheet said he was white or Latino, not black."

"Yeah," the other cop said, lowering his weapon. He went over to the guy in the chair. "Damn, call a bus."

Anwan took a glance at his arm as he lowered it. He had several tattoos up and down his left arm, including the one he got in the joint, but the cops were looking for a particular one. Looked like they'd stumbled on some shit that the cops was already on, which must have been why they came so damn fast.

The first cop also lowered his weapon and grabbed the radio clipped to his shirt and called for an ambulance.

When he was done, the first cop looked at Anwan and Cheese, who had come in after the cops. "You two need to stick around. We need to talk to you."

"This mask dude been around the block?" Cheese asked.

The cop shrugged. "Let's just say folks want to talk to him."

"Shit," Cheese said.

Anwan shook his head. "Lemme guess, he killed white folks, right?"

The cop ignored the question and asked one of his own. "So what were you two doing walking here?"

"Headin' to the train station." Anwan held up his canvas bag. "Got my books outta my storage unit down the street, headin' home."

Anwan and Cheese then gave statements. Cheese was reluctant, but they gave all the info the cops asked for, including the name of the storage place Anwan had his unit in, and what his unit's number was.

When he was done, Anwan added, "Also, y'all should know I'm on parole for GTA."

The cop smiled. "Nice of you to say so. You steal any cars while you were here?"

"Not today, no," Anwan said, rolling his eyes.

"Then we're good."

Another siren sounded in the distance. Anwan hoped that this was the ambulance, because this motherfucker needed help and now.

"Holy cow," said the second cop, who had clipped the zip ties. "This is Jean-Pierre Caspari."

"Okay," the first cop said in a tone that indicated that he had no fucking clue who that was. And neither did Anwan.

"Guy runs d'Artagnan Foods," the second cop said. "Trying to get the *foie gras* ban lifted. And this is the kind of rig they use to force feed geese and ducks to make the *foie gras*."

"The fuck is fwa grah?" Cheese asked.

The first cop said, "*Don't* get him started, for God's sake."

But the second cop went ahead and answered. "It's a delicacy among the upper classes made from goose and duck liver. They force feed the birds to make them *really* fat so the liver's all fatty and tasty for the *foie gras*. California banned the practice and the sale of it back in '04. This guy's company is one of the biggest exporters of *foie gras*."

Rolling his eyes, the first cop said, "Let's just get this guy to a hospital, okay, Mike?"

"Yeah, but—"

"This isn't the time for your Greenpeace crap, okay?"

Cheese was shaking his head. "So let me get this shit straight. They torture motherfuckin' geese and motherfuckin' ducks so they can use their fat to sell it to rich folks to eat?"

"Basically, yeah," the second cop said.

"You white people do some crazy-ass shit."

The second cop let out a laugh that sounded like a bursting pipe. "You aren't wrong."

Two paramedics came running in the door. "Over here!" the first cop said, sounding relieved.

Anwan shook his head. Two years in county, ten years on the streets of Compton before that, and he'd never seen *any* shit like this before.

CHAPTER TWENTY-TWO

Westin San Diego Gaslamp Quarter
San Diego, California, United States of America

IN THE DREAM, Michelle Halls was standing in an alley in Shanghai, surrounded by people who were speaking French for some odd reason, even though they all looked Chinese.

She stumbled down the alley, regularly bumping into people.

Then she saw the window, and the corpses of the dogs she saw in Atlanta as a teenager were hanging from hooks. As were Fredi Rodriguez and Alexander Lesnick.

Inside was their apparent suspect, Chanan Kayaan Carlisle, who was wearing the mask of a black cat for whatever reason, and had Chang in a headlock.

Then he dumped Chang's head into the boiling oil and Halls found she couldn't get in to save him.

She unholstered her nine-millimeter Beretta, but the weapon wouldn't fire. There was no door to the place, just the window that the corpses of the fighting dogs and of the MCD Meats victims were hanging in.

Chang was dying and her phone was ringing and the corpses started swinging back and forth in the window.

Her weapon jammed and she tried to unjam it and her phone was ringing and her feet wouldn't move for some reason.

Why couldn't she move or fire her weapon? Why was her phone ringing? How did she even get service when her plan wasn't an international one? Why wasn't anyone speaking Chinese in Shanghai? Why was her phone still ringing?

And then she woke up and saw her phone dancing across the nightstand of the hotel room while ringing out with one of the generic ringtones. Glancing over at the display, she saw that it was Amenguale calling.

As she snatched the phone, the small digital display on the clock on the nightstand said that it was two-thirty in the morning.

While she was grateful to be spared any more of that dream, she couldn't imagine why her sergeant was calling her at this hour.

"Wha's goin' on, Sarge?"

"Did I wake you?"

Halls blinked. "It's two-thirty on a Saturday fucking morning, whaddaya *think*?"

"Just checking. I guess you came back to LA.?"

"No, we're staying the night in San Diego. Don't worry, Interpol's paying for it." Halls had been impressed that Chang was willing to use his work credit card to pay for a hotel. It wasn't even a crummy hotel, to her abject shock, but a Westin in Horton Plaza not far from the convention center and the Gaslamp District. "After a day of chasing serial killers, I really didn't want to drive back up the 5 all night."

"Well, too bad, because you're gonna have to."

By the time Amenguale filled Halls in about Jean-Pierre Caspari being found in a warehouse in Vernon, she was completely wide awake. "Fuck."

"The ambulance took him to Huntington Park, but when they called his wife, she had a chopper take him to Cedars-Sinai. She was going batshit trying to find out what happened to him. He was supposed to be at some kind of party or other, but the limo that got him at his hotel never made it to that party. The wife was worried sick. Anyhow, Caspari's going under the knife as soon as the hot-shit surgeon the wife asked for shows up."

"Jesus. And it was our guy?"

"According to the Vernon cops, the two witnesses described him as wearing a goose mask. And he was force-feeding Caspari the same way they force-feed geese and ducks to make the foy grass he makes."

"That's *foie gras*," Halls said automatically.

"Whatever. Point is, it matches the whole animal cruelty thing you were telling me about on the phone before, as well as the mask. Oh, and before you ask, Albert Carlisle left the diplomatic service in 1989 and never worked for the government again. He died of a heart attack in 1993. Way before government employees and their families would have their DNA in the database."

Halls sighed. That was what she had expected, especially since Chang had said he had checked all biological residue at the scenes against all the available databases. If Albert Carlisle had been in the system, there would've been a hit from his son. "Yeah, that's what I figured. Thanks for checking. What about his mother and sister?"

"Abhaya Bhatnagar Carlisle died in 2004 of breast cancer, but Kiara—"

"Wait, when in '04?"

Amenguale sounded grumpy, probably because she interrupted him. "What difference does it make?"

"A lot, when in '04?"

A pause, then: "The third of December."

"Fuck me."

"I don't screw subordinates."

Halls snorted.

"And I was gonna say that Kiara Carlisle is actually living in Thousand Oaks. I'll text you the address, and maybe you can visit her after you get your ass back up here so you can talk to Caspari after he's out of surgery."

"That's what I love about you, Sarge, your subtlety."

"Just get up here, Detective."

"Yeah, yeah."

She ended the call, went to the bathroom, splashed some cold water on her face, then called Chang and filled him in.

Chang said nothing as she passed on the Cliff Notes version of what Amenguale had told her about Caspari. She didn't get into what she'd learned about Carlisle's immediate family, figuring that was better told in person, given his previous relationship with the suspect's sister.

His only reply was, "I will be in the lobby in ten minutes."

Halls hopped in the shower for a quick rinse-down, which was more to wake her up enough to operate a motor vehicle than to get clean. After throwing yesterday's clothes back on—she hadn't packed a change of clothes, since the original plan was to drive back in the evening—she went downstairs to see Chang at the front desk settling the account.

She wouldn't have credited Chang with being able to look *more* rumpled than he had been since she met him, but he managed it now. His button-down shirt and khakis looked like they'd been slept in. Perhaps they even had been.

While he was doing that, she handed the valet her ticket, prompting him to go off and fetch the department's Chevy from the parking garage for her.

Then she composed a detailed text message for Skolnick. With luck, his text notification wouldn't wake him up. One of them deserved at least a shot at a good night's sleep.

Chang finished up, took the receipt from the desk clerk, and stuffed it unceremoniously into his pants pocket before walking over to Halls. "Are you ready?"

"Sure." She blew out a breath. "Just waiting for the car."

Her phone rang again, this time with Skolnick's number, which she had entered into her contacts after they'd gone their separate ways following Chang telling them about Carlisle's childhood traumas.

Answering the phone, she said, "Sorry for waking you, Detective."

"Please, I couldn't sleep after that story your Interpol buddy told us. I've been sitting in the living room watching HGTV." Defensively, he added, "People being stupid about their houses relaxes me."

"Hey, I'm not gonna judge, I still listen to boy bands. Anyhow, Chang and I are gonna head back up north to talk to Caspari. We also have a lead on Carlisle's sister, Kiara."

Chang shot her a look at that.

"Good. Keep me posted, please? I'm gonna take another run at Atkinson's girlfriend tomorrow morning."

"You got it. And hey, try to get some sleep, San Diego."

"Fat chance, Monrovia. Drive safe."

As soon as Halls ended the call, Chang said, "You have found Kiara?"

"In Thousand Oaks."

The Chevy pulled up to the front door of the hotel. She tipped the valet two bucks, got in, fastened her seat belt, and drove up First Avenue toward the 5, all the while filling Chang in on the rest of her conversation with her sergeant.

"I gotta ask," she said after she finished, "when did you last speak to Kiara?"

"The last time we spoke was in 2001 over the phone, and she was living in southern California at the time, but I was not sure where."

Halls nodded. "Did you know that Abhaya Bhatnagar Carlisle died in December 2004?"

Chang shot her a look. "No, I did not."

"From what you told me and Skolnick, our boy was closer to his mother than his father."

"And closer to Kiara than either of them. What are you getting at, Detective?"

"You said the pattern up until 2004 was that he'd find some incident or issue and kill everyone involved. Gorillas here, elephants there, tigers there. Then it stopped. What if it wasn't because he feared detection like you thought? What if it was because he promised his mother he'd stop?"

Chang shook his head. "I doubt that Abhaya was aware of what

Kai was doing. She loved him, but she was quite skilled at ignoring that which she did not wish to see."

"And I doubt that she was that oblivious. She paid enough attention to send him to that monastery because she thought it would help him more than therapy would have. Frankly, the world would be a better place if she had let him see a shrink instead of turning him into a kung fu fighter, but whatever."

"Kai's victims are hardly people who have benefitted the world."

"Tell that to Fredi Rodriguez's wife and three kids," Halls snapped. "Look, the point is, Abhaya died of breast cancer. That means she probably had at least some warning. It's completely possible that Carlisle visited her when she was dying and she extracted a promise that he wouldn't kill anymore. You were the one who said he was principled."

"Then why begin killing again twelve years later?"

Halls shrugged as she merged into traffic on the 5 northbound. "Who the hell knows? This is a guy who made his first kill at age fourteen, for fuck's sake. Yeah, he's principled, but he's also obsessed. Any promise he might have made to his mother would've been swimming upstream against his need to keep reenacting revenge against the guy who killed his dog."

"You believe he is still killing Mr. Hongzhou?"

Shooting him a quick, incredulous glance, Halls said, "You believe he isn't?"

"His actions are more complicated than that, in my opinion. He wishes to achieve a form of justice for the animals who are harmed."

"Bullshit. His actions are *simple*: someone took his best friend away from him when he was five years old and destroyed his entire world, and he wants to get back at everyone who does that kind of thing to animals. This is *not* about justice. Oh, I'm sure he pretties it up in his head with nonsense about taking on the forms of the animals with the mask and all that other crap, but it's a smoke-screen. He's still, at heart, a five-year-old boy whose dog was taken from him in the worst possible way, and he's lashing out. That monastery gave him the discipline so that his lashing out is organized and thoughtful instead of random and stupid like a five-year-old, but that makes him *more* dangerous."

"Perhaps." He sighed. "Ultimately, does it matter?"

Halls chuckled. "Not really, I'm babbling about it so I don't fall asleep at the wheel. First thing Lieutenant Martinez told me when I made detective—he was my shift commander back then—was that motive doesn't make a goddamn bit of difference. When you're police, it's all about the who and how. Why is the perp's shrink's problem."

"Indeed." Chang sighed and lit up a cigarette, then pushed the button to lower the window so he could blow the smoke out. Talking louder over the wind now whipping into the car, he said, "He has never committed so many of his murders this close together when they were not related."

"Making up for lost time? He took twelve years off, after all."

"Perhaps. Or perhaps he is aware that the march of technology over the past decade is such that he is more likely to be seen by surveillance. As I said, he has never allowed himself to be caught on film as he was at SeaLand, and that is only more likely to happen moving forward."

"Maybe." Halls let out a long breath, blinking several times to keep herself awake. "I will say one thing—knowing he comes from a rich family puts a lot of this in perspective. That's a shit-ton of capital, which can buy you a lot of anonymity—and travel."

"As well as equipment. You said that he was force-feeding Caspari?"

She nodded. "Yeah, from what the Vernon cops told Sarge, he had a whole rig with a hose, a funnel, and a big-ass processor that ground up food and fed it through the hose."

Chang took a long puff on his cigarette. Halls longed to grab it from him and smoke it herself.

Then after he exhaled, he said, "That is identical to the manner in which ducks and geese are force-fed on the farms used by Caspari's company. He has denied it, of course, but it is difficult to credit that denial."

"Yeah." Halls shook her head. "I should have kept my fucking mouth shut."

"At what juncture?"

"My last case was a bunch of home invasions. Took me forever to write up the paperwork because it was *so* incredibly boring, and I kept hoping for my next case to be something with a little meat on it."

Chang almost smiled. "I believe we have once again come around to karma, Detective."

"Yeah." She hit the steering wheel with the heel of her palm in annoyance. "I officially hate this case—and not just because it's got more meat than I can stand. Half the time I'm right there with this guy. I mean, seriously, losing your dog like that when you're five? That's got to be the one of the worst things that can happen to anyone. And a lot of his targets are pretty much scumbuckets. But Jesus, what he does—I mean, torture on this level is beyond the pale, no matter *who* it is. That's where he loses me."

"As you say, it does not matter." Chang finished his cigarette and tossed it out the window. "He has committed multiple murders. The reasons are irrelevant. Your job and mine is to enforce the laws that he has broken multiple times."

Again, Halls could only say, "Yeah."

The drive continued in silence.

CHAPTER TWENTY-THREE

8 June 2019

Cedars-Sinai Medical Center
Los Angeles, California, United States of America

DOCTOR TONY KHALIL had been woken out of a sound sleep at three-thirty in the morning by a call from the hospital's trunk line.

"Doctor Khalil, it's Sanjay."

Khalil blinked the sleep out of his eyes. Sanjay was a trauma fellow, and he was obviously on duty in the ER. "Wha's goin' on?" he asked through a yawn.

"I'm sorry to wake you, but we've got a fifty-three-year-old male who was just chopper'd over here from Huntington Park. As soon as the chopper landed, he went into cardiac arrest."

Rubbing his eyes, Khalil said, "Sanjay, why the heck are you calling me for a cardiac arrest? You know I'm a surgeon, right? I mean, we've only known each other for two years, so you might not have caught onto that ..."

Sanjay ignored the dig. "He's got peritonitis, his face and neck are swollen—I've already secured an airway, and he's gonna need a tracheostomy—and his belly is swollen to the point where it looks like it's going to burst."

That got Kahlil's attention. "Say that last part again."

"The area between his thorax and groin looks like a balloon. He needs a surgeon."

"And what's wrong with the surgeon on duty?" Khalil asked testily. This sounded like an interesting case and all, but not worth losing sleep for.

"Myka said to call you. Apparently our fifty-three-year-old male's brother-in-law is a big donor or something. His wife is the one who had him flown here. Myka said he needed the best attending available."

"I'm gonna remind her of that on my next annual review." He sighed. "All right, have you done a CT?"

"We're taking him there now. How soon can you get here?"

"I have no idea, it's never taken the same amount of time to drive from here to the hospital twice. But tell Myka I'll get there as fast as I can."

"I will. Thanks, Doctor Khalil."

"Just get him to the OR and prep him after you do the CAT scan."

After kissing his wife—who, curse her, was able to sleep right through the phone ringing—and going into little Aditi's room and kissing her on the head, Khalil went to the garage and drove to Cedars-Sinai.

When he arrived, Myka was waiting for him in the entryway by the guard stand. Where Khalil had barely managed to throw a few clothes on, Myka was dressed as if she was attending a corporate meeting, her hair and makeup perfect. Which was impressive, given that she had probably gotten a rude wake-up call of her own when their VIP patient got helicoptered in.

"You got here fast," Myka said appreciatively.

"I've finally learned the secret to driving on the 405 without traffic—leave at four in the morning. Only time I've been able to go over fifty on that highway since I moved to LA."

A woman got up from a nearby couch and walked over to

Myka, saying something in a foreign language. It sounded like French, or maybe Italian.

Myka replied in the same language, which impressed Khalil.

Then she turned to Khalil. "I'm telling Madame Caspari that you're the surgeon who's going to save her husband."

Khalil winced. "I'll be operating on her husband, but please don't make promises I can't keep. I haven't even seen his chart yet, much less the man himself. I don't know the results of the CT, or much of anything."

Madame Caspari said something else, and Myka then said, "She says she knows you'll do your best." She added, "She understands English, she just can't speak it." Then she handed him a chart. "Here's the chart. Get to work."

While he rode the elevator to the surgical suite, he looked at the chart. It really did look like someone had taken every organ in his belly and blown it up like a balloon. Liver enlarged, though no signs of alcohol poisoning or hepatitis, the two most common causes.

Then he read the actual text—apparently the patient had been force-fed, which explained why the intestines were also engorged.

He quickly put on his gear and then got himself scrubbed so he was nice and sterile. The nurse was kind enough to hold up the chart for him to continue perusing while he cleaned his hands.

Entering the operating theater, he saw that Tobias Rosenthal was the anesthesiologist, and he had put in a central line and was starting an arterial line. The patient also had a chest tube already in.

That twerpy resident whose name he couldn't remember was assisting. He probably was the surgeon on call in the ER when the patient was brought in, which did a lot to explain why Myka ordered Sanjay to bring Khalil in. His nurses were Liza Weinshelbaum and Karen Lagdamen.

The patient himself was lying on the bed, sedated, with his outsized belly exposed. He had varicose veins on his stomach.

"Holy fudge, this is—bizarre."

Karen stared at him as she put his goggles on for him. "Holy fudge?"

"I have a five-year-old who's a near-perfect mimic," Khalil said. "It's played merry heck with my ability to be profane. Can anybody tell me what the CT said?"

The twerp said, "He had a right-sided pneumothorax—there's a bunch of holes on the right side of his chest that look like they track into the liver."

"Holes?"

Pointing at the patient's right side, the twerp said, "Yeah, take a look."

Following the twerp's finger, Khalil saw several needle marks on the right chest wall. "Geez Louise."

"His intestines are so engorged," the twerp said, "they could barely fit him into the CAT scanner."

"I assume Sanjay did the chest tube?"

Sounding annoyed, the twerp asked, "How do you know I didn't do it?"

Khalil stared at him.

"Fine, yes, Sanjay did it. He said he needed to decompress the pneumo, and then got him up here before he crashed."

"Good." Khalil then went over the patient's vitals with Tobias and Liza, verified with Karen that all the instruments he needed were at the ready, and then he requested the scalpel he would use to cut the patient open.

Slowly, he made a midline incision across the patient's abdomen.

As he did, the intestines came spilling out through the incision into the surgical field.

"Fudge, get this under control."

As he spoke, he and the twerp both gently shifted the intestines so they were stably sitting in the surgical field.

Khalil regarded the bloated intestines. "My little girl had a balloon twister at her fifth birthday party, and I swear this guy's intestines look exactly like the balloon animals that woman made."

"Geez, what happened to his liver?" Liza asked.

Khalil peered more closely at the liver and saw that it was indeed speckled with numerous tiny puncture wounds.

Shuddering, he said, "Yeah, those needle marks were for the liver. What was he trying to do, biopsy him?"

Karen said, "Story I heard is this guy was force-fed food the same way they force-feed ducks and geese. The companies that do that biopsy the livers to see if they have enough fat to make good *foie gras*." Everyone looked at her, and she shrugged. "What, I saw a thing on the Discovery Channel about it."

The twerp was shaking his head. "Sanjay and I really should've done this, they didn't need to drag an attending in."

"This guy's brother-in-law's a donor to the hospital, so they brought in the big guns." Khalil smirked. "Maybe you'll get to work on VIPs after your voice changes."

Both Karen and Liza were noticeably restraining themselves from laughing. And Khalil could see a pout forming under the twerp surgeon's surgical mask. Khalil supposed he really should learn the boy's name at some point ...

For now, though, he looked back down at the patient. "All right, give me more retraction, I can barely see what I'm doing."

To his credit, the twerp didn't hesitate, but adjusted the retractors to widen the incision even further.

As he did so, Khalil heard a popping noise and suddenly he couldn't see a damn thing. He felt something splatter his face and shoulders, covering his goggles completely. "What the fudge?"

Monitors started beeping, and the twerp cried out, "Fuck me, his intestine exploded!"

———

An Chang had not gotten a good night's sleep since he woke up in his tiny apartment in Beijing the morning of the day he flew to the United States.

Every attempt at sleep since—whether on the plane from Beijing to Los Angeles, in either of the hotels he'd stayed in since arriving in California, or in the car with Detective Halls driving—had been fleeting at best, an abject failure at worst.

Sooner or later, he was going to collapse and sleep for a week, but for now he was still going on adrenaline.

And he'd gotten a surge of it now, because for the first time in thirty years, he knew exactly where to find Kiara.

Not a day went by when he didn't think of her. Her passion, her musical laugh, her beautiful long, black hair that he'd put a viola into on the day that he learned he'd lose her forever. The way she would sit on that wall on campus, hugging her knees, bare feet on the top of the wall.

That visual of her on that wall was seared in his mind. He was hard-pressed to recall what he had for dinner four nights ago. He couldn't always be counted on to remember to feed his dog. But that image of Kiara sitting barefoot on the wall was always in his mind, often at its forefront.

However, he hadn't actually seen her since that day in 1989, and had only spoken to her a few times since then.

"You alive in there?" Halls asked.

They were sitting in the waiting room outside the operating theater at Cedars-Sinai. The trip back, done in the pre-dawn hours, was far faster than the trip down, but when they arrived, they were told that Caspari was in surgery and to wait here. Chang was seated on a vinyl couch, while Halls sat in a Naugahyde chair across the corridor.

"After a fashion," Chang said dryly.

"Yeah, me, too. I wish they'd—"

Halls was interrupted by the doors to the operating theater sliding apart and allowing a person in scrubs to exit. He had removed his headpiece and mask; the shoulders of his scrubs were stained a combination of red and ochre.

Chang quickly got to his feet, and Halls followed. They both flashed their badges. "I'm Inspector Chang of Interpol, this is Detective Halls of the Monrovia Police. Did M'sieu Caspari survive?"

"Hm?" The doctor took a moment to even acknowledge the presence of Chang and Halls, and then it took him a moment to process

Chang's question. "Um, I'm Doctor Khalil, Tony Khalil. I'm sorry, Inspector, I—" He shook his head. "No, he died on the table. His liver was engorged, and his intestines ruptured. We tried to get the bleeding under control, but he went into shock and there was nothing we could do. You know, I've been performing surgery for twenty-three years. Once I took a five-foot tapeworm out of a woman's intestine. I once watched another doctor remove every organ from a young girl's chest and excise cancers *ex vivo* and then put them all back—the girl's still alive today. But I have *never* seen anything like what was done to that man. His intestines just—just *exploded*. They were stuffed to bursting. I didn't think that was possible."

Impatiently, Halls asked, "Did he say anything before he died?"

"Hm?" Again Khalil seemed to be in a daze. "Uh, no, but he couldn't have. By the time I got here, he was already anesthetized. You should talk to Dr. Rosenthal or one of the nurses."

"And Dr. Rosenthal is?" Chang prompted.

"The anesthesiologist." Khalil looked around and behind him. "Tobias, you back there?"

Another doctor, whose scrubs were less stained, came through the door. "What is it, Tony?"

"These two are police—Detective Chang from Monrovia and Inspector Halls from Interpol."

"Actually," Halls said quickly, "it's the other way around. In any case, we need to know if Caspari said anything before you put him under."

"Yeah, he did, but it didn't really make any sense. He just kept saying *oie* over and over again. Given that his intestines were about to explode, I'm guessing he was in a lot of pain."

"I see, thank you, Doctor," Chang said.

Both doctors wandered off as if in a daze.

Halls watched their retreating forms and said, "I guess you don't see exploding intestines every day even in this place."

"Or in any place," Chang said. "But Caspari's words were not due to being in pain. He is a native speaker of French, and the word that the doctor quoted is the French word for goose."

Nodding, Halls said, "That tracks with what the Vernon cops

told Sarge, that our perp was wearing a goose mask. And that fits Carlisle's MO."

"We must find other incidents that might fit the *modus operandi*. It is obvious that Kai is—what is the expression, 'upping his game'?"

Halls smiled. "That's *an* expression, yeah. And sure, we can do that, but I really think our next step is to hop on the 101 and visit your ex."

"I would like to see Kiara alone, if I may."

"Oh hell, no," Halls said sharply.

Chang recoiled as if he'd been slapped by her. "I beg your pardon?"

"Um, do you not recall the part where you used to date this woman? Honestly, I *should* go talk to her without you. You've got conflict of interest all out the ass here, and I'm still not a hundred percent convinced that it never occurred to you in twenty-two years not to even *look* at the kid you met in Taizhou who ticked all the boxes of your mask killer."

"As I thought I made clear, Detective," Chang said testily, "Kiara and her family left Shanghai, never to return. My own life at the time was completely tethered to Shanghai. My only means of communicating with her were long-distance phone calls I could not afford, and I had no guarantee that her family would even allow her to come to the phone. To say her family disapproved of our seeing each other would be a grave understatement."

"All right, but why didn't you talk to her once you realized the mask killer was a thing?"

Chang hesitated and took a breath to compose himself. "By the time these killings became, as you say, a thing, I had had no contact with Kiara in almost a decade. When I thought of her at all, those thoughts were happy memories of our time together. Her brother was never part of those remembrances. It simply never occurred to me."

Halls shook her head and wandered over to the vending machine that was in the corridor. "I guess that makes sense. But I wasn't kidding about conflict of interest." She pulled some change out of her pocket and inserted it into the slot as she spoke. "I gotta wonder, though, how many people would still be alive if you'd remembered him in the first place."

Chang opened his mouth and closed it. He found himself unable to formulate a proper response to that.

"Whatever," she said as she fished a candy bar out from the machine's dispenser. "It doesn't even fucking matter anymore. Look, Interpol: either we talk to Kiara Carlisle together, or I talk to her alone, but those are the only two options."

Chang sighed. "I can understand that. I request your leave to join you for your interview with Kiara, Detective. It *has* been thirty years, and I would very much like to see her again."

She tore open the candy bar wrapper. "Fine, let's go. And I'm taking the lead on this. As far as I'm concerned, this is me following up a legitimate lead on my double, and you're just along for the ride."

"Of course," Chang said. "Let us proceed."

CHAPTER TWENTY-FOUR

8 June 2019

Carlisle residence
Thousand Oaks, California, United States of America

IN CHANG'S MIND, Kiara hadn't changed since that day in 1989 when they last saw each other.

Once it was a reasonable hour of the morning, Halls had called her on the cell phone number provided by her sergeant. Kiara said she was home, and that it was best to talk now, as she had appointments all afternoon. Chang had been able to hear her voice a bit, albeit quiet and tinny, over the speaker of Halls's phone. Even distorted as it was, though, it sounded the same as it did all those years ago. The three decades fell away, and he imagined he heard her saying the same words she'd said at the airport in Shanghai.

When they arrived at Kiara's house, Chang hesitated before approaching. This was a much more modest home than the palatial Bhatnagar estate in Shanghai, though still quite a large one. The yard was well-landscaped, with artfully arranged hedges and flower beds.

Chang looked around and was severely disappointed at the lack of violas.

Finally, he forced himself to follow Halls to the front door.

Much as he imagined it otherwise, the woman who answered the door *had* changed since he'd said his goodbyes to her at Hongqiao Airport all those years ago—but surprisingly little given the time frame. Her dark hair was thinner, and speckled with the occasional strand of silver, she wore makeup today that she had never bothered with—or needed, truly—as a young woman, and she wore a suit for this meeting with Halls and Chang. Though he supposed whatever engagement she had this afternoon may have required the suit and she put it on now to save time later.

"Ms. Carlisle," Halls said, flashing her badge as Kiara opened the door, "I'm Detective Halls, we spoke on the phone?"

"Yes, of course, Detective."

Stepping aside, Halls said, "And I believe you already know Inspector Chang of Interpol."

"You look as beautiful as ever, Kiara." His voice broke as he said it. Had that happened with anyone else, he would have felt shame at so emotional a response.

But now, he felt joy at seeing her. Remorse at it being so long. And disappointment at the reason why.

Kiara smiled, then, and Chang found himself transported back to the university when they were both young and in love. "And you look like absolute hell, An."

Halls chuckled. "I can't tell you how glad I am to hear that he didn't always look like crap."

"No," Kiara said mischievously. "Once upon a time, An was actually attractive."

The good-natured teasing only made Chang feel the agonizing pull of thirty-year-old memories more strongly.

Halls smirked. "I'll have to take your word for it." Then she grew serious. "Unfortunately, our business here isn't to reminisce about old times—exactly. This involves your brother. May we come in?"

Nodding solemnly, Kiara said, "Of course."

They walked through a well-appointed foyer, with a curved stair-case leading up to the second floor. They moved past that, through a living room filled with lush furniture to a kitchen with a sliding glass door to a back patio that had a lovely view of the Santa Monica Mountains. A pitcher and three glasses sat on the patio table.

As she sat in one chair, Kiara said, "I hope you like iced tea. Aside from water, it's all I can offer you to drink, since I assume you cannot consume alcohol while on duty."

"Thank you," Halls said as she sat next to her.

Chang took the other chair and poured iced tea first for Kiara, then for Halls, before pouring for himself.

"Still the gentleman, eh, An?" Kiara asked.

He simply inclined his head.

"Ms. Carlisle," Halls said after sipping her tea, "when did you last speak to Chanan?"

She chuckled. "It's funny, as a boy, he always hated that name. As an adult, he took to it, but I always thought of him as Kai. And Father, of course, kept calling him Colin, because that was what he wanted to name him. Mother wouldn't allow it, of course, and our parents—" She blew out a breath. "They seemed to exist in a perpetual impasse. There were never arguments, only tense disagreements."

"Not much love lost there?" Halls said.

"No." Kiara took another sip of tea. "I'm afraid I may not be of much help with regards to my family, Detective. I stopped talking to my mother and my brother shortly after our father died."

"That was in 1993, yes?"

Nodding, Kiara said, "Mother wished to return to India after that. She tended to make decisions and expected the universe to go along with them. She was very cross when Kai and I refused to move with her, as we wished to stay in America. I moved here to California, while Kai moved to New York. Kai and I lost touch with each other after a time, and Mother refused to even speak to me. I only found out that she died when a lawyer contacted me with regard to my inheritance."

"All right," Halls said, "but you and Chanan lived together with your parents prior to your father's death, yes?"

Again, Kiara nodded. "After he lost his diplomatic post, Father became a lobbyist, so we lived near Washington, DC. Chanan attended school there, and he got excellent grades, though he didn't seem to make any friends. He spent a lot of time volunteering at the National Zoo, and also studying martial arts, although he never stuck with any art for very long. Six months doing kung fu, a year doing aikido, three months doing karate, another year doing kendo. He never really talked about it much. In fact, the only thing he did talk about was the animals he worked with at the zoo."

"Do you think that was because of what happened to his dog?" Halls asked.

Kiara looked at Chang. "You told her about Nandita?"

Chang nodded.

Halls said, "There have been a series of incidents involving cruelty to animals over the past two decades, and we think Chanan may know something about them. We need to question him, but we don't really have any idea where to find him."

"Wait—does this have something to do with what happened to Jean-Pierre?"

Chang blinked. "You know Jean-Pierre Caspari?"

"I work with many charities, and d'Artagnan has donated food for fundraisers I've been involved with. I've known Jean-Pierre and Hélène for years. She called me this morning and told me about what happened to her husband." She shook her head and stared at Chang. "You're saying Kai might know something about *that*?"

Chang hesitated. "We do not know if he does or not. That is why we wish to question him."

Kiara shook her head. "My brother is a suspect, is he not?"

"Like the inspector said—" Halls started, but Kiara cut her off.

"You do not need to prevaricate with me, Detective. I have not spoken to my brother in very long, but I do know him. Or, at the very least, know who he was." She put her head in her hands, then wiped the tears that were forming. "Kai had so much anger in him.

I had hoped that the Sifu at Hé Ping would give him a way to channel his anger positively, but it seems he failed at that."

"We don't know what he's succeeded or failed at," Halls said.

"Perhaps." Kiara sipped more iced tea. "The only time I ever saw him even show an emotion after he came back from the monastery was related to animals. He was only ever angry when someone mistreated the animals at the zoo, and he only ever smiled when he was volunteering there."

"You said you and he lost touch," Halls said. "Why is that?"

"We were on opposite sides of the country, and the attempts were all one way. I would call him, but on those rare occasions when he answered the phone, he said almost nothing, and when he didn't answer, he never returned my messages. After a time, I simply gave up."

"I am sorry," Chang said. "I remember how close you were."

"Emphasis on the past tense, An." Kiara smiled. "I love my brother, but I have had no contact with him in over twenty-five years. I don't know what might have happened to him in that time, and I have no means of contacting him. My life has almost nothing to do with my parents or my brother anymore. Mother and Father are long dead, and Kai and I have no connection. I focus my time and money on helping people. I'm on the board of several charities, and I do a great deal of outreach to the less fortunate."

Halls frowned. "You said 'almost nothing.'"

With a chuckle, Kiara said, "Well, the money I am spending is my inheritance. My father had considerable wealth, and that is as nothing compared to the Bhatnagar fortune. Even with Kai receiving half, I came into a considerable sum after my parents died, and I have tried to put that to the best possible use."

They spoke for a bit longer, though Chang remembered nothing of what was said from that point until they left.

As they walked back through the house toward the front door, Halls handed Kiara a business card. "I know it's a long shot, but if you do hear from Chanan, please call me right away, okay?"

"Of course, Detective. And An?"

Chang had already made it to the front door, but he stopped. He did not turn, for he felt that if he faced his former love, he would break.

"When this is over, please get back in touch? I would very much like to catch up."

"I would like that as well," he said without turning around, and he continued out the door.

As they headed to Halls's car, the detective smacked his arm.

"What is that for?"

"Lying. You don't have any intention of calling and getting together, do you?"

"What would be the point? When this is over, I will have captured and incarcerated her brother. She will hate me."

"I doubt that. She isn't the twenty-year-old girl you knew back then who loved her brother. She's moved on."

Chang stared at her incredulously. "Did you not see her tears?"

Halls waved that off. "That was for her childhood memories. And maybe for the fact that, when we arrest him for these murders, she'll become known as the sister of a serial killer. But emotionally? She has *no* connection to him anymore."

Now Chang smirked, forcing himself back into the here-and-now instead of allowing his mind to be mired in the past. "*When* we arrest him?"

"Oh yeah. We're going back to Monrovia and we're gonna comb through every bit of the world wide web and we're going to figure out who his next victim is."

"You believe he is using the internet to find his targets?"

"Why not? It's the most efficient way to do it. And he's obviously going after as many people in southern California as he can, so we'll focus on that. Let's go."

They got into the car, and Halls gunned the motor and drove out of Kiara's driveway at a faster-than-was-truly-safe speed.

CHAPTER TWENTY-FIVE

8 June 2019

Homicide Unit, San Diego Police Department Headquarters
San Diego, California, United States of America

SARABETH MONTGOMERY LOOKED like she wanted to be anywhere else.

J.D. Skolnick was used to people sitting at his desk having that look. Nobody wanted to be in the Homicide Unit offices; they were usually there because someone close to them had died and/or they were a person of interest in the investigation of that death. It was never a fun place to be.

"I'm sorry, Detective, but I can't really tell you that much about Jim in the first place. We have a bunch of mutual friends, but last Friday was our first real date. He'd just broken up with his girlfriend, I'd just broken up with my boyfriend, we're both divorced, both in our forties, it seemed like a good fit. Besides, I used to love going to SeaLand as a kid, so I figured going on a date with the CEO to a staff party would be a dream come true."

Based on the tone in her voice, Skolnick had to smile. "Not so much, huh?"

She shrugged. "It was like any other office party—a bunch of friends and colleagues getting drunk and stupid at the same time. And nobody there was drunker or stupider than Jim. Honestly, if you want to know who might want him dead, it would be anybody who saw him guzzling his way through that party."

Skolnick hadn't actually asked that, but he let it go. "The last time the two of you were together was when he went into the rear section and you were stopped by a security guard, yes?"

Nodding, Sarabeth said, "Yeah, I was just trying to get out of an uncomfortable conversation by saying I wanted to go in back. But once that guard started up, I didn't want to keep going. Jim insisted, so he went back. I walked away." She swallowed and looked away. "I never saw him again."

"What can you tell me about the guard?"

She looked back at Skolnick again. "I'm sorry?"

"The guard. What did he look like?"

"Um—" Sarabeth stared at the far wall and grimaced. Then she shook her head. "I couldn't tell you. I mean, he wore a uniform and a big ballcap—he had dark skin, like he was Latino." She shrugged. "Sorry, I don't remember."

"Did you notice any tattoos on his arm?"

"A tattoo? No, he—" She frowned. "He had long sleeves on, actually. I think he was the only person in the whole place who did." Shaking her head, she said, "Look, I'm sorry, but I don't remember anything about him."

Skolnick's phone buzzed and danced across his formica desk. Grabbing it, he checked the display to see that it was Halls. He swiped across the display and said, "Hold on for a minute, Monrovia." Without waiting for a reply, he put the phone down and said, "I have to take this. I think we're done here. If you remember anything, about Jim or about the guard, you have my number."

Rising to her feet, Sarabeth nodded. "Thank you, Detective—I'm sorry I couldn't be of more help. I hope you catch whoever did that to him."

"Me, too. You okay to get home?"

"I'll get an Uber. Thank you."

She walked toward the exit, and Skolnick picked his phone back up and said, "Sorry, was talking to a witness. What is it?"

"We have a couple of really good possibilities for the next target, and one of them is in your neck of the woods. I just e-mailed you a link to a Facebook page."

"Okay. Hang on."

Skolnick put the phone down and called up his e-mail. Sure enough, there was something from Halls's Monrovia Police e-mail account. He opened it, clicked on the link, and saw a Facebook page belonging to Deena King. Her profile picture was of her holding a rifle while kneeling next to a dead cheetah, and her cover photo was of her in a similar pose next to a dead rhino. He also saw that she lived in Escondido and all her recent posts were about how much fun she'd had hunting. At one point she even referred to herself as "King of the jungle."

He picked the phone back up and dryly said, "I'm starting to see why you think she might be a target, yeah."

"She's not the only one. Chang and I spent the last several hours combing the web for people who mistreat animals in Southern California. Swear to God, I'm sending half my paycheck to PETA after this shit."

Skolnick let out a bitter chuckle, as he'd been having similar thoughts ever since they watched the footage of Atkinson's murder.

"Anyhow, King did a Reddit AMA last week. Please tell me you know what that is."

"Means 'ask me anything,' and it's basically a fancy name for a scheduled chat session on Reddit."

"Sorry, I just had to spend ten minutes explaining it to Chang."

"I'm sure he'll be begging for those ten minutes back on his deathbed. I know I'll be begging for all the time I spent on Reddit back."

Halls snorted. "Anyhow, that AMA got some decent publicity, and she's actually been advertising on Facebook to get more likes, *and* she's local to Southern California, so she could very easily be on Carlisle's list. You should try to get ahold of King and warn her."

"Like, say, by calling her on the phone number she put in her Facebook profile?"

There was a brief silence before Halls said, "Are people still dumb enough to *do* that?"

"Apparently. Something my lieutenant always says: money, resources, and intelligence are all well and good, but the thing that makes police work succeed more than anything else is people being stupid."

"Amen to that. Keep us posted. We found two other possibilities, one in Anaheim, one in Corona, so we're gonna check them out."

Skolnick ended the call, then looked up Deena King's full address online, as the profile only said that she lived in Escondido. That was a slight problem in and of itself, as Escondido was out of his jurisdiction. Still, she counted as a person of interest in his homicide, so he could fudge it.

Besides, he had some friends up there. He quickly found a number on his phone and called it.

"Escondido Police, Sergeant Genevka."

"Hey, Joe, it's J.D. Skolnick."

"Oh, sweet fuck, what'd I do this time?"

Skolnick laughed. "Nothing, you're just paranoid."

"With reason. Last time you called me out of the blue I wound up hanging from a scaffold on Centre City Parkway."

"It's nothing that bad, I promise. I need one of your patrol cars to go by a house." He read off the King family's address. "Girl named Deena King lives there, and we think her life might be in danger."

"Why do you give a shit?"

"Because the person who wants to kill her is responsible for my homicide in SeaLand."

"Oh, fuck me backwards, you caught that one? Didn't they find the guy's leg in a whale or something?"

"Or something. Can you help me out, Joe?"

"Yeah, sure."

After making all the arrangements, Skolnick wished his friend well, and then ended the call so he could try the number on the Facebook page.

It went straight to voicemail without ringing, so he left a message saying to call him immediately, giving both his cell number and the number of the Homicide Unit. A call from the murder police usually got a pretty quick response.

He headed toward the motor pool while composing a text to Guerra. His partner had already checked out and was at his daughter's piano recital, so his phone was definitely off, but he'd want the update at intermission.

As he retrieved the keys to a Ford from the motor pool sergeant, his phone rang.

"Detective, this is, um, Officer Adler of the Escondido Police. Sergeant, um, Genevka said to call you."

"Yes, Officer, what can I do for you?"

"Well, Detective, I'm, um, I'm at the King house. The sergeant sent me and my partner here, and the mother just, um, just informed me that her husband and daughter are at a shooting range over on Ash Street and Ohio Avenue called, um, Arms and the Man."

Skolnick couldn't help but chuckle. "Shaw's getting dizzy in his grave right now."

"What was that, Detective?"

"Uh, nothing, Adler." The last thing he wanted to do was explain that the store name was best known as an 1894 play by George Bernard Shaw, and also the opening line of Virgil's *Aeneid*. "Can you go over there and try to find her and her father? I'm about a half hour or so away, but I can meet you there."

"Um, will do."

He ran to where the Ford was parked, got in, started it, and headed toward the 15. He used his siren and lights to get through the worst of the traffic, eventually getting off at Exit 28—the exit for the very same Centre City Parkway that Genevka had been referring to.

Skolnick really didn't think that incident was his fault. How was he supposed to know the guy they were after would climb up the scaffolding? And Genevka only spent a few days in the hospital.

After turning right at Felicita Plaza, he drove for a bit before turning left onto San Pasqual Valley Road, where there was a sign that said the San Diego Zoo Safari Park was to the right.

"I can't get away from animals on this case," he muttered. He was still having trouble sleeping after Chang's stories of murdered dogs and faces in boiling oil and such.

San Pasqual Valley turned into Ash Street, and he soon arrived at Arms and the Man.

As he pulled into the gun range's parking lot, he noticed that there was a Methodist church across the street. "I love this country," he muttered.

An Escondido Police patrol car was parked in front of the range, and he saw a man with a shaved head approach. His nametag said ADLER, so Skolnick figured this to be who he talked to before.

"Welcome to, um, to Escondido, Detective."

"Thanks, Officer. What's happening?"

"Um, dead end, I'm sorry to say. Bob and Deena King were scheduled for, um, target practice at eight. It's about nine-thirty now, and they haven't showed. They aren't answering their phones —I tried both of them myself, while we were waiting for you. Straight to, um, to voicemail."

"You think you can get your people to ping their phones?"

Adler blinked. "Um, I can ask, but does this even connect to a case?"

Skolnick sighed. Damned jurisdictional nonsense. He could probably get Genevka to give the order, but there'd still be hoops to jump through, and there wasn't time.

"You think they been kidnapped, Detective?" Adler asked.

"Given who we're dealing with, I'd be grateful if it was only a kidnapping. This girl has been posting pictures online of her with the animals she's hunted and killed, and our killer goes after people who torment animals, usually by—" Then his eyes widened, as he recalled the sign he saw as he turned onto San Pasqual Valley. "Sonofabitch."

"Detective?"

"Officer Adler, I need you to radio in for backup to meet us at the Safari Park."

"It's, um, closed at this hour."

"All the more reason to get over there. Our perp may want to give the animals an after-hours feeding."

He hopped back into his Ford and called Chang's cell, since he figured Halls was driving.

It went to voicemail, so he quickly said, "Inspector Chang, this is Detective Skolnick. I think we hit paydirt. Deena King and her father didn't show up for an appointment, and nobody's answering their phones. That appointment was only about five miles from the San Diego Zoo's Safari Park, which has both cheetahs and rhinos. I think he's doing his *Mikado* act there, with the punishment fitting the crime. If you want in on the collar, get your asses down the 5 and meet me there."

He left the same message on Halls's phone, and then drove the five miles to the Safari Park, Adler and his partner in tow.

They were met at the parking lot by two other units, as well as another car that contained Joe Genevka.

"What are you doing here, Joe?" Skolnick asked as he hopped out of the Ford.

"Keeping an eye on your commandeering my cops for your case," Genevka said. "This turning into a kidnapping?"

"I think so—with the distinct possibility of another murder or two if this goes the way the others have gone. Our perp likes to kill people who hurt animals, usually by some means that he finds appropriate. The SeaLand victim was the CEO, and his little amusement park mistreats the orcas, so the perp mistreated him the same way—whipping him with barbed wire and stuffing his gut with rocks."

"Cute," Genevka said. "What about the Kings?"

"Well, the daughter posted pictures of herself after killing a cheetah and a rhino. They've got both here, so we need to check wherever they stow those animals at night and make sure our perp didn't bring them here for some of his brand of justice."

"God, I hate this serial shit. I like my murders simple, over money or love or something like that." Genevka shook his head. "All right, let's see if anybody's in the damn park."

They headed toward the hut-like structure that served as the park's front entrance. It was gated shut, but the gate had a door in it, and someone was walking toward the gate from the inside. Skolnick figured that the person was a night security guard or some such who heard all the people milling about in the parking lot when it should have been empty.

As they approached, Skolnick could see that it was indeed a security guard, and he looked an interesting combination of surprised and scared.

"Wow, you guys got here *fast*."

Genevka frowned. "Excuse me?"

"I only called you guys, like, a minute ago."

Skolnick and Genevka exchanged a quick glance. "Called about what?"

"There's some weird noises in the cheetah run."

Now Genevka stared at Skolnick. "I really didn't want you to be right about this."

"Me, either. Unfortunately, I'm almost always right about this kind of stuff."

"That's why I want to be on your bar trivia team." Genevka turned to the security guard. "So you gonna let us in, or what?"

"Huh?" The guard seemed to be in a trance of some sort. Then he reached for the keychain on his belt. "Yeah, yeah, of course. Sorry, been working here ten years, and never heard *anything* at night when we weren't doing one of those Roar and Snore overnight things."

He opened the small gate that was embedded in the big gate, and Skolnick led the way through, followed by the others.

As he led them through the hut-like entrance past the carousel and around the lagoon, the guard said, "At night, when there isn't an event, the animals all go into little indoor shelters. We've got a caretaker on call in case something goes wrong, but I've been trying her cell for twenty minutes, and nothing. I'm worried she's the one in there, 'cause the screams have been pretty bad."

Skolnick stopped, stared at the security guard, then pointed to Genevka. "Call for backup, *now.*" Back to the guard, he said, "You didn't mention screams! Where is this place?" He started jogging ahead.

The guard did a quick double take, then jogged to catch up. "This way."

They ran down a service road to the cheetah run. Along the way were several closed-up pavilions, quiet bodies of water, empty petting areas, and so on. It was very eerie, especially thanks to the only light coming from flashlights carried by the guard and the Escondido uniforms.

As they passed a small stadium and a picnic area, Skolnick started to hear the screams the guard had mentioned. He also could hear Genevka calling for backup, including a call for their Tactical Operations Unit. Skolnick was grateful that he was calling in TOU, as he didn't really have the authority to call in the local SWAT team, nor was he sure that Genevka would do it for him if he asked. The fact that the sergeant was doing so without his asking meant that Genevka believed that *something* bad was going down.

Skolnick hoped it wasn't too late for the Kings.

A man wearing a blue fleece jacket with the Safari Park logo over a red polo shirt and khakis approached. The latter two articles of clothing were the standard outfit for all San Diego Zoo volunteers, both here and at the main zoo downtown. The volunteer wore a gray safari hat. It wasn't, in Skolnick's opinion, nearly cold enough to justify wearing the jacket or hat, but different people got cold at different temperatures. Besides, it was a bit chillier here in the park than it had been out on the street.

"What is going on?" the man asked with a slight accent that sounded vaguely Indian.

The guard was frowning. "Where's Mara?"

"Called in sick," the volunteer said. "I'm filling in."

More screams. Everyone turned their heads. Skolnick saw Adler go for his weapon.

"Okay, I believe I know why you are here. Let me go in first, make sure it's safe for the animals."

"Those are human screams," Skolnick said, "so it's not really their safety I'm primarily concerned with."

"You should be concerned with your own, Detective—if the cheetahs have been disturbed, they could be dangerous."

Skolnick had to admit that he had a point. "Fine, you go first."

The volunteer went ahead toward the indoor shelter, the entry to which was in a back corner of the cheetah run. This was a three-hundred-foot track where the cheetahs could do what they were most famous for—run fast—for the enjoyment of park patrons.

The screams got louder, and now all the cops had their weapons out. The volunteer herded the cheetahs out, and Skolnick said, "Keep them secure."

"They won't leave this enclosure," the volunteer said confidently.

As they came outside, Skolnick saw blood on the teeth and paws of several cheetahs.

"Shit." He ran in, and found a grisly scene: amidst the bedding and food dishes and other amenities for the big cats, against the wall were a middle-aged man whose throat, chin, and chest were drenched in blood, and a young woman who was also bloody, and also screaming. Skolnick also noticed that they were both covered in bits of ground meat. Both of them had their hands behind their backs, and their ankles were secured with zip ties.

While Genevka got on his radio and called in an 11-41—a call for an ambulance, to add to the backup and TOU—Adler checked on the older man, who wasn't moving, while Skolnick checked on the girl, who was definitely Deena King. "Easy, Ms. King, I'm Detective Skolnick of the San Diego Police Department. We're here to rescue you."

"Oh God, it was horrible, the man took us and tied us up and covered us in meat and it was *awful*, Daddy, are you okay? Daddy? *Daddy!?*"

Adler looked over at Skolnick and shook his head.

He looked at Deena. "I'm sorry."

That started her screaming again.

Adler cut the zip-tie that was restraining Deena's hands behind her back. Skolnick, for his part, thought he heard something else besides the teenager's cries of pain and grief.

He went to the back of the shelter and heard a muffled noise behind a small door.

Opening it, he saw a woman in a red polo shirt and khakis, who was also secured the same way the Kings were. She was making a muffled "Mmmmmm!" noise, but she wasn't gagged.

"Mara I presume?" Skolnick said.

"Mhmm!" She made the noise, but didn't nod.

Another uniform moved to free her. Her arms and legs still didn't move, though, even after the zip ties were cut.

"Dammit, he must have given her curare or something. She's completely paralyzed. Which means she can't tell us who did this until it wears off."

"I don't get it," the uniform said. "He was trying to kill those two, why not kill her?"

"He's principled."

"Huh?"

Skolnick shook his head. "Nothing. I—"

Then everything clicked in his head. Hat that obscured his face. Jacket to cover the tattoo. The Indian accent. Claiming that Mara called in sick, when this was obviously Mara sitting before him paralyzed.

Running toward the door, he cried out, "Stop that volunteer!"

He ran outside, followed by Adler and several other cops, only to find cheetahs milling about, and one uniform on the ground, clutching his belly.

Skolnick knelt down to check on the officer. "You okay?" He also heard helicopters overhead, which was probably the backup Genevka had asked for.

"Bastard sucker-punched me. Never saw it coming." The officer coughed twice. "Fucker's *fast*, too. Ran off."

Instinctively, Skolnick reached for his radio, but it was on the wrong frequency for Escondido. He looked over at Genevka. "We gotta get this guy. He's still gotta be in the park, and we can't let him leave."

Nodding, Genevka called in for TOU to secure the safari park.

"He's an Indian male," Skolnick prompted him, "about six-two, shaved head, distinctive tattoo on the inside of his left arm of the sign of Shiva."

Genevka stared at him. "I'm only gonna say 'tattoo,' okay?"

Skolnick nodded as he helped the officer to his feet. "Let's find this guy; he just added to a very lengthy kill list."

An officer stuck his head out from inside the shelter. "Guard says he needs to let the ambo in."

"Go with him," Skolnick said without thinking, but cut himself off at a glare from Genevka.

The sergeant then said, "Stay here, Cornwell, and keep an eye on the girl and the real volunteer. And find a blanket to cover the body, maybe the girl'll stop screaming. Adler, go with the guard, keep your eyes peeled. This guy took out Rostonkowski with one punch."

"Um, yes, sir. C'mon."

The guard and Adler moved off through the cheetah run in the general direction of the front entrance so they could escort the paramedics back, while Cornwell went back into the shelter. The remaining half-dozen or so uniformed officers started a search of the immediate vicinity. Skolnick told them, "Don't go too far. Our perp has navigated the African Congo and Chinese mountains, he'll run rings around you if you get too deep in here. Just go about five hundred feet in each direction and report back."

Within a few minutes, there were half a dozen helicopters in the air over the safari park, one of which landed in the cheetah run. Skolnick also heard the siren from the ambulance in the distance.

A uniformed officer with lieutenant's bars came out of the helicopter and ran over to where Genevka and Skolnick were standing. The helicopter took off again as soon as the lieutenant was clear.

Genevka immediately said, "Detective J.D. Skolnick, SDPD, this is Lieutenant Dave Kupfer, CO of TOU."

"M-o-u-s-e," Skolnick muttered in a singing tone. "Sorry—crazy day. Hell, crazy *week*. Pleased to meet you, Lieutenant."

"The same, Detective," Kupfer said. "I got the whole park surrounded. Ain't nobody gettin' in, ain't nobody gettin' out."

"Good." Skolnick ran a hand through his hair. "Don't underestimate the target, Lieutenant. He's been killing people for twenty years in multiple countries, and we only figured out who he is yesterday. He's a trained fighter, and his kills have all been meticulously planned and executed. He's smart, and he's skilled."

Kupfer nodded. "Bully for him. I got fifty guys and six helicopters, I like our odds. This ain't tee vee where they say they put up a perimeter and then the bad guy gets through it anyhow. Don't nobody get out of our perimeters. We'll get 'im for you, Detective."

"Not only for me, I've got an Interpol inspector and an LA cop coming down for him, too."

"Great, we'll have a party. I'm tellin' you, I'm glad you ain't callin' him the 'unsub.' Fuckin' tee vee, man."

Frowning, Skolnick asked, "Why would I call him that? 'Unsub' is an abbreviation for 'unknown subject.' We *know* who he is—his name is Chanan Kayaan Carlisle, he's the son of a former US ambassador to China and his very rich wife." His felt his phone buzz in his pocket. Pulling it out, he saw that it was Chang. "Excuse me, this is our Interpol inspector now." He swiped his finger across the display and put the phone to his ear. "We got him, Chang."

There was a pause. "A moment, while I put you on speaker." A second later, Skolnick heard a click followed by a great deal more background noise. "Repeat what you said, please?"

"I said we got him. You guys were right on the money with the Kings. He kidnapped them, took them to the Safari Park, tied them up, and poured ground meat on them so the cheetahs would chew on them. Killed the father, and the daughter's in bad shape. Paramedics are almost here. He's escaped into the park dressed like one of the folks in red shirts who work here, but we've got a perimeter, and I'm assured by the lieutenant in charge of TOU that he won't get out. And I already gave the lieutenant the 'don't underestimate him' speech."

Halls said, "Nice work, San Diego!"

"Hey, if it wasn't for you two, we wouldn't have even been looking for them until it was too late."

"Yeah, we're one big happy law-enforcement family. We'll be there in about half an hour."

Skolnick frowned. "You gonna teleport?"

"We were already in Corona when we got your message, so we've been hauling ass down the 15."

"Okay, good. With any luck, we'll have him in cuffs by the time you get here."

Chang said, "That is a conclusion to be greatly hoped, Detective."

Then both Genevka and Kupfer's radios squawked with a voice crying out, "11-99!"

Even as the details were yelled out over the radio, Chang asked, "What is an 11-99?"

Escondido used the same signal codes as San Diego, so Skolnick answered without hesitating: "Officer in distress."

CHAPTER TWENTY-SIX

8 June 2019

San Diego Zoo Safari Park
Escondido, California, United States of America

Officer Juanita Perez moved slowly through the empty safari park, slowly working her way past a rest room and around a closed food stand.

It was supposed to be a quiet shift.

It had been an exhausting few weeks for Perez. She was going for her black belt in karate, at the same time as her daughter, Perlita, who was going for her junior black belt. They had joined as a bonding experience after Perlita's father smoked and snorted his way out of their life. After five years of hard work, they were preparing for the three-day promotion. She'd already scheduled the next two weeks off, starting after this shift ended, so she could focus. As it was, she'd spent every off-duty hour either training, reviewing, or not getting enough sleep.

So what happened two hours before the shift was supposed to end? A call to the Safari Park—the very same place she had promised to take Perlita after the promotion—to track down a serial killer.

At least she hadn't actually seen the guy yet, which suited her fine. Every time she turned a corner, she expected to see him. If she actually made the arrest, she'd be doing paperwork into the next shift, and while she didn't mind the overtime—mixed with time-and-a-half, since the next day was Sunday—getting involved in a big case like this would probably mess with her off time. And the promotion.

Praying to a God she was only occasionally on speaking terms with since she found Armando's drug stash in the closet, she peered around the food stand. There was a big picnic area on the other side of the stand, which was wide open. There was only a half moon in the night sky, which wasn't enough to provide significant light, especially with all the trees in the park. Still, the picnic area looked deserted, answering her prayer in the affirmative.

Keep it up, God. I may even go back to church someday. Her plan was to check this picnic area, at which point she'd have gone the five hundred feet she'd been ordered to check out. After that, she'd haul ass back to the cheetah run, which had become the command post. TOU was here now—their helicopters were flying overhead—and *they* could handle this shit. She needed to get back to the quiet part of her shift.

Then she heard a voice cry out, "Over there!"

Two seconds later, she saw a man running into the picnic area on the far side, right under a tree. He was wearing a red shirt and khakis—which meant he'd ditched the fleece and hat. She couldn't blame him for that, it was much too damn hot out for that crap, and besides, he was trying to move fast. From what she'd heard, the hat was to hide his face and the jacket to hide a distinctive tattoo. At this point the cat was out of the bag, so why bother?

Two TOU guys were running into the picnic area behind him, and yelling, "Freeze, police!"

Instead of freezing, the perp jumped up into the tree. Perez thought he had something in his hand, but it was too dark, and the perp too far away, for her to be sure.

The two guys from TOU moved into position under the tree. "Please come down from there, sir. We've got you covered, and there isn't anywhere to go."

Perez was pretty sure that was Sweeney who said that. It sounded like his voice, and besides, he was always polite.

She slowly moved across the picnic area to back up Sweeney and his partner. On the one hand, those two were trained for this tactical stuff. They had AR-15s and did this sort of crap every day. She was a red belt with a Beretta, and she was a couple of hours away from two weeks off the clock.

But she was still a cop. Cops backed each other up. So she headed toward Sweeney and his partner, Beretta ready, keeping an eye on the tree the perp had jumped up.

"I *said* come down from there, sir," Sweeney said, "or we *will* be forced to open fire and—"

Suddenly, the perp leapt out of the tree and—somehow—executed a double front snap kick while falling downward, getting both Sweeney and his partner right in the face, knocking them to the ground. And then he landed smoothly on his feet, bending his knees. He gripped what appeared to be a long bamboo stick like it was a *bo* staff and quickly swung it like a baseball bat to knock a still-dazed Sweeney to the ground, then whirled it over his head to do the same to his partner.

For several seconds, Perez stood there, dumbfounded. The person who ran her karate school was a seventh-degree black belt who had participated in about fifty international fighting tournaments over the decades, and placed first in about two-thirds of them. On his best day, he could never do what the perp just did. Certainly not that *fast*.

Then she shook off the shock, and started running. She couldn't throw a shot from this distance. The visibility was for shit, and there was too much risk of hitting Sweeney or his partner.

So she closed that distance. As she ran, she activated the radio clipped to her shirt and called in an 11-99.

While the other TOU officer struggled to move, Sweeney got

right to his feet and tried to get a grip on his rifle, which was attached to his Kevlar vest via a bungee string.

This time the perp used the improvised *bo* to sweep out Sweeney's legs, and the officer once again tumbled to the ground.

The perp somehow managed to hook the rifle with the bamboo staff—he was still too far away for Perez to figure out *how* he managed it, exactly—and yank it from Sweeney's chest, tossing it aside.

Then he stomped on Sweeney's groin. Perez winced and she could hear Sweeney's agonized cry.

By this time, though, she was close enough to line up a shot. Steadying herself, thumbing the safety off her Beretta, and aiming it right at the sonofabitch's head, she yelled, "Freeze, asshole! One move, and I shoot!"

Sweeney had whipped out his own Beretta, which all the TOU guys had as backup weapons, and pointed it at the perp from the ground. "You heard the lady. Don't budge."

Perez smiled. Looked like they were gonna get this guy. And Sweeney could take the arrest, thus saving her from paperwork hell.

Then the perp whipped the bamboo stick so fast Perez barely saw it, slamming one end of it into Sweeney's hands, causing the officer to yell out in pain.

Perez didn't hesitate. She squeezed the trigger.

Blood sprayed out of the perp's shoulder, but it didn't even slow him down. He ran toward a small stadium where they held shows and things. Cursing, she ran after him.

She hesitated and looked at Sweeney and his partner, but the former waved her on. "Don't worry about us, Juanita, just *get* the guy!"

Perez ran around the stadium. It looked like he was heading for Elephant Valley. Like all the other exhibits, it was empty, with the elephants off in some shelter somewhere for the night.

As she rounded the stadium, she caught a stick coming at her face out of the corner of her eye. Raising her arms to block it, she still wound up falling on her back, slamming into the dirt, her fore-arms now sore from the impact of the staff.

"Impressive reflexes," the perp said as he stepped in front of her.

Perez scrambled backward away from him and quickly managed to get to her feet. Only when she was upright did she realize that somewhere along the line, she'd dropped her weapon.

Unfortunately, she couldn't afford to take her eye off the perp in order to look for it in the dark. Instead, she raised her arms in a defensive posture.

"You seem to have some training," the perp scoffed. "You Americans play at the martial arts the way you play at everything else."

"Karate's a hobby—this is my job, and as someone who's pretty good at her job, I'd say your smart move is to surrender. You can take down two guys who didn't realize how fast you are, and you might be able to take me, too, but there's dozens more in this park, and that fake *bo* ain't gonna help much against that many AR-15s. Surrender now, and nobody else gets hurt."

"The only ones who should be hurt are those who harm the helpless."

"Little late for that, given what you did to those two back there."

"They will recover. As will you."

And then he twirled the staff over his head, and Perez raised her hands and leaned back to protect herself—

—leaving her wide open to be kicked in the stomach.

She doubled over, trying to catch her breath. Recalling her training, she struggled to raise her arms, to continue to protect her head.

But she wasn't fast enough. The perp brought his improvised *bo* down right onto her skull, and she fell to the grass.

———

Halls didn't think Chang was going to wait until she hit the brake before he leapt out of the car.

They'd driven down the 15 as fast as they could and pulled into the Safari Park's parking lot. The locals had set up a cordon to keep people out of all save the outer edge of the lot.

Not that there were too many people to keep out, given the somewhat remote location of the park and the fact that it was after hours.

As she pulled in, Halls said, "Will you take a gander at *that*? No looky-loos, and only two cameras. The local press doesn't seem to be on the ball. I'm surprised, this many helicopters flying over one location up here, you'd think the press would be all over it. I mean, in LA or San Diego proper, that'd be one thing, but this is the suburbs."

Chang said nothing. He had been staring intently out the passenger-side window and hadn't said a word since they got off the phone with Skolnick. Sure enough, Chang barely waited for her to bring the car to a full stop—and didn't wait for her to put the car in park and turn the ignition off—before hopping out of the vehicle.

A cop in tactical gear approached them. "Excuse me, ma'am, sir, but you'll have to—"

Halls didn't even wait for him to finish before showing her shield. Chang was doing the same with his credentials. "Detective Halls, Monrovia Police. This is Inspector Chang of Interpol. We're expected."

The officer called behind him. "Cornwell! The out-of-towners are here."

A uniformed officer from the Escondido Police approached. "Inspector, Detective, I'll take you to Lieutenant Kupfer."

Halls frowned. "Who?"

"He's in charge of this operation now, ma'am. Head of TOU."

"Ah. Did you catch him yet?"

"No, ma'am, but it's only a matter of time. He's been wounded."

On the other side of the cordon, there were two ambulances. Halls saw four officers in tac gear being treated and a uniformed officer with a bandage on her head.

"One of the TOU guys got him?"

Cornwell shook his head. "Actually, no, it was Juanita there." He pointed at the uniform with the head wound. "He took down two of the TOU guys with a bamboo stick, believe it or not, but then she threw a shot into his shoulder. He conked her on the head and took off. Funny thing, though—the perp actually dressed her wound before he ran off. Not," he added quickly, "that bandage, the EMTs did that, but the bad guy stopped the bleeding. Might've saved her life."

"Yeah," Halls said wryly, "that's what happens when you go up against a principled serial killer."

Chang said nothing, but continued to walk forward, stone-faced.

Halls went on: "And sounds to me like he endangered her life, he didn't save it."

"Yeah," Cornwell said. "And she did better than TOU did."

"That part's hilarious. Y'know, for shits and giggles, when I was in uniform, I applied for LA SWAT. I got laughed at." She put on a good ol' boy voice. "'Oh no, little lady, don't even *think* about it, you'd never pass muster.'" Then back in her normal voice, she said, "And now this badass serial killer is surrounded by dozens of these guys, he takes down two of them with a fucking stick, and the *woman*'s the one who put a shot in him."

"Maybe," said a deep voice from a few feet away, "but it's gonna be my guys who take his ass down."

Halls saw another cop in tac gear, along with a plainclothes detective and Skolnick.

"Glad you guys could make it," Skolnick said. "Lieutenant Kupfer, Sergeant Genevka, meet Detective Halls from Monrovia, and the Ahab to our bad guy's white whale, Inspector Chang of Interpol."

"Good to meet you guys," Halls said. "No luck capturing him yet?"

"No," Kupfer said, "but it's only a matter of time at this point."

Chang finally spoke. "Your confidence is unwarranted, Lieutenant. He has eluded capture for twenty-two years."

Skolnick shook his head. "No, he's eluded *detection* for twenty-two years. He's been detected now, and he's trapped. There's nowhere for him to go, plus he's wounded."

"He took the time to dress the officer's wounds," Chang said. "I'm sure he did the same for himself. You cannot rely on that working in your favor."

Kupfer snorted. "Maybe not, but it ain't gonna be dark forever, and this chucklehead can't hide from the sun. It's a 'when' thing, not an 'if' thing. So sit tight, and we'll capture him for you, 'kay?"

With that, Kupfer turned and started talking on his radio to his people.

"C'mon," Genevka said, "let's go over here."

They were in a big open field that had a couple of small bodies of water. A bunch of floodlights had been turned on, and several uniforms and one or two TOU guys were standing watch. A few stone structures were on the other side of one of the ponds, probably a place for the animals to hang out when they weren't outside. For all Halls knew, they were in there now. Beyond the structure were trees and grass and open mountains that probably had buffalo roaming or some such during the day.

Genevka led them to one of the wooden fences. "We can wait here until Kupfer's guys take him down."

"If they take him down." Chang sounded almost petulant.

"You heard Kupfer." Genevka turned to Skolnick. "He always like this?"

"Hell if I know, I only just met the guy." Skolnick looked over at Chang. "We'll get him, Chang, trust me. You look like you're gonna jump out of your skin."

"Go easy, San Diego. This has been twenty-two years of his life," Halls said. "Hell, it's been more like thirty."

Chang shot her a look.

So did Genevka. "What's that supposed to mean?"

Realizing she was speaking out of turn, Halls waved a hand back and forth. "Never mind. Long story, and it's not mine to tell."

Genevka's cell phone buzzed, and he looked at it. "Fuck. It's Sternquist." He touched the screen and then put the phone to his ear. "Yeah, boss? Um, we kinda had to call in TOU. I know, but this guy's killed a whole lotta folks. Hell, he took down four of Kupfer's guys and Perez without breaking a sweat. What? Detective Skolnick from San Diego. Yeah, he's here with me. Hang on." Genevka looked at Skolnick as he put the phone to his chest. "My boss is pissed 'cause he got woken up out of a sound sleep and now he wants to talk to you, me, and Kupfer."

Skolnick shrugged. "Sure."

Halls was impressed with the detective's *sang froid*, as she herself always found conversations with bosses to be frustrating. Just dealing with Amenguale was usually enough to give her a headache.

Glancing at Halls, Genevka asked, "You two'll be okay?"

"Of course, go," she said, waving him off.

Genevka and Skolnick headed back the way they had come, in search of Kupfer.

Halls stared at Chang. "Skolnick's right, you are gonna jump out of your skin."

"I believe my anxiousness is justified, Detective."

She held up both hands. "Easy. I don't blame you. But Kupfer was right, it's only a matter of time. I don't care how good he is, the only way he's leaving this park is in bracelets or a bag."

"Intellectually, I know you are correct. Emotionally, I cannot help but recall how often Kai has escaped justice prior to this."

"Like Skolnick said, nobody knew who he was before. Hell, you were the only one really chasing him before. Now, though, he's got half of southern California's law-enforcement on his ass."

"Of course, but—" Chang cut himself off and looked out toward one of the stone structures. "Did you see that?"

"See what?"

Chang suddenly ran off toward one of the structures.

"Oh, for—" Halls sighed, turned, and realized that she had no way of getting anyone's attention. There were TOU guys and uniforms, but they were looking away. Her radio wasn't on Escondido's frequency and she forgot to ask for it.

She could either run after Chang, who was rapidly running out of sight toward the stone building—and soon would be out of the range of the floodlights, making it impossible for her to find him again by sight—or try to get the attention of the Escondido cops who were all too busy to pay attention to her.

Deciding that it would be better not to lose Chang in the safari park, especially since the idiot wasn't armed, she ran after him.

She caught up to him as he was moving slowly around the stone structure. As she approached, he put his finger to his lips. Then he pulled out his phone, made a show of turning the volume down, and then pointed at his phone and then at her pocket.

Pulling out her phone, she also turned the volume down, and then he sent a text: "Saw something behind this building."

Her right index finger moving rapidly across her phone's screen, Halls replied, "So you just ran off? WTF?"

Before Chang could reply, he started running around to the other side of the structure. Halls snarled and followed him.

Back here, there was almost no light, as the floodlights the Escondido cops had set up were directed the other way, and the structures just cast more shadows. Chang activated the flashlight on his smartphone and in that light Halls caught sight of a flash of red.

Recalling Skolnick saying that Carlisle was wearing a red shirt, Halls realized that this was their perp.

Chang kept running.

Halls texted Skolnick: "We see him behind the stone buildings!" Once that was done, she pocketed her phone and unholstered her Beretta.

The floodlights cast shadows that plunged the rest of the park into near-total darkness, so Halls could barely make out the red-shirted figure that was now running quickly away from them.

"Come!" Chang said, and gave chase.

"You've gotta be fucking kidding me," Halls muttered.

The perp was running speedily away from them. Chang was soon no longer running; he had stopped and was wheezing, bent over, hands on knees.

Pointing her Beretta at the red blur that she didn't have a chance in hell of hitting if she fired, she nonetheless yelled out, "Freeze, police!"

All that did was cause Carlisle to dart to the side, behind a copse of trees. Halls lost him completely at that point.

"Shit," she muttered, then checked on Chang.

"Forget me," he got out in a ragged whisper between labored breaths. "Go after him, *please!*" Then he let loose with a phlegmy coughing fit.

She heard movement behind the trees.

"Shit," she muttered and ran toward the trees, weapon raised, and very grateful for her decision to stick with sneakers for footwear.

A flash of red caught her eye as she ran, and again she yelled, "Freeze!"

Closer and closer, and the vague red form started to look a lot more like a torso.

"Don't move, Carlisle! It's over!"

He moved slowly out from behind the tree. Halls could still barely see him, but she kept her Beretta raised. One thing she was able to make out was that he had torn off one of the short sleeves of the red shirt to use as an improvised bandage on his shoulder wound.

"Hands behind your head, interlock your fingers. When you're past that tree, get down on your knees."

He did none of those things, to her annoyance. Instead, he was staring over her shoulder. Halls could hear footfalls behind her, and figured it was Chang joining the party.

Sure enough, the perp said, "It has been some time, An."

"Yes," was all Chang said in reply from behind her.

"It's over, Carlisle," Halls said. "Cuff him, Interpol."

"I cannot allow myself to be captured."

"You don't really have a choice," she said.

"Yes, I do."

With that, he turned and once again ran.

But this time, she had a shot. Halls squeezed the trigger of her Beretta twice.

Blood sprayed from Carlisle's stomach and his forward motion ceased, his arms splayed outwards.

The perp fell to the ground.

Halls lowered her weapon.

"Motherfucker!" she shouted, her words echoing off the trees and the hills.

Chang jogged over to the prone form of the person he'd been chasing for two decades.

Again, Halls said, "Motherfucker." The Beretta felt absurdly heavy in her hands. At once, she felt the cool of the metal grip and the heat of the barrel from the weapon being fired. She wanted to just drop it or throw it away, but it was evidence in a police-involved shooting now.

As Chang knelt down, Halls heard the perp say in a hoarse whisper, "Tell Kiara—"

Then he gurgled and didn't say anything else.

Putting a finger to his neck, Chang said after a moment, "He is dead."

Reaching into his back pocket, Chang pulled out a pair of gloves and snapped them on. Then he picked up the dead body's left arm.

Halls thought he acted and sounded remarkably calm and controlled, all things considered. For her part, it was all she could do to keep from screaming. They were supposed to capture him, not kill him.

There on the dead body's forearm was the same ink they'd seen in the SeaLand security footage.

"This is the tattoo that Kai obtained at the monastery," Chang said. "And while it has been some time since last I saw him, this looks very much like him."

"And he recognized you," Halls said. "Looks like it is him."

She heard more footfalls from behind her, akin to a herd of elephants. Given where they were, it might have been a herd of elephants, which would've just been the perfect capper to the evening.

Turning, she saw that, no, it was just Skolnick, Genevka, Kupfer, and a bunch of TOU guys and Escondido uniforms joining them too late.

"You guys okay?" Skolnick asked.

She shook her head. "Not even a fucking little bit. I had to shoot the bastard."

Skolnick winced. "Damn."

"I've never shot anyone before. Fuck, I've never discharged my weapon outside the range before."

Genevka got on his radio to inform the rest of TOU that the perp had been brought down. Halls knew that the area was going to be a madhouse pretty soon.

"Jesus, who do I turn in my weapon to?"

"What?" Skolnick asked.

"I'm out of my jurisdiction. Hell, so are you, San Diego. Fuck, I discharged my weapon and the perp's dead and I'm a hundred miles from home and I have no idea what the procedure even is, and—fuck!"

Skolnick put a hand on her shoulder. "Easy, Monrovia, you're okay. It's over, and it was a clean shoot."

"Who judges that? Escondido? Monrovia? San Diego? Fucking Interpol, who?"

"We'll figure it out. For now, let's—"

"Detective."

Chang's voice was like a lifeline to Halls. She walked over to where the inspector was looking over the body. He was still using his smartphone as a flashlight, though the lights attached to the barrels of TOU's weapons were providing more illumination.

While trying very hard not to think about the fact that she was responsible for it being a dead body instead of a live perp, she asked, "What is it?"

"Look at this." Chang had turned over Carlisle's wrist to reveal a small scar between the wrist and knuckles on the back of his hand.

Skolnick was right behind Halls. "That's a scar from where they put IVs in. Our guy's been in a hospital recently."

"Maybe that's why he's stepped up his game," Halls said. "If he was sick or dying or something, he might try to get as many kills in as he could before the end. Or, at least, before he was too sick to go on."

Snorting, Skolnick said, "He took down several highly trained officers, I don't think he was any kind of too sick."

Chang pointed at the upper arm that was exposed by the ripped sleeve, which was covered in discolorations. "These appear to be tumors on his skin."

Halls shuddered. "Could be a sarcoma from having cancer." She glanced at Skolnick. "Your friend Pooja's gonna have a *lot* to look at in the autopsy."

"It doesn't matter." Chang stood up. "As you yourself said, Detective, motive is of no consequence. What is important is that Kai's reign of terror is at last at an end."

Chang walked away.

Halls did not follow, still staring at the body.

Again, Skolnick asked, "You okay?"

"No. This isn't how I wanted it to end. It may have been easy for him to take lives, but I'm not him. And on top of that, now I can't even *talk* to him. After listening to Chang babble about him for the last few days, not to mention seeing first-hand what he did to Lesnick, Gonzalez, Atkinson, and Caspari ..." She blew out a breath. "I know motive doesn't matter, and now all three of us have closed cases under our names, and that *is* what matters, but—"

"But what?"

Halls stared right at Skolnick. "I wanted to know why. I'm sorry, but one Golden Retriever being turned into a casserole isn't a good enough reason for *this*. Even if a lot of those shitheads deserved it, it's not a good enough reason for their families to have to suffer their loss, it's not a good enough reason for them all to be tortured, and it for *damn* sure isn't a good enough reason for me to have had to kill the sonofabitch."

———

An hour later, the San Diego County medical examiner had taken the body away. Genevka had taken Halls's weapon pending instructions from on high. The case was a jurisdictional nightmare, since the operation in the Safari Park was technically an SDPD case—the

Atkinson murder—with the Escondido Police assisting. Halls and Chang were both official consultants to the SDPD investigation. But, according to Amenguale when she gave him the low-down over the phone, it was an open question as to whether or not Halls was even allowed to discharge her weapon outside Monrovia.

It would probably take weeks to figure it all out.

For now, she was getting a once-over from an EMT. She hadn't been hurt, but it was standard procedure after a shooting.

Skolnick walked over to her with an evidence bag. "You okay?"

"Can you please stop asking me that? I'll be okay when it's next year and this case is a memory."

"Fair enough. Found something on the body that might interest you." He held up the clear plastic bag.

Halls saw a key attached to a diamond-shaped piece of plastic with a stylized "N" and a stylized "M" poorly etched into it, along with a number 207.

"I haven't seen a hotel key like this in over a decade," Skolnick said. "Even the shittiest motels have key cards these days."

"The shitty ones do, the shittiest ones don't." Halls actually smiled. "And trust me, this place is the shittiest in all creation. It's a dump in Van Nuys—I think every cop in LA County has been there at least once to pick up a perp, stop a drug deal, or some damn thing. Crossroads of the dregs of humanity, mostly because they *don't* have key cards, so you can stay there without there being a record of it."

Skolnick nodded. "Smart. Well, we'll process this and then get it up to you so you can check Room 207 out."

"Not to me. I'm gonna be riding a desk until they figure out whether or not I still get to be a cop after this."

"Oh, stop that, Monrovia. It was a clean shoot."

"If your pal Genevka had shot him, it would've been a clean shoot. Me shooting him, though, is a clusterfuck of epic proportions."

"Maybe. But at least it's over."

Halls sighed. "Yeah."

EPILOGUE

"WITH THE LATEST on the incident at the Safari Park last night, here's Marisol Calletano."

"The San Diego Zoo's Safari Park is often the sight of exciting adventures involving its animal population, but last night after hours it was the scene of a major manhunt. The Escondido Police Department has released a statement confirming that their Tactical Operations Unit had tracked a suspect in the murder of SeaLand CEO Jim Atkinson. According to the statement, the suspect is also a person of interest in the murders in the Los Angeles area of two other CEOs, Alexander Lesnick of MCD Meats and Jean-Pierre Caspari of d'Artagnan Foods, as well as MCD employee Fredi Rodriguez. The suspect resisted arrest and injured several police until one officer—whose name was not released to the press—shot and killed the suspect. In addition, the suspect kidnapped two Escondido residents, Internet celebrity Deena King and her father Robert. Robert died on the scene, while Deena is in the ICU at Palomar Medical Center.

"The suspect was not identified by name, but a source who requested anonymity has informed KUSI that the suspect's name is Chanan Carlisle, and he's suspected in several other murders around the world. An investigator from Interpol was sighted on the scene at the Safari Park, in addition to Detective Michelle Halls of the Monrovia Police, who is the lead investigator on the MCD Meats case.

"We'll have more on this story as it develops. For KUSI, I'm Marisol Calletano."

9 June 2019

Nelson's Motel
Van Nuys, California, United States of America

Halls stared at the wall of the cruddy room in Nelson's Motel, wondering why Carlisle left all this stuff here.

And also really really wishing he hadn't.

Technically, she wasn't supposed to be here. As she had predicted to Skolnick, she was riding a desk while the bosses in Escondido, San Diego, and Monrovia all figured out what to do with her.

However, Caren Howie, the LAPD crime scene investigator who had been sent to process Carlisle's room at Nelson's, used to work at the Monrovia lab. She was willing to let Halls look at the scene and not tell Amenguale or any of his bosses that she was doing so, as long as she didn't touch anything.

When she'd arrived, she'd been hoping that she might find some of the answers that her having to shoot Carlisle had denied her.

Instead, she had the same questions, only intensified.

It had been difficult enough to not feel a certain lack of disgust with what Carlisle was doing. One could almost view it as right-eous. Most of the victims Chang had described to her were people that, if Halls was honest with herself, the world was probably better off without.

But that didn't make what Carlisle was doing right, either.

Still, that was hard to keep to when this was his cause.

All over the wall were printouts, photographs, and clipped articles about horrible things being done to animals. On top of that, there was a fresh newspaper article about Atkinson's death and a printout of an article about MCD's recall.

There were, she noticed, two gaps in the wall, and she

wondered if they were pieces about Caspari and King, since those were his latest kills, and they weren't represented elsewhere.

The three photos on top made Halls's heart beat like a triphammer. Two were the first signs she'd seen that Carlisle had feelings for any other humans: one a picture of a much younger Kiara Carlisle, the other a picture of a bunch of men in crew cuts and matching brown robes with white sashes that looked a lot like how Chang had described the Hé Ping Temple in China that he'd visited. She saw a younger version of Carlisle on the far right.

But the third was the kicker: a very old picture of a dingy little storefront in an alley, with animals hanging in the window. Halls couldn't tell where the storefront was, but it had a definite Asian feel to it. Sure, it could've been in almost any big-city Chinatown, for example, but she knew in her bones that it was the place where Carlisle's Golden Retriever met her end.

"Just had to leave that behind, didn't you?"

"What was that, Michelle?" Caren asked.

Halls shook her head. "Sorry, nothing."

Caren shook her head. "This place is a mess. Dust everywhere"—she pointed at the desk—"except for this void here on the desk."

Following her finger, Halls saw a rectangular void in the dust pattern that was the right size to be a laptop.

"Yeah, that figures. Also explains why he didn't take his wall of shame with him—he's probably got it all on his computer."

Her phone buzzed, startling her. Pulling it out of her pants pocket, she saw that it was her own lab.

Confused, since LAPD was processing this scene as well as the warehouse in Vernon and SDPD was handling SeaLand and the Safari Park, she slid her finger across the display. "Halls."

"Hey, Michelle, it's Sunana. I've got news."

"Hi, Sunana. Is it good news or bad news?"

Sunana hesitated. "I'm honestly not sure. I got the DNA back on that white coat your guy left behind at MCD Meats."

Halls blinked. She had totally forgotten about the coat. "That's great! You need to match it against the corpse. It's in San Diego County's morgue right now pending autopsy, but—"

"Way ahead of you, Michelle. This is a press case, so everything's happening fast now. We've got DNA from SeaLand, DNA from this coat, and DNA from the warehouse in Vernon. They all match each other."

"Good."

"But they don't match the body. In fact, the only DNA that matches the body is what they found in the Safari Park."

"Say that again, slowly."

"The guy who got killed in the Safari Park isn't the guy who killed all those people. Well, except for Robert King. He killed him and hurt his bitch of a daughter, but the others? Different guy. Oh, and when I talked to the San Diego ME, she told me something interesting—the guy you shot had stomach cancer. Had maybe three months left."

"So I was right." She sighed. "About some of it, anyhow. Okay, Sunana, thanks for that."

After ending the call, her eyes drifted back up to the three pictures on top of the wall.

She looked at the picture of the temple, seeing Carlisle in the center front.

"Holy fuck."

Snatching it off the wall, she peered at it more closely.

"Hey!" Caren cried out. "Stop contaminating my scene, Michelle!"

Halls ignored her.

On first glance, she'd seen Carlisle on the far right in the picture, but the guy in the center front also looked a lot like him.

"Son of a goddamn bitch."

10 June 2019

Vista Atlantic Flight 47
In the air over the Pacific Ocean

Chang watched the screen in the back of the seat in front of him as CNN Headline News did a brief story on the incident in the Safari Park in Escondido. It was light on details, though he was sure that would change soon. Too many jurisdictions, too many different police departments and laboratories handling too many different pieces of evidence.

Normally as the Interpol investigator, he would be coordinating, but that was before Superintendent Zhou sent him a very terse e-mail ordering him to return to Beijing. He was being taken off the case and was to go before a review board upon his return.

He supposed that was an inevitable consequence of the superintendent learning that the chief suspect in the case was the brother of his ex-girlfriend.

But he had no regrets about how he'd comported himself. He had followed the investigation as best he could; he had followed the evidence that presented itself.

Conveniently, none of that evidence pointed to Kai.

At least, not until they saw the tattoo on the inner left arm of the person who killed James Atkinson. That was the first evidentiary indication that Kai might be the suspect.

Of course, Detective Halls had been correct in her accusation made in the hospital waiting room. From the very beginning, he had suspected that Kai might be the mask killer.

But to pursue it further without any physical evidence to it would have required him to break more than one promise.

7 January 1989

Hongqiao Airport
Shanghai, People's Republic of China

Chang stood before Kiara on the tarmac, the cold wind slicing through his chest, and he found himself wishing he'd worn something thicker than the windbreaker—which was very much not living up to its name.

Kiara, of course, wore a fur coat. She *was* an ambassador's daughter, after all. And she had put the viola he'd given her into her thick hair, securing it against the wind with a bobby pin.

Her eyes were welled up with tears, though they evaporated in the wind before they could get any further. "I will call you," she said.

"You will have to." Chang could not help but smirk. "I am afraid that the long-distance charges are beyond the means of what the police pay me."

She choked out a laugh. "It isn't funny, An. We'll never see each other again. My mother hates it here, has hated it ever since what happened to Nandita. I doubt she will ever set foot in China again."

"Perhaps your father's work will take him here, and you may accompany him."

Sighing, she said, "That is not very likely. After all, we lived in Shanghai so Father wouldn't have to deal with us while working in Peking. Besides …" She trailed off and looked away.

"Your parents do not approve of me."

"They approve of you as a person." She looked back at him. "But they do not approve of you as a match for me."

"That does not mean we may not speak on the phone when the opportunity presents itself. Or write letters."

Kiara smiled. "I would love to write you letters."

"As I would to you."

He said the words knowing full well that neither of them would ever do so. The Carlisles would not tolerate the long-distance charges on their phone bill and neither Chang nor Kiara would actually get around to writing a letter—a truly archaic practice in the age of the telephone in any case.

So, since he knew he would never see her, and probably never talk to her again, he said what he had debated whether or not to say.

He put his hands on her fur-coated shoulders. "Kiara, there is one last thing we must discuss. Right now, there is an open investigation into the death of Donghai Hongzhou."

Kiara stared at him blankly. "I don't understand."

"He ran a small butcher shop in Wufu Alley. He was flensed and what was left of his face was boiled in cooking oil. It was a particularly brutal death."

"That's horrible, but why—"

"Hongzhou owned the shop that Kai's dog was taken to."

Eyes widening, Kiara backed away. "No."

"Witnesses saw a very tall young man. Not much of a physical description, but everyone remembers the bike he was riding."

"Many young men ride bikes in Wufu," Kiara said defensively, looking away from Chang. "It's the only way to get around in the crowds."

"Yes, but most of the bikes are old and battered and well used. This was a well-kept, expensive bicycle that very obviously belonged to a child of wealth and privilege."

"What are you saying, An?" Kiara stared intently at him. "Is Kai in trouble?"

Chang gave her a dubious look. "With the police? Of course not. Hongzhou was not particularly well liked, he had no family, and while his shop was moderately successful, there are others, and one will replace his as well. We are unlikely to expend sufficient resources to investigate his death—certainly not enough to track down the son of the outgoing US ambassador who is about to leave the country forever." He stepped closer, trying to speak more softly, though the wind made it necessary for him to speak up a bit. "My concern is with Kai."

"You don't know it was him."

"I doubt too many other young men riding so pristine a bike would have reason to kill Hongzhou so brutally."

Kiara said nothing.

"Remember how he nearly broke my back when I tried to step on a rat? And that was, to be blunt, a *rat*. It's not exactly a stretch to think that he'd have a much more brutal response to the person responsible for his beloved dog's death."

Kiara closed her eyes and sighed. Then she reopened them, and Chang saw a pleading expression there that had superseded her sorrow at having to leave him. "No, it is not a stretch, An. In fact, I fear for what will happen to him. He has so much anger—and also so much love that is then turned into anger. You have to promise me that, if the worst does happen, you will do the best you can to keep him safe."

"Kiara—" he started. How could he make such a promise? He was a mere junior officer. Who knew where Kai would even wind up?

But then he saw the expression on her face, and she plaintively cried out into the wind, *"Promise* me!" The viola in her hair vibrated with the intensity of her passion.

He could not resist the pleas of one who loved him.

"I promise," he whispered.

It was the last thing he would say to Kiara in person for thirty years.

10 June 2019

Vista Atlantic Flight 47
In the air over the Pacific Ocean

At the time he had made that promise to Kiara, Chang had never imagined that he would wind up working as an inspector for Interpol.

However, when he learned of the meticulous killings of people who harmed animals, with—as Skolnick had so adroitly pointed out—the killer emulating the title character in *The Mikado* by letting the punishment fit the crime, he soon realized that it had to be Kai.

He continued to work the case, but he did not investigate Kai. There was no evidence that pointed to him. There were only Chang's own memories of Kai, and as long as those memories stayed in his head and out of the file, he could plead ignorance—or forgetfulness, as he had to Halls.

As long as he told no one of Kai, he could fulfill his long-ago promise.

So he stayed away from Kiara to avoid even the possibility of implicating him. He did not call. He did not write.

At least not until Detective Halls noticed the tattoo and forced his hand.

However, he still fulfilled his promise to her. He had no idea if Kiara was aware of it or not, but that mattered not a whit to Chang. She may not have known that he kept his vow, but *he* knew that he had, and that was what was important.

That was why he had lied in the Safari Park.

Oh, the body looked very similar to Kai. But though it had been three decades since he'd last seen the two of them, and gotten them mixed up when he met them at the Hé Ping Temple in Taizhou, he could tell the difference between Kai and Ajay.

But they had the same tattoo, so it was close enough for an ID. Chang suspected that Kai was counting on that.

The last piece of e-mail he'd gotten before the superintendent took him off the case was the preliminary autopsy report from the San Diego County Medical Examiner's Office, which revealed that the body that was still being tentatively identified as Chanan Kayaan Carlisle had stomach cancer, which explained the sarcoma that they'd noticed at the scene.

Ajay and Kai had been comrades at Hé Ping. If Ajay was dying anyhow, Chang wasn't at all surprised that he would be willing to put what was left of his life on the line so that Kai could continue his work.

Going forward, Chang would have a much harder time fulfilling his promise. He was unlikely to be let anywhere near the case, once they figured out that the corpse in San Diego wasn't Kai, once Kai started killing again.

He'd be on his own.

For Kiara's sake, Chang wished him well.

3 September 2019

Hotel Nagisaya Wakayama
Taiji, Japan

Chanan sat in the lobby of the hotel, catching up on e-mail.

Most of it was material from various animal-rights mailing lists he subscribed to, as well as mailing lists related to hunting, poaching, and other acts performed by people who specialized in being cruel to the helpless. Sifu had always told him that knowing your enemies was as important as fighting your enemies, and that indeed knowing them gave you the best path to fighting them.

There was also an e-mail from his sister.

"Kai:

"I received another visit from Detective Halls today. First time in a month, though I found out why I stopped hearing from her in August—she is no longer on the case, because she no longer works for the Monrovia Police Department. She not only was cleared of any wrongdoing in killing poor Ajay, her work on the case against you apparently impressed someone. She now works for the LAPD's Robbery-Homicide Division. That's quite a kudo for her. I know this is of little interest to you, but I liked her, and An obviously respected her, so I'm glad to see her do well.

"I still have not heard from An, even though Michelle told me that he was off the case and was suspended due to his conflict of interest. I have reached out to him, but he has not answered. I do not understand why—he obviously kept the promise I rather stupidly made him make thirty years ago, even though I never imagined he'd be able to actually do so. I know you don't like to be reminded of this, Kai, and I know you think that Ajay truly deserves the credit, but the fact of the matter is that you owe An your life at least as much as you do Ajay for taking your place in San Diego.

"I hope you are continuing to lay low. The authorities all know who you are now. An won't be able to protect you, and neither will I. The bank account in the Caymans is still viable, of course, but you should use that to remain off the grid. If you start your crusade again, it will end badly.

"I love you.

"Kiara."

In addition, he got a notification of new videos uploaded to YouTube that might have been of interest to him, and one in particular caught his eye: a news story from KUSI in San Diego about SeaLand reopening their new arena.

The video was dated the previous Friday, the 30th of August, and it started with a Latina woman standing in front of the entrance to SeaLand.

A caption identified the woman as Marisol Calletano. "Sea-Land's Arjun Keshav Arena is finally reopening this weekend, with a grand ceremony that new CEO Arren Ordover promises will be less eventful than its initial opening in June of this year, during which parts of previous CEO James Atkinson were found in the mouths of the performing orcas."

The image changed to that of a tall, slim man with short brown hair and a pleasant smile, identified by a caption as the aforementioned new CEO. "There were obviously a lot of problems here, ones that went deeper than the fact that this arena was a crime scene. The manner of Jim's death forced us to really take a good hard look at our policies and our practices. I can tell you that SeaLand is joining other California water parks in no longer having orca shows, and Sid, Nancy, Pixie, Sasha, and Malia are in the process of being acclimated back into the wild where they belong. That process is being overseen by the Institute for Conservation Research. Jim's death was indeed a tragedy, but I hope that some good can come out of it as we phase out some of his more unhealthy practices toward our attractions."

The image returned to Calletano. "The arena's grand reopening will include an all-new dolphin show, the park's popular sea lions, as well as the Dancing Pet show, in which clients can bring in their pet dogs, cats, and birds to cavort in the water park."

Back to Ordover. "We're hoping this reopening will remind people that we're still a place for the whole family to have fun."

Back to Calletano, who was now walking along the entrance to the Keshav Arena. "The death of SeaLand's CEO led to a statewide manhunt for those responsible for the murders, not only of Atkinson, but also of two other CEOs, Jean-Pierre Caspari of d'Artagnan Foods and Alexander Lesnick of MCD Meats, both killed in the Los Angeles area. One of the alleged perpetrators, who has been identified as Ajay Mehta, was fatally shot by police while resisting arrest in the San Diego Zoo's Safari Park, where he had kidnapped and imprisoned Internet celebrity

Deena King and her father Robert. Robert was Mehta's last victim, while Deena remains in a coma. Police have stated that Mehta worked with an accomplice, Chanan Carlisle, who remains at large, and continues to be sought by authorities around the world for these murders, as well as others throughout the United States, and also in Africa, Asia, and Europe. Carlisle is the son of Albert Carlisle, who served as US ambassador to China under both Jimmy Carter and Ronald Reagan. For KUSI, I'm Marisol Calletano."

The video stopped and Chanan closed the tab.

From the front desk, a voice called out, "Mr. Raj Patel?"

Chanan quickly closed the laptop and got to his feet. The person Kiara had hired to create his false ID had given him one of the most common Indian names. The assumption was that he would be able to blend in more easily that way.

"Yes," he said as he put the laptop in its case and went to the front desk.

The clerk was running a key card through the machine. "Your room has finally been cleaned, Mr. Patel. We can complete the check-in procedure now."

"Excellent."

"Are you in Taiji for the dolphin hunt?"

Chanan nodded. "Yes. I have heard many things."

The clerk got a sour look on his face. "Be wary of protestors. They sometimes disrupt the proceedings." Making a clicking noise, the clerk shook his head. "They have no respect for tradition. Or for our economy. The dolphin hunting is why people come here. And besides, it's not like the dolphins care one way or the other. Personally, I've never believed that nonsense about how they're as intelligent as us. If they were, would they let us kill and eat them?" The clerk chuckled and gave Chanan his key card inside a folded piece of cardboard. "The room number is written on the inside, as is the Wi-Fi password."

"Thank you." Chanan took the card and then gave a small smile. "I'm looking forward to seeing those responsible for hunting the dolphins. I hear they are quite impressive."

"Oh, yes, sir, very impressive. I'm sure you'll be quite taken with them."

Chanan simply nodded, picked up his laptop bag and satchel, grabbed the handle of his wheeled luggage, and headed toward the elevator.

He had taken Kiara's advice and had lain low for almost three months now.

But the helpless were still being tormented and killed needlessly. Nandita still cried out for vengeance. He had sacrificed everything for his crusade: the love of his family; the respect of his Sifu, who had cast him out when he realized what Chanan's intentions were; even the life of his only friend, for all that Ajay was dying in any event. For that matter, he appeared to have inadvertently sacrificed An Chang's career, a service Chanan would not have expected.

Those sacrifices could not be in vain.

He arrived in his room, and removed the dolphin mask from the satchel.

There was more work to be done.

ACKNOWLEDGMENTS

Munish: The idea of this book was the confluence of experiences I had over many years and my evolution into understanding that animals are sentient beings. That evolution has been further perpetuated by my son Ayaan, who at the age of three decided he was not going to eat meat and became engrossed in the well-being of animals. Most of us have a visceral reaction in seeing the senseless torture, abuse, and killing of animals. We abhor the people who perpetuate these crimes, such as killing a majestic lion or a rare endangered sheep or giraffe for sport. But our lives go on. We must as a society protect these creatures.

I would like to thank my wife Pooja, who has provided support, encouragement, and three beautiful children, Ayaan, Kairav, and Kiara. My wife also says I should thank our dog, as she feels that Laila has taught me a lot, and who am I to argue?

I also want to recognize my parents Raj and Nirmal Batra who, despite the challenges they faced in life, always prioritized our education and sense of security, and my siblings, Rajnish, Sunana, and Lori, who have been a source of inspiration and family support.

Finally I want to recognize my uncles, Satpal Mahana, Sudesh

Dua, and SatdevDua. Though they have passed on, their life lessons live with me.

Keith: I would like to thank the Wildlife Conservation Society (of which I am a very proud member), San Diego Zoo Global, the World Wildlife Fund, *National Geographic*, and other online resources too numerous to mention, which provided useful (and appalling) background on the mistreatment of animals all over the world. In particular, Wikipedia and its "external links" section was invaluable—it wasn't my only reference source, but it's a great place to start your online research on a subject. In addition, many thanks to *Shuseki Shihan* Paul and the other folks at my karate dojo, where I have been studying for a decade and a half, and which informed a lot of the martial arts stuff. My own experiences and research writing police procedurals also came in handy, and I'd be remiss if I didn't mention my favorite book on that subject, David Simon's *Homicide: A Year on the Killing Streets* (the inspiration for two of the finest cop shows in the history of television, *Homicide: Life on the Streets* and *The Wire*). Also thanks to my family, both human and feline, for love, support, and other cool stuff.

Both of us would like to thank author Jonathan Maberry, who brought us together, and film producer Tony Eldridge—both are all-around magnificent human beings, and their feedback was invaluable. Thanks also to Jonathan Hadaya, who has been instrumental in connecting us with various high-profile animal lovers. Gratitude also to Lucienne Diver and Lane Heymont for their efforts on our behalf; and finally many, many, many thanks to Kevin J. Anderson, Marie Whittaker, and all the other fine folks at WordFire Press for taking us on.

ABOUT THE AUTHOR

Munish K. Batra, MD, FACS was born in Kanpur, India on Halloween in 1965, which he always felt was fateful. His family emigrated to the US in 1972. He devoured J.D. Salinger and Kurt Vonnegut in high school, and entered Ohio State University with the goal of becoming a writer. However, he eventually gave in to parental pressure and studied medicine, attending medical school at Case Western Reserve University in Cleveland. During his third year of med school, he joined the US Army as a reservist.

He entered a general surgery and trauma residency at St. Luke's Medical Center, and during that time he assisted with military operations for Operation: Desert Storm at Fort Ord in Monterey. This led him to seek out California as his new home. After his general surgery training, he completed a plastic surgery residency and a craniofacial and pediatric plastic surgery fellowship.

Dr. Batra's extensive experience in trauma and reconstructive surgery and craniofacial surgery has been put to charitable use at missions overseas, and he has lent his services during natural disasters such as the tsunami that struck southeast Asia in 2004 and the earthquake that devastated Nepal in 2011. In his new hometown of San Diego, he has started Doctors Offering Charitable Services (DOCS), which provides charitable surgeries to the less fortunate in Southern California.

His cosmetic practice is one of the busiest in the nation, and Dr. Batra has been featured in *People*, the *Los Angeles Times*, and many other national media outlets, as well as on *The Oprah Winfrey Show*. He is active in developing multispecialty medical practices that put patient care and the doctor-patient relationship at the center of health care.

Dr. Batra is currently collaborating with Keith R.A. DeCandido on other fiction projects, and is also working on a nonfiction book called *Medical Madness*. He also enjoys Brazilian jiu-jitsu, yoga, and meditation. His wife Pooja and their three young children, Ayaan, Kairav, and Kiara, offer him constant encouragement and support.

Keith R.A. DeCandido is the award-winning, best-selling author of more than fifty novels, almost a hundred short stories, a smattering of comic books, and a ton of nonfiction. Some of it is in thirty-plus licensed universes (*Star Trek*, *Alien*, *Doctor Who*, Marvel Comics, *Supernatural*, *World of Warcraft*, *Cars*, *Resident Evil*, *The X-Files*, *Orphan Black*, etc.), others in worlds of his own creation, from fantastical police procedurals in the fictional cities of Cliff's End and Super City to urban fantasies in the somewhat real cities of New York and Key West. Some of his most recent fiction includes the *Alien* novel *Isolation*; his long-running fantasy police procedure series, the latest novels of which are *Mermaid Precinct* and *Phoenix Precinct*; an urban fantasy series set in his native New York City that debuted from WordFire Press in 2019 with *A Furnace Sealed;* and which will continue in 2021 with *Feat of Clay*; short stories in the anthologies *Across the Universe*, *Bad Ass Moms*, *Pangaea* Book 3: *Redemption*, *Footprints in the Stars*, *Horns and Halos*, and *Release the Virgins!*; and scripting the graphic novels *Icarus* and *Jellinek*.

His nonfiction about popular culture can be found in a variety of sources, most prominently on the award-winning website Tor.com, and also in magazines (*Entertainment Weekly*, *Star Trek Magazine*) and anthologies (the *Outside In*, *Smart Pop*, and *Subterranean Blue Grotto* series). Keith is also a third-degree black belt in karate (for which he both teaches and trains), an editor of more than twenty-five years' standing (for clients both personal and corporate), a professional musician (currently with the parody band Boogie Knights), and probably some other stuff he can't recall due to the lack of sleep. Find out less at DeCandido.net.

IF YOU LIKED ...

Animal, you might also enjoy:

Selected Stories: Horror and Dark Fantasy
by Kevin J. Anderson

Band on the Run
by D.J. Butler

River Runs Red
by Jeff Mariotte

OTHER WORDFIRE PRESS TITLES BY KEITH R.A. DECANDIDO

A Furnace Sealed
Feat of Clay (coming in 2021)

Our list of other WordFire Press authors and titles is always growing. To find out more and to see our selection of titles, visit us at:
wordfirepress.com

facebook.com/WordfireIncWordfirePress
twitter.com/WordFirePress
bookbub.com/profile/4109784512